P9-DMK-335

LINES OF POWER—

must always be maintained, and on Darkover, where power comes through the strength of one's *laran* skills, marriages are planned to breed true to these talents. But not all are willing to sacrifice love for lineage, and not all have talents that are easily recognized or tamed.

This all-new collection of stories set on the world of the Bloody Sun takes us on a fascinating expedition from Dry Towns to Domain . . . from the childhood of Regis Hastur to dangerous Aldaran and Alton experiments with the powers of the Overworld . . . from a fateful journey to Thendara House to a city endangered by a pathmaster's tragic loss . . . from a handfasting where a thirst for vengeance must finally be quenched to a lady on the way to her own wedding whose destiny may be changed when the Ghost Wind blows. . . .

**Other DAW titles
by Marion Zimmer Bradley:**

Novels:

HUNTERS OF THE RED MOON
THE SURVIVORS
WARRIOR WOMAN

Collections:

LYTHANDE (with Vonda N. McIntyre)
THE BEST OF MARION ZIMMER BRADLEY

Anthologies:

GREYHAVEN
SPELLS OF WONDER
SWORD AND SORCERESS I
SWORD AND SORCERESS II
SWORD AND SORCERESS III
SWORD AND SORCERESS IV
SWORD AND SORCERESS V
SWORD AND SORCERESS VI
SWORD AND SORCERESS VII
SWORD AND SORCERESS VIII
SWORD AND SORCERESS IX

A Reader's Guide to DARKOVER

THE FOUNDING:

A "lost ship" of Terran origin, in the pre-empire colonizing days, lands on a planet with a dim red star, later to be called Darkover.

DARKOVER LANDFALL

THE AGES OF CHAOS:

1,000 years after the original landfall settlement, society has returned to the feudal level. The Darkovans, their Terran technology renounced or forgotten, have turned instead to free-wheeling, out-of-control matrix technology, psi powers and terrible psi weapons. The populace lives under the domination of the Towers and a tyrannical breeding program to staff the Towers with unnaturally powerful, inbred gifts of *laran*.

STORMQUEEN!
HAWKMISTRESS!

THE HUNDRED KINGDOMS:

An age of war and strife retaining many of the decimating and disastrous effects of the Ages of Chaos. The lands which are later to become the Seven Domains are divided by continuous border conflicts into a multitude of small, belligerent kingdoms, named for convenience "The Hundred Kingdoms." The close of this era is heralded by the adoption of the Compact, instituted by Varzil the Good. A landmark and turning point in the history of Darkover, the Compact bans all distance weapons, making it a matter of honor that one who seeks to kill must himself face equal risk of death.

TWO TO CONQUER
THE HEIRS OF HAMMERFELL

THE RENUNCIATES:

During the Ages of Chaos and the time of the Hundred Kingdoms, there were two orders of women who set themselves apart from the patriarchal nature of Darkovan feudal society: the priestesses of Avarra, and the warriors of the Sisterhood of the Sword. Eventually these two independent groups merged to form the powerful and legally chartered Order of Renunciates or Free Amazons, a guild of women bound only by oath as a sisterhood of mutual responsibility. Their primary allegiance is to each other rather than to family, clan, caste or any man save a temporary employer. Alone among Darkovan women, they are exempt from the usual legal restrictions and protections. Their reason for existence is to provide the women of Darkover an alternative to their socially restrictive lives.

THE SHATTERED CHAIN
THENDARA HOUSE
CITY OF SORCERY

AGAINST THE TERRANS
—THE FIRST AGE (Recontact):

After the Hastur Wars, the Hundred Kingdoms are consolidated into the Seven Domains, and ruled by a hereditary aristocracy of seven families, called the Comyn, allegedly descended from the legendary Hastur, Lord of Light. It is during this era that the Terran Empire, really a form of confederacy, rediscovers Darkover, which they know as the fourth planet of the Cottman star system. It is not apparent that Darkover is a lost colony of the Empire, until linguistic and sociological studies reveal that Darkovans are of Terran extraction—a concept not easily or readily acknowledged by Darkovans and their Comyn overlords.

    THE SPELL SWORD
    THE FORBIDDEN TOWER

AGAINST THE TERRANS
—THE SECOND AGE (After the Comyn):

With the initial shock of recontact beginning to wear off, and the Terran spaceport a permanent establishment on the outskirts of the city of Thendara, the younger and less traditional elements of Darkovan society begin the first real exchange of knowledge with the Terrans—learning Terran science and technology and teaching Darkovan matrix technology in turn. Eventually Regis Hastur, the young Comyn lord most active in these exchanges, becomes Regent in a provisional government allied to the Terrans. Darkover is once again reunited with its founding Empire.

    THE HERITAGE OF HASTUR
    SHARRA'S EXILE

THE DARKOVER ANTHOLOGIES:

These volumes of stories written by Marion Zimmer Bradley herself, and various members of the society called The Friends of Darkover, strive to "fill in the blanks" of Darkovan history, and elaborate on the eras, tales and characters which have captured their imagination.

    DOMAINS OF DARKOVER
    FOUR MOONS OF DARKOVER
    FREE AMAZONS OF DARKOVER
    THE KEEPER'S PRICE
    LERONI OF DARKOVER
    THE OTHER SIDE OF THE MIRROR
    RED SUN OF DARKOVER
    RENUNCIATES OF DARKOVER
    SWORD OF CHAOS

Marion Zimmer Bradley
Four Moons Of Darkover

DAW BOOKS, INC.
DONALD A. WOLLHEIM, FOUNDER
375 Hudson Street, New York, NY 10014

ELIZABETH R. WOLLHEIM
SHEILA E. GILBERT
PUBLISHERS

Copyright © 1988 by Marion Zimmer Bradley and The Friends
of Darkover.

All Rights Reserved.

Cover art and border design by Richard Hescox.

DAW Book Collectors No. 761.

If you purchased this book without a cover you should be aware that
this book is stolen property. It was reported as "unsold and destroyed"
to the publisher and neither the author nor the publisher has received
any payment for this "stripped book."

First Printing, November 1988

4   5   6   7   8   9

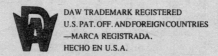

DAW TRADEMARK REGISTERED
U.S. PAT. OFF. AND FOREIGN COUNTRIES
—MARCA REGISTRADA.
HECHO EN U.S.A.

PRINTED IN THE U.S.A.

Contents

Introduction

Well, it's been another year and a new crop of stories. Not too long ago, a well-known writer, whom I will not characterize further than to say that he seems to think we should all be making a couple of hundred thousand a year before we're allowed to know anything about writing, remarked that slush—those unsolicited manuscripts we all get so many of—were about ninety percent garbage, and lamentable garbage at that. I ventured to remonstrate with him, saying that most of what I got was pretty good, and he accused me of being "disingenuous." I told him that if he called me dishonest in print again I would have his head on a platter, and he sent me an elaborate letter saying he had chosen the world carefully and it did not *mean* "dishonest." Well, I don't know what they taught him in school, but where I grew up, the difference between *dishonest* and *disingenuous* was pretty minimal. Look them both up in the dictionary sometime.

Now, granted, some people are taking up writing who are, to say the most charitable thing possible, better qualified to be readers than writers. They do not know how to make their views known in good English and don't show themselves to have a great deal of talent for doing so. They write blank verse epics which, to put it politely, are very far from showing promise as a successor to Tennyson. They are having fun, and far be it from me to say that if they want a hobby they should take up crocheting or collecting stamps. If I sometimes wish they would spare me their efforts, that's just the risks of the game. I could have been a plumber, and no one would ever have sent me any bad fiction to read.

And so could my colleague. In fact, he could have stuck to writing, and he would have been spared the effort of reading all these bad stories by people who don't come up to his exalted standards. We have all of us—yes, even him, and even me—written bad stories before we wrote good ones. Sometimes we have even done it on purpose; but more often we do it because we don't know any better. And if we produce something which, if printed, would bring shame on a fanzine printed by a thirteen year old, well, all the worse for me and my colleague that these have not been taught better. After all, we have to get the stories we print from *somewhere*.

But as a matter of fact most of what I get—for these Darkover anthologies anyway—is pretty good. This year especially, I could have used about seventy-five percent of what I got.

So do I sit back and congratulate myself, or what? Have I weeded out the worst writers by a tough-minded policy of not encouraging anyone but the very best? I hope not. I am proud of anyone who starts out by imitating me, of course; I started out by imitating— sometimes pretty shamelessly—C. L. Moore and Leigh Brackett. Once, in a conversation with C. L. Moore that I still recall, I found out that she was aware of how near I had come to plagiarizing one of her books with one of mine, and I asked her why she had never done anything about it. She replied—most generously— that, first, the amount involved was pretty insubstantial anyhow; second, that I was probably too young to know any better; and third, that in its way, it was a form of flattery—imitation being the sincerest form of same.

Well, she was right; and when I start chiding someone for imitating my work, I seldom do more than encourage them to write in their own voice; because I wonder where I would have been if Catherine had lit on me like a ton of bricks at the beginning of my career. Probably teaching second grade somewhere on Staten Island, and none of the Darkover books would ever have been written.

My friend—and I hope we are still friends in spite of all this—has said publicly that I shouldn't encourage these people. One can't help wondering if he is simply trying to stifle the competition. I'm not; when I'm too old to write, I would like to think there were still some writers coming up there. He and I appeared once together on a panel of "young writers"—fans turned pro. We were not far out of our teens then; I was a housewife in Texas, and he was holding down some scutwork job somewhere in publishing to keep beans on the table. As it happens, we both became well off and equally well known; he has devoted his life to talking about the horrors of reading slush, while I—much better known as an editor and teacher than he is, fortunately—have spent a lot of time working out what divides the good writers from the yet-unpublished and encouraging the latter to become the former. I still have a little of my sense of wonder about the "slush pile"—you never know when you're going to discover, say, a Jennifer Roberson or a Mercedes Lackey—to name only two—at the bottom of the heap, or in the next envelope you open. I'd like to think there will be a lot more before I get done with this business. What would the fantasy world be like if H. P. Lovecraft had not encouraged half a dozen of his friends, including Robert Bloch and Fritz Leiber, to write? What would it be like if—say—I had actively discouraged Jennifer, Misty—or Deborah Wheeler, whose work you will read herein? I wonder if my friend would like to take that responsibility?

And I wonder—which one of us is having more fun?

Of course it means I have to think of some reason for rejecting all those stories I don't get to print. In this particular anthology, it means I have to write and tell people over and over how inelastic typeface is—a lovely phrase I picked up in my kid days from Sam Merwin. I get more stories than I can use, and a lot of them are, all things considered, pretty good. So what do I do with the blank-verse epics and the really awful stuff? (Yes, there is some written by people who ought to take up crocheting.) Sometimes I tell the truth and say that it just isn't up to a professional standard. But every year there are stories I regret having to turn down. I still remember a good story about an *emmasca*, and wonder if some day I'll get it back again when I have room enough to print it. But then I'd have to reject someone else's story. . . .

There seems to be no end to it. So onward—let's open the next envelope. Maybe it will be another dreadful blank-verse epic and I'll have to think up some way of telling the hapless author that I am not the right market—if there *is* one, which I doubt. But maybe it will be the next story by—well, maybe *yours*.

And maybe not. But that's the risk you take. Nobody told you not to be a plumber.

I think if I had one minute left to tell everybody everything I know about editing, that's what I'd say: "Nobody told me not to be a plumber."

And all things considered, I'm glad.

—*Marion Zimmer Bradley*

The Jackal

By Vera Nazarian

Vera Nazarian was the youngest writer ever to sell to me. I have heard of young beginners in the science fiction world, including the fourteen-year-old Con Pederson; but he never did anything as an adult. Still, in a world noted for youth (Bob Silverberg sold his first novel while still in his teens, and so did Harlan Ellison), I was, though a young beginner, not a particularly early seller. I did write my first published novel at eighteen (THE WEB OF DARKNESS), but it wasn't printed for many years after.

I have heard of many prodigies; when a teenage girl wrote A CERTAIN SMILE, a well-known literary critic quipped that girls were writing books they wouldn't have been allowed to read when he was a boy. (If true, so much the worse for him; censorship never did anyone any good. I am—as I am very well aware—the product of a large uncensored library, and so is every writer worth reading.)

What's all this got to do with Vera's story? Nothing; she's now in college and is no longer particularly young as writers go. But it gave me a good chance to sound off on a subject dear to every writer's heart; censorship, and the importance of not discouraging the young. (MZB)

"*Vai dom*, legend speaks of an old curse, a disfavor laid upon the Harksell Keep and its lord by the Dark Sisterhood of Avarra," said the man. "I strongly recommend—no, that's not the right word—I urge you, I *beseech* you reconsider this madness. Our men are too few in number, we are—"

"Your words carry no sense, Dorian," said the dark feral man whom the other had addressed as lord. "If this *gre'zuin* Ridenow is so accursed, as it is befitting such filthy spawn to be, then it is only to our advantage to attack him, even though we be few in number, as I'm well aware. I'll take him and his not only by virtue of surprise, but also by that very curse hanging over their heads."

"Oh, but *Dom* Jaqual, this curse does not discriminate. It affects, they say, anyone within sight of the Keep. And besides, you have their blood. . . ."

"Yes. Their blood. Their filthy *nedestro* blood," spat Jaqual, reclining in the single chair within the makeshift tent around which his feeble mercenary band made camp for the cold night. Jaqual called them "his army," and planned with all earnesty, curse or no, to storm Harksell, that old holding of black stones, in the Serrais lands.

High overhead, the four jewel moons were waxing full, and aligning, one against the other—an event the possibility of which happening fell but slightly outside the realm of randomness, so unusual it was in astronomical terms.

"Tell me, then, of this curse," said the lord who was no lord. Dorian, standing before him, a thin blond older man, shifted his weight from one foot to the other. As always, he was made uneasy by directly meeting the canine-yellow eyes of Jaqual mac Naella, *nedestro* son of the very same Ridenow lord whose Keep he now plotted to take for his own.

"Men say, my lord, that the one who is your father,

and whose name you forbid us to use, had sinned against Avarra. That was long before you were born, and I was very young then."

"What else did the *filth* do, besides what he'd done to my luckless mother?"

Dorian would not meet his eyes.

"Speak, Zandru strike you!"

"He—*vai dom*—he is said to have been to Avarra's place, forbidden to men—the Island of Silence, where *her* Priestesses are said to reside, they who are the Dark Sisterhood, I think. Your father had gone there, on a boyish whim, on a bet over a lost game of dice."

"Indeed. And I am Carolin Hastur of Carcosa! There has only been one man who'd ever had the insolence to trespass upon the Goddess, and that was, but recently, the king of Asturias' strange twin-paxman. Men know of this happening only because the Priestesses allowed it to be known—"

"My lord, believe me, I do not lie. Your father has done this deed, and came back to boast of it—I remember well—although little did he tell us about what he'd actually seen. Then, I was still his man. I remember he told us, half-jokingly, that he'd had a dream afterward, in which the Goddess came to him. And he somehow knew then that he *was* cursed."

The yellow eyes became slits in the handsome face framed by hair like burning coals. "You speak much, tossing empty words around, yet so far you've told me nothing of the curse itself. What is it?"

"That, I don't know. . . ."

"Yes. I can see that you really don't," whispered Jaqual after a moment, while Dorian shivered, thinking how the other could read his mind.

A smirk came to Jaqual's lips, while his eyes remained like Hellers ice. "No matter. You've alerted me to the possibility of danger, that is all. I do not fear. My hate burns deeper than any threat of woman-sent affliction." And then his smirk deepened into a grin, baring white teeth. "In fact, *I* might be that very curse personified, for by my hand *he* will fall, ere I die. Tomorrow, by the will of the Lord of Light."

The fire burned bright in the great hall of Harksell Keep. A boy whose own hair was several shades darker than the flames, sat and watched, hypnotized, how they danced fluidly, and there was a light smile on his lips. It seemed, within the flames there were tiny beings of light, whirling endlessly, dizzily, and he tried to catch their true form, fix it in his mind. . . .

"Garrik! Stop idling like that, or, like Dame Lisea says, your whole life will fly by before you even know it. Didn't I tell you Master Veynal would like to speak with you regarding that ill-done lesson?"

The boy looked up, starting, and gave an angry look to his sister Xiella Ridenow. So absorbed he'd been in the flames, that he never sensed her mental approach. He frowned. "You spoiled it, Xie. I was about to *understand* them, at long last, and you spoiled it! Zandru's ice-hells, but one second more and I would have seen—"

"I don't know what you're talking about, Garrik." Xiella cut him off sharply. "I wish you'd stop doing that." Her voice was stern, while her mental barriers hid a great worry for her brother. *Staring into the fire for hours.* . . . Lately he'd been taking this whole men-in-the-flames business too seriously. It had an unhealthy feel to it; it stank to heaven of old matrix witchery. And therefore appearing so unnatural, it seemed the more terrible.

In their family they no longer meddled in such things. Children were tested and given a matrix, but more for reasons of family honor than any desire to tamper with the unknown for the sake of gaining power.

Xiella thought of her own light-spangled blue stone

hanging around her neck. Why weren't *she* or Keithyl inclined to odd things, like Garrik, to look into flames, or other such? Was her brother somehow different from them all?

You worry too much for me. I know what I'm doing. I'll never do anything careless to hurt anyone. If all of you could just understand this. . . .

So, he'd seen through her barriers again and read her thoughts. "You! It's about time you learned that despite your abilities, it's rude to pry like that!" she said, an edge to her voice. "I should tell father on you."

"I'm sorry. I couldn't help it." Garrik looked at his sister, standing hands on hips, taller than him by a head, although he was already eleven. Everyone said that she was getting to be so pretty now, her golden hair with its red berry highlights, her great blue eyes, and slender ripening figure. Somehow he just couldn't quite see her as grown up, and to be handfasted to Piedro Ardais. Piedro had been fostered here with their older brother Keithyl, and was tall and handsome, with laughing eyes, and now he'd several times taken Garrik hunting, with the adults.

"Go and talk with Master Veynal, Garrik. I don't want to hear another word about *that*, now." She pointed nervously to the flames, "Or else I'll really tell father."

You're beginning to boss me around like an old dame!

I heard that!

"All right. Then I'll go and watch the moons in the sky. Forever! Until I petrify and die!"

"You do that and I tell father *and* mother, and you won't get any dessert for dinner, and I'll tell Piedro so that he won't—"

An angry knot was tightening in his throat. "I really

don't care!" he threw at her, and then got up, biting his lip, and ran out of the hall.

Xiella's hands fell helplessly. *Cassilda knows, I was only half-serious! Couldn't he at least pick up that much?* What had gotten into the boy? It was as if he'd been possessed by some old menace lately. And she inadvertently remembered what people said about the Harksell Ridenow, what supposedly lay upon their blood, and smiled nervously to herself. Old superstition, all.

She heard the sound of a shutter banging and came to a window to fasten it. The weather was cold for this early in the fall, and the strong wind blew chill into the great room. Outside, the night was violet, silvery-light, except for the clouds strewn across the sky, racing like dark shadows. All the moons were nearly full.

How odd, she thought, *I have never seen them to be so synchronized, or positioned thus, in such a straight line. Only Idriel, the color of sea-foam, is trailing off to the side slightly.*

And now I am behaving like Garrik. . . . She almost recoiled, averting her eyes from the enchanted and somehow sinister vision, closing the shutters tightly.

Where was everyone, at this hour? And had she no better things to do but stare out of the window?

Only her *laran* hinted with a prickling that something was not right. There was, it seemed, a taint to the air, of foreboding.

Jaqual mac Naella got his name when at the age of fifteen he'd tamed two wild jackals and kept them with him, like oddly faithful dogs, ever since, until their natural death. Before, he'd had another name, but it he chose to let go together with his childhood. It was now twenty-five winters since Rafael Ridenow had raped and beat his mother near unto death, and had left his seed in her. And Jaqual wanted, most of all, to forget. What he wouldn't give to harbor no other awareness of the time! No memories to associate with it, not even the name his mother gave him. One thing he wanted only, and that was hate, to bear hate toward his father the Lord Ridenow and toward the whole filthy clan. Hate had driven him thus, helping him to live each minute, to become a fierce mercenary soldier, and to rally men to his cause.

"I shall be Lord Ridenow!" he told them, and they believed, seeing how, normally, despite all odds, all he ever attempted came to pass. Jaqual's men were all equally desperate, seasoned by years of sorrow and deprivation, yet all knew that this particular cause was as hopelessly impossible as if conceived by someone straight out of a Ghost Wind. Nevertheless, being aware of this, they remained loyal, out of love for this man. Jaqual, bitter and driven, was always good to them, fair when it came to arguments and dividing things, like a *bredu*, almost.

Jaqual sat sleepless in his tent that night, listening to the wind outside, feeling the chill drafts come in, and thought, *He sits before his fire, sleeps in a warm bed with a woman next to him who should have been my mother. The whimpering whey-faced* gre'zuin *had tortured Naella, beat her senseless. And when later the unfortunate bitch whelped me, she died like a beast of the gutter, only having given me a name. I want no name of her choosing. I bear her own only to remind me of my revenge, long overdue. They had borne me into the world which never wanted me. And I never wanted even their love, anything of theirs. . . .*

He cringed, for a moment feeling an old pain of a wound so very near his heart. He didn't even clearly remember how he got it, there were so many others. A close miss, that one. And always it would plague him with the changing weather.

He was so scarred. So scarred was Jaqual mac Naella, for one so young in years. Indeed, there was no curse upon all of Darkover that might wreak any greater harm on him.

Dom Rafael Ridenow glanced only once at the glamour-filled night outside his window, before having the shutters closed. "Oh, Arielle, something lies heavy on my heart," he said to his wife, coming to lie beside her under the soft warm coverlets and furs.

"Peace, beloved," she smiled, and he saw the warm love in her eyes just before the candle had gone out. "It's but the wind. I sense it, like an old friend. All the way from the Hellers it must come." And she gave a soft laugh in the dark. "Probably looking for me, on my father's bidding."

She had always said this to him in consolation, did this no longer young, gentle-eyed woman who had Aldaran blood in her. Once from beyond the Kadarin, plain folk claimed, it never lets you go. And Arielle had never forgotten, having come here against the will of her kinfolk who were in a quarrel with the other Comyn—but that is another story.

I don't know what is bothering me. It's more than something in the chill wind.

Her thoughts in response were like warm caresses. Even after so many years of marriage, and three children, their love remained firm, had even deepened.

"You have no reason to be upset, dearest." she whispered, "You must be simply tired. And worries you have, many worries for the well-being of our children, the estate."

A moment of silence, and then he laughed, weary indeed. "Even the moons, Arielle, appear odd. Have you looked outside, tonight? It's as if they're lining up for a ring-dance, and their faces are all full!"

"And you fear that portends something? Rafael,

I've seen odder sights in the Hellers, when I was a little girl, believe me. Indeed, I think the sight is lovely."

She paused, seeing him in her mind's eye the way she had always seen him—a dark-haired, graying, thin man with such kind deep eyes that they wrenched her soul with his utmost understanding of her. So deep they were, she thought, holding some sad secrets of the past. And she felt, as always, such tenderness, that she wanted to rip the worry out of him, the eternal sadness, stamp it out, then soothe him, love him. . . .

In answer, he embraced her tightly, and said, changing the subject: "It makes me more happy than anything to see Xiella and Piedro together. I love him like my own son."

"Yes, and our daughter has grown. So hard to believe that only a while ago I held her in swaddling clothes!"

"And tomorrow, she is to be handfasted. Sweet Evanda, how time flies."

They lay for a while, listening to the wind, then *Dom* Rafael, sleepless, murmured: "Maybe it's the thought of Garrik that bothers me so. The boy is too sensitive. I believe he's coming to be more fully aware of his *laran* now, and that gives rise to those moods of his. The way he looks at things, stares so."

Arielle sighed. "I noticed that he holds a strange fascination for fire. He told me only the other day that there are little men dancing in the flames. How is one to take that? And Xiella and Sabrynne both complained about this oddity. Master Veynal says Garrik ignores his lessons, daydreams—"

"Now that is odd indeed. I remember Veynal told me what an excellent student he'd found in Garrik, how he is so eager to learn, always so inquisitive."

"Rafael. I know you don't like it when I speak of this, but this time, I think you should hear me out."

Dom Rafael knew what this was leading up to.

"I think you should really, seriously, consider my brother-in-law Kyril's offer. He was first to notice Garrik's inclinations, even before we thought anything of it. He should know, being a technician at Dalereuth Tower. Besides, I think Garrik would find it fascinating at Dalereuth, enough to supply himself with adequate patience to learn the proper skills. It's being ignorant of these skills, that makes him so soul-sick now."

Dom Rafael sighed heavily. "Garrik has shown no signs of the empathy which runs in my line."

"Yet he is a telepath! He picks up thoughts, already well enough to make us keep our barriers shut tight around him. He needs to be taught, Rafael, you know that!"

"He is still a boy. He knows nothing of—"

"He knows enough! Please, my husband, your son is grown enough to be well aware of what he's doing. And now he must be taught not only control, but *laran* courtesy. Besides, I suspect that he might have something of *my* heritage, not of the Ridenow."

"Arielle . . . eventually I might allow him to go to Dalereuth, but not yet. Give him two years at least."

"But can't you see that even *now*, he's going through some *laran*-related phase? Let him be examined, at least, by a professional."

"*No.* Arielle, not yet. Let us end this useless talk, it is late. I am tired and—I still sense some foreboding."

"But—oh, Rafael, Rafael." She grew silent then, closed her eyes. *I wish you would only see!*

He moved closer to her, under the warm covers, and she huddled against him. She knew that gesture was the only manner of asking for pardon that she'd get from the proud Ridenow. Yet he *knew* how she felt; his empathy was so strong for her, that he inadvertently asked her forgiveness with his touch, sensing, if not being actually aware with the mind, that he was in the wrong.

That feeling. As if we are imminently to be attacked.

"By what?" Arielle replied with startled words, as again she was disturbed from the warmth of their embrace, by his unrest. "Surely there's no one that might attack us, that's ridiculous! Why? *Why* would anyone want to attack us? You are overexcited—"

And then, she could almost imagine the sardonic curve of his lips, as his unspoken thought trailed off: *You, who do not have Ridenow blood, cannot understand. Not even now, not ever, is there peace for me. I feel it! This place, the Harksell Keep, is cursed, in truth.*

And then Arielle, lady of Harksell, knew fear.

Jaqual was a man eaten by memories. The empathy passed on to him by his hateful sacrilegious father (whose own *laran* was infinitely weaker than that of his son) forced him to relive, over and over, endlessly, the scenario of his mother's rape, and then, his tortured birth which almost killed her. Those were *her* memories, imprinted upon him, so that he could have no peace, ever, lived through her torture with all its exact intensity, knew her hate for *Dom* Rafael, and built upon it his own hate. And then he knew her own helpless hate for him, the unwanted child of rape, knew how she wanted to tear him out of her swollen belly prematurely, had even wanted to use the women's herb that causes miscarriage. She had screamed with the pain of birthing him, and had unconsciously forced it, all of it, including her former pain, upon his sensitive empathetic mind, in that instant of entry into the world.

Jaqual remembered—for he *was*, then, Naella—the lewd advances of her lord. She, Naella, was but a serving wench, and the Harksell Keep's young lord had laid his eyes on her buxom fine figure and desired her immediately. Known for his heavy-handedness, because he had so little of the Ridenow gift, so weakly developed, and even less tact, he had from the start frightened Naella. Soon she found herself having to hide in the women's quarters, when not at her chores, so as to avoid him. But one night, drunk after some minor military victory (for those were hard times), he sought her out and forced her, and when she struggled in terror, he beat her with his razor-sharp whip, until bloody skin peeled off her back, and her throat was hoarse with screaming. And when they found later, that she had conceived, Naella was named a whore and thrown out. Before Jaqual was born, Naella had been, for months, a tattered beggar, going from village to village in Serrais lands.

Her beautiful hair, full and dark as the eyes of a chervine, had gone lanky, while her yellow-golden eyes, like the goldenflower, had become bleak and empty of reason. Jaqual had inherited those eyes, and his somehow always carried in them that hidden pain, only turned fierce and wild and proud.

Pain, pain . . . Searing mental pain. Not only was it a physical pain that Naella had felt, but there was also an unspeakable terror of being mauled to death, and a destroyed self-respect (for he forced her to see herself less than a woman, subhuman).

Mad banshee bitch! Dirt! Over and over had Rafael Ridenow hoarsely thrown at her these epithets and endless worse others, all from the gutter. There were many she did not understand, but could sense the meaning of, by the waves of gloating fury which came from him. It had all lasted for an hour, no more, but had felt to her like an eternity, a million bloody sunsets, and the sun had set, over and over, in a sea of her own lifeblood. . . .

Jaqual heard it all in his brain, felt the blows descending upon his weeping body, the tearing, the fire-agony in his loins. . . . And tears rolled silently from his eyes. Always, tears came when he was alone.

And as the hoarse voice continued pounding in his mind, his hate grew, eternally, until he burned like all Zandru's hells, wanting to tear his father apart with his two bare hands.

And then, there were his own memories. Jaqual remembered, from the eyes of a small boy, his mother dying, swollen from malady and hunger, and leaving him alone. That in itself constituted an unspeakable fear, for he was a child, and had no one, and was starving. Jaqual had then to become a man prematurely, or die. . . .

With difficulty he shut off the flood of *memories*, for several minutes. Here, in the coolness of the rational night, reality came to him again. For his own sake, for the sake of his inner peace, he had to destroy that man. Really, he could no longer even help it. It had been "inbred" in him now, stronger than any *laran*, a geas. His mind's protective mechanism was at work.

Yet something human, some deeply buried awareness, made Jaqual pause, wanting to understand Lord Ridenow, to actually *understand* his father.

Jaqual knew that what he'd planned was hopeless. All along he had been so harsh, so cool and confident with his men, when telling them of his plans, yet that in itself was unfair. He had been closing his eyes to the facts. Jaqual knew that to force his ragged band of mercenaries to storm the nearly impenetrable Keep would amount to nothing except their deaths. Truly, the act of an obsessed madman. Harksell was well fortified, and even his hardened men—were there thrice as many—were no match for its defences. If only they had *clingfire*. . . .

Oh, but I am mad. What I plan is suicide, and to be fair to my soldiers and my honor as a man, I should

*attempt this thing alone. To kill my father is my only
hope and desire. I want nothing of this Keep. It would
only be taking his curse upon myself. And I am cursed,
as it is. . . .*

And then a new thought came to him. Those he'd
recently sent to spy on the Ridenow, had returned to
tell of the approaching feast day where a handfasting
was to be held. The *Dom* himself will be present,
surely, and so would a crowd of other people. When
else would a better opportunity arise to slip in unnoticed among the crowd of kinfolk, and to plunge a
good knife in the black heart?

*Tomorrow is their day of joy. And on the morrow I
had planned to strike. It is fated then, since this opportunity falls to me, that I take it. I shall venture alone,
leaving orders for my men to wait until midnight. If I
do not come back, they shall leave this hateful land, to
disperse and seek another leader and cause to rally
under. I will not make my hopeless revenge their sure
death. My brothers, my loyal only brother jackals.
Long have we fought in the same pack. . . .*

*They say my half sister is beautiful, the one who will
be handfasted. And my half brothers are strong and fine
of face. I know so much about them . . . I hate them
yet bear a strange interest toward them, like my own
flesh.*

*Yet they don't even suspect my existence. And why
should they? Pups whelped of a self-satisfied dog. He
would never tell now, not anyone, what dark secrets his
youth held.*

*Avarra, Dark Mother, help me destroy him! Help me
vanquish him who had committed the sacrilege, to ef-
face whatever evil he had wrought, to you and yours,
and to myself.*

And later, when dawn painted the sky deep lavender, Dorian the right-hand man, watched—outwardly
restrained, but his heart bleeding, after having heard

his instructions—the silent leave-taking of the young jackal. In the end, just as the older man thought he would, knowing his just nature, he had heeded Dorian's early words only too well. Jaqual left them now, in all fairness, with their own peace, while he went to settle his own quarrel. Whether he would come back or not. Dorian had no *laran*, yet he knew somehow, hating and fearing, and in a way loving him, that this one's was now a road apart.

So many kin had come to Harksell in the middle of Serrais land—other Ridenow and Serrais, the Ardais, to see Piedro handfasted, and several other Hastur-kin. Early evening it was, and the dark Keep of black stones blazed with lights of festival night. The sun of blood had sunk like a stone beyond the horizon, and the four chill faces of the full moons lined up over-head, to witness.

Dom Rafael, lord of Harksell, in his House colors, greeted his guests with a smile on the lips, and a secret heaviness in his heart. At his right hand stood Keithyl, his son and heir, tall and strong-limbed, and as well-formed as a true son of Ridenow. His hair, like fire-gold, put the lights to shame, and his blue eyes, they said, were never forgotten by a maid since first he'd meet her glance.

Next to him, Piedro Ardais, whose eyes never stopped throwing sparks, a laughter waiting to burst out, wore the colors of his House. And it seemed the colors did not suit the brightness of him, just as his own dark hair and swarthy complexion appeared in odd contrast to his ready smile. Rarely was there a happier bridegroom.

"Stop smirking, *bredu*, or your teeth'll fall out." Keithyl winked at his foster brother. "They say it's bad luck to be too happy at your own handfasting, else the wedding will give you tears."

Piedro shook his head, grinning, and half-whispered,

in a like tone: "Wait till it's *your* turn, brother. You just wait." His glance meanwhile, searched the hall for signs of his betrothed.

Garrik came running, his pale face having more color in it than usual, his eyes sparkling. "Piedro, Xie looks beautiful! She's wearing—but never mind, I'm not supposed to tell yet. You'll see for yourself. She told me to—to—" Here he paused, blushing in embarrassment for his sister, as Piedro picked up.

"Told you what? How about giving Piedro a kiss from her? Delivered by such a pretty *damisela* as you, why, he wouldn't mind a bit it's not Xie herself!" teased Keithyl.

"Shut up!" Garrik's eyes flared in real anger at his older brother, remembering how, when he was little, they used to say he was as pretty as a girl. "Don't you ever call me that again!"

Easy, bredu . . . came Piedro's mind-touch to Keithyl, *you are being too hard on him. Remember, he's not been himself lately. No jokes like that.*

"All right, *chiyu*, don't mind me. Look now, are you all right?" Keithyl grew serious for a moment, looking with concern at the boy.

"Don't call me *chiyu*, either," said Garrik sadly, sullenly. "I'm not a child." And then, gathering his dignity, and still angry at his brother, he said stonily to Piedro: "Xie told me to give you her love. That's all."

"Thank you, *bredu*," said Piedro seriously to the boy, with such tact that Keithyl, usually the more sedate of the two, stared at him. And then his eyes warmed. "I'll take her love with all my soul, and if you see her again before I do, give her mine own, in return." And then he winked. "Now go, have a honeycake! You deserve it for the hard work of running messages between me and my Xie."

Smiling again with sadness, Garrik nodded and moved away. *Have a honey-cake. Even Piedro still takes me for a babe.* The light of the nearby torch momentarily caught his eye, and he paused, fascinated.

Across the hall, Sabrynne, cousin of Piedro, stood next to some older womenfolk, and looked with enchantment in her eyes, about her, at the dancing kinfolk, the lights, the finery. She was being fostered here like Piedro had been, with girls of the household. Sabrynne, a thin pale twelve year old with introspective eyes, had only now helped Xiella, her foster-sister, dress, and now dreamed of her own glittering wedding in the future. She was only a budding girl, naïve, yet dreams as such were not alien to her imagination. She thought of some handsome, kind-eyed stranger, who would come and sweep her away to his castle, a mighty young lord, like in those ancient tales. . . .

Across the room, she suddenly met the gaze of two golden intense eyes. She did not even realize the strangeness of their gaze, but met them honestly with her childish blue ones. The eyes, never blinking, followed her, and there was in them something so ardent, so burning, an emotion Sabrynne had never even known. And because the nature of the look fascinated her, she noticed the rest of him. A tall dark man—so dark that he was like a bit of the night torn out and dislocated to be here, in the midst of the bright-lit hall—stood some space away from her, wearing clothing that struck her as odd somehow, not belonging to the festival night. And he himself, hawklike, seemed both to stand out and drown in the crowd, a paradox. There was something so fierce about him. . . .

Impulsively she pulled at the sleeve of the nearest woman, an odd thrilling fear gripping her, and asked, pointing: "Who is that man, Milda?"

The woman looked as directed, squinted, then said, "Nonsense, child, what man? There's only old dames I see."

"No, over there, next to the green-clad *dom* and his lady, in violet—"

"There's no one there, *chiya*!"

"But Milda, you are blind, truly! Over there, the one in the dark clothes—"

"Oh, stop it, girl. I can't see anyone like you're describing. Go instead, make yourself useful, don't gawk at strangers."

And indeed, when next she looked, Sabrynne found him not there.

Dom Rafael spoke with Piedro's kinfolk, but never did the load on his heart lighten. *Something must happen. Tonight.*

Keithyl took one drink from a tray being carried around, and proposed a toast: "To Ardais and Ridenow!" he exclaimed loudly, while smiles and the clinking of glasses filled the hall.

And then came a hush, and all dancing stopped, for the bride came into the room, escorted by her women. Xiella wore a radiant gown of lavender, like the dawn had been that morning. Yet Piedro never saw the color of it, for he was looking at her face.

In that instant, Keithyl at his side, looking at the loveliness of his sister, almost felt a prickling of some foreboding, and held his breath superstitiously. She was simply too beautiful. . . .

In the far corner of the hall, where the musicians sat, Garrik peeked from behind a column, his mind in a daze, flames whirling in his vision, both outer and inner. He was only half-aware at that moment, of his sister's entrance.

Dom Rafael watched his daughter approach, but on a different level he shivered, for two golden eyes had seen him, and he was suddenly aware. . . .

And he continued being thus aware as he put together the hands of his daughter and his foster-son, and blessed them, in the name of the gods.

And then, when officially they were made a handfasted couple, and the music resumed all around, *Dom* Rafael had no strength in him to dance, not even as custom decreed, with his daughter. His limbs felt like lead, and he was weak, oh so weak. . . .

"Go dance with your Piedro, *chiya*. You must forgive me now, I feel tired all of a sudden. I promise you a dance, later."

"You are ill, father?" the bride whispered, her smile leaving her. Indeed, despite the happiness, her mind had lain uneasy the whole night.

"No, my dear, just tired. Go, now." He smiled in reassurance, yet she somehow knew he was worse than he claimed. But Piedro whirled her away before she could say another word.

"I must've had too much to drink, so early in the night. I am sick already," came from a few feet away, as some near cousin of the Harksell Ridenow complained loudly. "What else would weigh me so?"

Sabrynne looked up at the man with yellow eyes. "What is your name, sir?" She was no longer afraid of him, of his odd manner, or his darkness. There was a smile both on her lips and in her eyes, as she met his, innocently.

For a long moment he said nothing, and she was beginning to fear again, momentarily. The golden eyes were so piercing, so burning. She almost felt he disliked her for some reason, or why else would he stare so? And there was pain in him, deep, she was beginning to realize. If only she could look deeper into those eyes, maybe she would know. . . .

"Change partners now, Piedro! For shame, you've been dancing with my sister all night! What of the other young men who want some of the bride's luck? At least let her own brother have a go, will you now?" said Keithyl, laughing, and snatched Xiella away from her betrothed.

"I'll get you for that! Why so spunky all of a sudden?" But the two were dancing out of hearing range.

Domna Arielle went to sit with the women, breathless from the last dance with a relative she couldn't politely refuse. *How worn out he looks*, she thought, watching her husband from where she sat. *Something worries me now . . . something he said.* And then it was as if her own Aldaran gift stirred in her, and she saw that *something. . . .*

Dom Rafael felt a prickling down his back, and knew *someone* was approaching him. And to escape this, he quickly walked across the room, making an excuse that he needed to talk with a distant cousin on the other side.

"Are you all right, Garrik, my boy?" asked Darryl, the old *coridom*, as he passed the youngster hiding in the shadows of a corner, near a balcony. The old man neared, grinning. "Had, by any chance, too much of the stronger stuff, eh? That which you're not supposed to have at all, boy?"

"No, sir." came a faint cold voice, and Darryl knew the other did not lie.

He frowned. "Maybe you should get to bed, then? 'Tis getting too late for one your age, almost midnight—"

"No! Please, Darryl, I'm just getting a breath of air from the balcony here. It's so hot inside."

"If you're sure—then all right. But careful now. Get to bed soon, you hear?"

"Yes, sir."

And then Xiella found herself dancing with a man whose eyes were golden like the *kireseth* flower. He was dark, and there was something at the same time fierce and ethereal about him, like the night. Staring into his eyes, ensorcelled, she whispered, "Who are you?"

And at first he did not answer her, only looked, with a fierce longing of some inexplicable thing. Xiella felt herself melting suddenly. The awareness, spreading through every cell of her body, was of him only, in a way that only a woman who had known desire, could be aware. Yet she was virgin.

All thoughts, tenderness, infatuation with Piedro, flew out of her head, were gone, like the wind. Truly, in those moments she forgot Piedro's very existence. "Are you—a kinsman?" she whispered, trembling, as his hand came to lie at her waist, whirling her in the dance. Its pressure dizzied her, clouded her thoughts.

"I am—a kinsman . . ." came his voice for the first time, like an echo, low and intimate, and sweet like agony.

Yes, agony, pain can be sweet . . . it occurred to her in the madness of those moments.

"Oh, I am so hot!" she exclaimed then, unable to bear his gaze, "take me to the balcony, *kinsman*. I need some air to breathe—so hot here, suddenly."

His mouth—so feral, she realized—curved suddenly into something of a smile.

"Yes." he said, "Come."

"No!"

They turned, to see *Dom* Rafael standing before them. Never had Xiella seen her father's eyes flash so, nor felt such a stirring of *laran* all about them. Yet she was englamored by the golden-eyed man, and all this impressed her only as a second thought.

"No," repeated *Dom* Rafael, while the dark one was impassive, regarding him. "Let my daughter go, whoever you are! I have sensed trouble for a long time now, and it drove me mad with worry. But now I know—it signified you. What do you want, to come and disrupt my daughter's handfasting? *Who* are you? What evil is it I sense?"

Silence. The wind was audible, howling from the outside, so silent became the hall. There was a glamour on all of them.

And then, a voice, like a whisper, came inside his head. *True. It is only you I want. Only* you *I have come to destroy. . . . Fiend from hell, you shall die!*

Why? Who are you?

I am Jaqual.

And then the dark stranger moved, pulling the nearly limp girl close to him, and whispering. "You! You who are of my blood, my sister, look into my eyes. Look within me! Before I kill him who fathered us both!"

And as she looked with her soul, falling into the strange absolute rapport that only two of the Ridenow blood can accomplish, merging, becoming the other, Xiella *saw* what he held in him. And seeing, she gave a bloodcurdling scream, and went into a dead faint.

With odd gentleness, Jaqual lowered her to the floor, then stood and faced *Dom* Rafael.

"And now," he said, his voice like fate and the wind, "it is only fitting that you see also, what you have wrought."

And before *Dom* Rafael's maddened eyes could blink, a wave of searing absolute mental and physical pain came over him, and he saw and felt and remembered all the terror that he had done. . . .

With an effort, he wrenched his mind away, and then his body doubled over in pain. "What . . ." he began, "what are you? You are no man. What nightmare is this?"

But Jaqual said nothing, only slowly took out a dark slender glinting knife from his belt, and neared the man whom he knew to be his father.

And now *Dom* Rafael was under the glamour also, unable to move, only his thoughts, still reeling from the *agony*, raced wildly. *Is this Avarra's curse then, the one my great-grandfather brought upon Harksell? Oh, merciful Avarra. . . . He is—*

A weak childish scream, the only sound except for the wind, interrupted the falling of the knife.

Jaqual! No! came the mind-cry of Sabrynne, *you are mistaken, Jaqual! This is not the one whom you seek to kill! No!*

And as he, only an instant ago relentless, turned to her with a strange look coming to the pained golden eyes, she went on, her *laran* crying to him, while physically she sobbed, convulsing, sobbed with pity for *him* and with absolute empathy, without being Ridenow—for Sabrynne had shared *his* rapport with Xiella.

In a matter of instants, the little girl had matured into an adult woman. There was a stamp of wisdom and agony on the thin, no longer young face.

No, Jaqual mac Naella, do not strike this man, she went on, *he is not the same Dom Rafael that you so justly hate. The one you seek died—more than a hundred years ago. . . .*

He died, Jaqual, by your hand. But his paxman struck you down also. Look at the wound in your heart, the one that always pains you so—it is real, not a miss! You are dead, Jaqual! You have been dead for almost two centuries!

And as the blue eyes of the girl met the suddenly stricken golden ones, she continued, only softly, gently, her thoughts caressing. *Oh, Jaqual, poor Jaqual. How I wish I could take your pain for my own, your lonely awful pain. . . . Oh, I love you, my poor Jaqual. Peace! Go from hence, this is no longer your place! Have peace, unfortunate one!*

And in that instant of truth, the entity once called Jaqual mac Naella remembered everything. He remembered how those long ages ago he'd stolen alone into the Harksell Keep on the festival night when his father's daughter was being handfasted, how, sparing his own men, he alone sought Rafael Ridenow out among the crowd. . . . Their searing, screaming mo-

ment of rapport. . . . The knife that he twisted and
tore through the flesh of his hateful father, and in a
moment of inadvertent empathy, felt *his* death pain.

And then, among the whirling tumult of the tragedy-
broken festival night, a guardsman's face loomed before him, as he was torn away, too dazed with mind-pain
from the rapport with the still twitching body, and a
different knife was plunged into his own heart—

Somewhere, a bell struck midnight. And thrice there
came the calling of crows. As the ghost of Jaqual
began to fade, slowly, the pained consciousness shim-
mering and fleeing deeper into the long-sought peace
of the overworld—at last—people all about the hall of
Harksell Keep were given an instant of *sight*. Many
thought later, that in the dream they saw the face of
her who is Avarra, and a new sadness was in the
unknown eyes of the Goddess.

"She never meant to curse *him!*" sobbed the woman-
child Sabrynne, breaking the dreamlike silence, for his
golden eyes had met hers last of all, softening, with a
new longing upon them, just before his complete ef-
facing into the mercy of Avarra, "I know it, she spoke
to me! There had been no curse upon Harksell! Never
had *Dom* Rafael Ridenow of long ago even set foot on
the ancient Island of Silence, it had been a lie he'd
fabricated out of his own insecurity and false pride.
But he had been cursed in another way, later, when he
had violated with such animal-evil the woman Naella.
Avarra would never stand such a crime against her
own. Thus, the first Rafael Ridenow was meant to die
by his son's hand.

"Only Jaqual was oversensitive, as if compensating
for his father who barely had a smattering of *laran*,
much less compassion. Having borne his mother's pain
all his life, he then easily 'took upon himself' not only
his father's death-pain, but also his *guilt*. Guilt for
everything that confused evil man, his father, had ever

done. And being triple-burdened thus, for his parents and for himself, Jaqual's consciousness virtually fractured, and he became three people at once."

Dom Rafael finally found himself able to speak again. "No wonder the poor soul could not leave this place," he whispered, as others began nearing him. "His mind was too confused to know that he had died, too obsessed with the pain. And there was no *leronis* around to help him know better, to free him to go his proper way."

Dom Rafael moved quickly to Xiella's side, who was in a faint, on the floor. "Quickly," he said to those nearest, "get the *leronis* Valdia, my cousin, here!" And he added, to all in general: "The three of us have been touched by the terror, we need to be examined."

Not just touched, he thought, *we could have died. I would have died, at least, under the knife, which although immaterial in one sense, was wrought of his concentrated psi energy of hate, and would have been just as lethal. His will had given him a kind of material body. . . .*

And then the last adrenaline left him, and he collapsed from weakness, to sit on the floor next to his senseless daughter.

Sabrynne, half-faint herself, was held by *Domna* Arielle, and her hysterics would not cease. "Jaqual!" she continued to cry out, so piteously that Arielle wept with her, "Jaqual, I love you, if no one else, then I love you! Oh, Jaqual!"

"Get the *leronis*, quickly!" someone said then, "Hush, dear child."

We are cursed then, nevertheless, thought *Dom* Rafael weakly, *if only by that which just took place here. And if Jaqual has finally found peace, then there's still the guilt, that general human guilt, for everything, to lie on someone's heart, on all of our hearts.*

Avarra is kind and merciful. That poor disembodied

soul's plight was not the work of her will, but man's wrongdoing coming back on itself. The law of cause and effect.

In that moment Xiella came to her senses in Piedro's arms, and screamed in terror of her father. *She* still was under the same delusion that the ghost had shown her, thinking her father a murderer.

Valdia, the redheaded older woman *leronis*, arrived at last, took out her matrix, beginning her ministering on them.

This will take quite some time now, thought *Dom* Rafael, as he slowly eased under Valdia's probing. *We shall be scarred, for a long time. . . .*

And for a ridiculous irrelevant instant, he thought for some reason of the four full moons outside, and how odd a thing it was to see them thus, and how, after all, they had portended nothing.

"Lord of Light, where's Garrik?" Keithyl remembered suddenly. "I haven't seen the boy. Something might've happened—"

Domna Arielle gasped in worry, and in a rush men were sent to look for the youngster. They found Garrik after a quick search. He had been sitting straight as a statue in a chair, in one of the outer rooms, in a kind of *laran* trance, his gaze focused upon a brightly burning fireplace.

"Don't touch him!" cried Keithyl to the surrounding men. He then took out his own matrix stone, concentrated into it, and called inwardly, *Come back, brother. Please, Garrik!*

As if plucked from somewhere far away, the awareness returned, the slight body started, then an expression came to the boy's eyes.

"Oh, thank the gods, *bredu*, you're all right," exclaimed Keithyl, "Come, this has gone far enough, we'll get you to the *leronis* so she could see what—"

"What—happened?" whispered Garrik, seeing so many around him, "Has the ghost left us at last?"

Keithyl frowned. "You—*knew* about that?"

"I knew all along. I just didn't know how to tell father. Especially seeing that all of you think me a child. I've *known* this would happen, for almost a fortnight now. And many other things."

"Then why didn't you *say* so—"

"Because," said Garrik, stopping his brother's rising, angry words, "it was meant to be. For things to happen that way was, surely, the best. Besides, no one would've believed me *then*."

"And now," spoke Keithyl, looking with new awe at his younger brother's sad composed face, seeing something there that wasn't there before, "now what?"

Suddenly startled, he remembered, "What of those little men in the flames, Garrik? Are they real then, also? Are they?"

A sad, wise smile came to the boy's lips. "No, brother," he said softly, after a pause, "that was but my threshold sickness, the way it manifested in me."

"Threshold sickness! And we had no idea!"

They were interrupted when *Domna* Arielle, followed by the *leronis*, came in.

"Are they all right, mother?" said Keithyl quickly, thinking of the others in the hall.

"Yes, for now," she nodded, thinking, *Gods grant. . . .*

"I am fine also," said Garrik, rising somewhat stiffly, and looking into his mother's eyes.

"We'll see about that," said Valdia. "But at least you can walk, which is more than I could say for the others. Come along then, boy, I must check you."

"I knew you'd have the Aldaran Gift," said his mother, taking him into her arms, her voice trembling with the overload of emotions for that evening.

"Come, Garrik!" said the *leronis*.

Garrik threw one last glance around the room, then

suddenly gave a light smile and said, "You probably don't know it, but I know it, that father will now let me go to Dalereuth. In fact—"

"Hush now, come along," came Valdia's kind voice, and he did not need to read mentally, but saw in her eyes, that she hoped he'd not say any more.

And as Garrik turned to go after her, his eyes caught the glint of the flames in the fireplace, and he remembered that *something* in it that he'd seen.

And Garrik shivered with a moment of horror, thinking, *Yes, I have been wise not to say anything. I am learning already. Most of the time it is best not to tell others what I know with my Gift, in order to spare them the many horrors, the pain, not to burden them. . . . After all, what comes to pass should come to pass.*

Somewhere high overhead, the four moons of Darkover had reached the apex of their incidental alignment, and waning, began to swing along their own destined paths. Almost, it seemed Avarra's laughter could be heard to hang in their wake—if such were the Goddess.

But since she isn't, all is well, thought Garrik, thinking far ahead to his life, and to the so many endless wonderful things—

But not too far. In the back of his mind, hidden deep under the self-protective layering of *laran*, where lay the things that the mind chose to forget, Garrik knew the horrible shadow that was real and that he'd seen in the flames, the one which would spring up to plague the generations to come. . . .

For burning deep, behind the golden-red face of the flames, he had seen the horror that was to be Sharra.

Death's Scepter

By Joan Marie Verba

Joan Marie Verba is no stranger to these anthologies; her first story for us was in FREE AMAZONS OF DARKOVER. This story arrived too late for us in the last of these anthologies—RED SUN OF DARKOVER— and I could not find room for it. I told her, however, that it was worth resubmitting for the next of them.

I am sure it has happened many times on Darkover that brothers, especially twins, should be rivals; and I am a sucker for stories which deal with this as an idea; perhaps because my last attempt to deal with this idea did not come off too well. Of course I have, and had, a good excuse; I started it when I was busy with something else, and was interrupted too often for a good story. But it was (and is) a good idea; twins separated in childhood but remaining in close telepathic contact. This idea is not new; it was used by Alexandre Dumas for THE CORSICAN BROTHERS; but it still strikes me as a very Darkovan idea, and some day I'll do it.

Meanwhile, I like this one. (MZB)

Regis Hastur, *tenerezu* of the old Comyn Castle Tower, looked at his younger brother, King Stefan, with kindly concern. Sitting on an upholstered chair opposite him in the visitor's room, Stefan could not meet his eyes. Both strongly *laran*-gifted, Regis could not help but catch Stefan's thought: The gods help me, I may have to kill you, *bredu*.

Immediately, Stefan lifted his head, so that Regis could see his gray eyes. "I didn't really mean that."

"I know." Regis' gaze strayed to the hilt of Stefan's knife. Emblazoned on it was the Hastur crest with the crown above it. Most thought that was Stefan's own knife; only Stefan and Regis knew that they had exchanged knives, taken the oath of *bredin*, when Regis was heir-designate of Hastur, and that the crest had been his, then, as crown prince. In a world of kin-strife and blood feud, it was unusual for sons of the same parents to be so close in affection that they would bind themselves to a pledge of mutual protection.

Stefan sighed. "I was beginning to think, at the end of the last council season, that they were starting to accept me at last as the rightful king, not as someone who usurped the throne from my older brother, the one with the Hastur Gift."

"Are you telling me that your healing Belhar Ardais of that mortal wound was not sufficient to impress them? Shall I sit in council again and tell them once more I forfeited the crown of my own free will?"

Stefan shook his head. "It is no use, *bredu*. Any demonstration of *laran* skill seems to satisfy them only as long as the memory is fresh. When that begins to fade, it pales against the stories of grandfather Rafael IV and the spell sword, or great-great-grandfather Carolin of Hali and his confiscation of so many wild matrixes when he enforced the Compact, or our more distant ancestors wielding the *laran* weapons in the Hastur rebellion. I tell you, without the Hastur Gift, I think sometimes I could impress them only if I passed the two veils at Hali and took up the Sword of Aldones myself!"

Regis smiled. "I have to remind you, *bredu*," he

said softly, "that to manage the Sword of Aldones you would have to have the Hastur Gift."

Stefan nodded. "I have had thoughts, on occasion, of going to Castle Hastur for the Sword of Hastur, except unless an affair involves the honor of the Hasturs, I would be known henceforth as Stefan One-hand."

"Perhaps I should look into the matter to see if the honor of the Hasturs is at stake on questions of the succession."

"Would that it was!"

Regis thought for a moment. "The council season is just beginning . . . what is it this time? Are the independent fiefdoms putting up a fight again?"

"No, at least, not at present. It's beginning to look like we may eventually be a kingdom of Seven Domains instead of many little territories. Lord Serrais managed to settle with a few more on his borders during the winter. In fact, it's the Leyniers' and Lanarts' struggle for the Alton domain that's the biggest threat at the moment, but for now they're behaving themselves."

"Then it must be the Compact."

Stefan settled back in his chair. "Sometimes I wonder if great-great-grandfather Carolin did us a favor. On one hand, it's clear that the large matrix weapons are forbidden under the Compact, which is good . . . and everyone can agree that swords and knives are allowable. But there are a lot of cases in between, like last season when we argued whether longbows were allowable. And what did Callista of Arilinn bring up the first day of council season but the question of whether the Compact allowed healing outside a Tower."

"What *could* have made her think of that?"

"She challenged my competence to judge such a matter. I, who worked in a Tower six years prior to Father's death."

"You could have been *tenerezu*, if you hadn't been crowned, and she well knows it."

". . . and then, it started all over again. Council split, not on the merits of the issue, but by who in council considers me to be the rightful king and who considers me a usurper."

"You know I will help you in any way I can, majesty."

"I know. I know." He rose from the chair. "In truth, I didn't come for advice, but for a sympathetic listener. Thank you, *bredu*."

Regis followed him to the door. As he walked away, Regis again sensed the anguished thought: *Will I have to kill you, bredu, in order to keep my throne?*

Regis plodded down the hallway, to the room where the matrix screen was. The keeper of the second circle, Gabriela Lanart, would come soon. They would bring Alastair Aillard through to be the new Keeper of the first circle of the new Tower at Comyn Castle. Gabriela had the Alton Gift; she was one of the growing number of women who served as Keepers in the Towers. One day, Regis suspected, most Keepers would be women. For one thing, it had been found that women had more positive energon flows—and they could hold them longer; for another, it was one of the few occupations outside the home open to women.

Regis smiled to himself. Just as there were few occupations open to the eldest son of the Hastur king, he thought.

He leaned back against the wall, smoothing his red mustache. At thirty-two, he thought that he had made the correct moral choice. He did not have the skill to rule, did not have the instinct to know when to leave things alone and when to assert authority, as his brother had. Regis was convinced that no other king could have ruled five years with the contention in Comyn Council, without the extraordinary political acumen that Stefan had. Then again, if Regis had been crowned, there would not be as much friction as now. It had briefly occurred to him that he might have done as well if he had been crowned, naming Stefan his chief adviser. Many rulers before had managed in a similar manner. But to Regis, it seemed right that those who did the work should have the credit; he thought it only fair that if his brother would rule in fact, he should rule in name, as well.

Besides, Regis found, when sent for a few years of training in the Towers, that this was the life he was born to: he enjoyed it, and he was good at it, particularly after his father had awakened the Hastur Gift in him. Stefan had enjoyed it, too, even after Father had failed to awaken the Gift in him, but Stefan seemed to like any task he was good at, whether hawking, training cadets, monitoring matrixes, making babies, or speaking in council.

Regis stood when Gabriela entered the room. Like many Comyn women, she was tall and thin, with bright red hair. Mutual recognition required only a moment for a thought to pass between them.

Gabriela motioned to the screen. "Shall we?"

Within minutes, Alastair Aillard stood between them, brushing off his robe. "I tell you," he said, "no matter how many times I go through these screens it's always unsettling. I check my fingers and toes to see if they're still there." He held up his hands. "Good. Six each. I'll count my toes when I'm settled in the old Tower. I presume my baggage preceded me?"

Gabriela smiled at him. "It arrived yesterday. Don't worry."

"Speaking of worry, old friend," Alastair brushed the back of Regis' hand with a fingertip, an intimate greeting among telepaths, "I have a warning for that brother of yours. Denita Elhalyn came back from wintering at the castle and told me her scruffy little brother, Valentine, is plotting something. He was very secretive about it, especially around his Tower-trained big sister, but she's certain that it's not a trifle. She says he mutters things such as if the Hastur of Hasturs won't put the right man on the throne, the Hasturs of Elhalyn will."

Gabriela inhaled sharply as Alastair was speaking. When he finished, she said, "I saw my cousin Cyril Leynier yesterday. He said he was worried that his friend Valentine was late for the council session. I didn't think much of it at the time, but. . . ."

Regis nodded. Cyril and Valentine were younger relations of their domain lords, grasping for attention by making nuisances of themselves last season. They were prominent in Stefan's reports last year when he unburdened his problems with Regis. "I'll give him the message."

"Good," said Alastair.

"I'll send for someone to escort you to your rooms," said Regis. "Since there is nothing on our schedules for tonight, I hope you'll come back here and dine with Gabriela and me."

"Delighted."

After Alastair was gone, Regis went to his room. There, using his individual matrix, he contacted Stefan.

"Cyril and Valentine," mused Stefan. "No, that's not a surprise. Whatever they've planned, if it appears to the others that it has a chance of working, every Comyn in the council who opposes me will join them to supplant me, weak as the Elhalyn claim to the throne might be. You have no idea exactly what they're up to?"

"None."

There was a pause. "Thank you, *bredu*. I will handle it."

"If there is some way I can help. . . ."

"I know."

Contact was broken. Regis rewrapped his matrix in

its insulating fabric and let it fall back to his throat.
Although he often offered to help Stefan, Stefan rarely
took him up on his offers. Not that he could blame
Stefan: in political matters, Regis had made embar-
rassing mistakes, as heir-designate, that Stefan had
helped him set right again. Not for the first time,
Regis wondered if the best solution all around might
be for him to take his own life. What had stopped him
before was the thought that Stefan might be accused
of killing him and making it look like suicide, which
could make matters even worse. On the other hand, if
the thought crossed Stefan's mind, to kill him, maybe
it would make matters better. Then again, maybe he
should just get lost. He could easily teleport to a
remote area and travel by foot to one of those isolated
communities near the Wall Around the World. In
searching for unmonitored matrixes following the Ages
of Chaos, the Towers had records of known or suspected locations. But could he get far enough away so
that the Towers or Domains would never find him?
He wasn't sure.

Dinner was in a small room next to Gabriela's.
After the meal, each of them sat back sipping hot
spiced cider. Regis looked over to Alastair, who, in
the dim light of the room, seemed more like a wood
spirit then a man. His red hair was going gray at the
temples; his craggy face was furrowed by a network of
wrinkles. He was a head shorter than Regis, and many
years younger.

"You look far more worn than I, my friend," said
Alastair to Regis as if guessing Regis' thoughts. "Been
stalking the wild matrix again?"

Gabriela groaned. "After last year, I don't want to
see another one."

"Nor I," said Alastair. "But I fear we shall. Our
ancestors seem to have had more matrix weapons than

there are leaves on the trees in the forest. Varzil the Good and his colleagues gathered up all the large ones, very many of them. In the years since then, we've found many more. But ever since I was a lad in the towers, it seems that every summer, a farmer finds another while tilling a field or a pair of friends finds one while fording a stream. A guardsman found one while sheltering on the road in a woodsman's house— the family had no *laran*, and they thought it a pretty trinket for their fireplace mantel. I daresay we'll find more before we're through."

"At that rate, we'll go on finding them for generations untold!" said Gabriela.

Alastair smiled. "Even the leaves of the forest aren't limitless. No, I think finds will become ever more rare until we find all those not deeply hidden. In my time, most discoveries have not been very powerful matrixes. Well-insulated, high-powered ones *may* escape notice a few more generations, but I think it will not be long before we find all those of consequence."

"Just the same, I could stand one or two more years of quiet before finding another one," said Gabriela.

Alastair held out his glass in Regis' direction. "As long as we have friend Hastur, here, I think we need not worry. He's a powerful matrix all in himself. And enjoys it, too, don't you, my friend?"

Regis recalled the fear and exhilaration he felt as he acted as focus for the Tower circle. It was not the first time had had made use of the Hastur Gift, but it was the first time he had faced so deadly a challenge. Even now, he still did not know which had been greater: the thrill of accomplishment, or the dread that he might fail, be burned to a cinder, or thrust out of the world forever.

"It is good for your brother that no one outside the Tower saw you then," said Alastair. "The Hastur glamour was about you for certain. The common folk, even

some of the Comyn, are superstitious still—expecting
their king to display incredible powers."

It was a quiet evening, though this was ordinarily
the time the Towers were at work. Probably Neskaya
and Arilinn were, Regis thought as he looked out the
window of his room. Tonight, however, in deference
to Alastair's arrival, and because of no pressing needs
in their vicinity, the two Towers of Comyn Castle were
at rest. Drizzle fell outside; through it Regis could see
lights in the Hastur suite. Stefan playing with the
children before bedtime, or Stefan wondering what to
do about Cyril and Valentine? Probably both, guessed
Regis, knowing his brother.

Turning, he saw the barracks area and two adjoin-
ing courtyards. Beyond them, the night watch pa-
trolled the walls. Over the wall, Regis could see lights
from the city. He wondered what the people thought
of Stefan. Were they split in opinion, like the Comyn
were? He regretted he did not know. Regis rarely left
the Tower, rarely stepped outdoors, except when Tower
work demanded it. He preferred living that way. Was
he wrong to have done so?

Regis woke gasping, hand at his throat. No one had
taken the insulation off his matrix and touched it,
though it felt as if someone had. He slipped out of
bed, reaching for . . . not the red robes of a *tenerezu*,
or the blue of a matrix technician, but the blue embroidered shirt which matched his eyes, the black pants
with the silver trim, black leather boots, silver-gray
cloak lined with blue—the Hastur colors.

Slowly, softly, he went down the stairs. No other in
the tower was awake. Was it a false alarm, or something attuned only to his *laran*? In either case, it was
directional, and he was going in the right direction.
Out the door, through a gallery . . . Regis knew the

castle from boyhood, but it had been some years since
he had explored it extensively. And now, a door to the
courtyard. Hearing voices, Regis kept close to a wall
in the shadows. The drizzle had stopped. It must be
near dawn, he thought. As the clouds broke, the light
of two moons outlined five figures, and glinted off an
object. It looked like a gold-plated rod.

"I found it last autumn, when I camped in the ruins
of an old castle," said one of the figures.

"How does it work, Valentine? Have you tried it?"
said another.

"Yes. You take the insulation off, point it at something, concentrate, and it kills whatever you aimed at.
I brought down a wild chervine that way."

Regis already had his matrix out, contacting Alastair,
then Gabriela. They could alert others.

Almost there, said Gabriela in his mind. *I heard you
walk past my bedroom.*

"Let's try it on something," whispered a voice in the
courtyard. "There's a bird perched on a wall, over
there."

"No!" said Regis, stepping forward.

He heard the sounds of swords being drawn. "Who
goes there?" shouted a figure.

"Regis-Mikhail Hastur of Hastur!"

"Vai dom," said Valentine. He held out the rod.
"Take this and assume your rightful place among the
Comyn."

At first Regis was startled. Did this mean Valentine's motive wasn't to try to claim the throne for
himself or his lord? Then, without stopping to think
how Valentine might react, Regis answered, "I will
not rebel against the rightful king." He sensed someone step behind him. *Gabriela*, she whispered in his
mind.

Valentine pulled the rod back. "If you will not, we
will!"

"Fool!" said Regis. "You'll destroy yourself."

He ran forward to snatch at the rod, but Valentine stepped back. His companions blocked the way. Regis felt, rather than saw, Valentine take the insulation off the rod. Instantly, there was enough light to see by.

"Hey!" said Valentine. "It didn't act this way before!"

"Drop it!" said Regis. He and Gabriela linked to oppose the power coming from the artifact. Valentine screamed and let go, but it was too late—the thing was activated. When his gift was in use, Regis' awareness was limited to telepathic forces. He knew Valentine's companions had fled only because of low, receding thought impressions. The thing's power had burst forth like a column of flame. Regis shielded himself and Gabriela, then reached out to contain the alien force. He succeeded in preventing it from spreading, but to force it into quiescence, he needed more help. The thing was bleeding reserves from him, from them.

Then . . . ah! a solid, steady strength joined them, one they could lean against, one that stood fast: Alastair, probably. At the center of the resistance, Regis coordinated the forces, using the additional energy to quench the fire, insulate the matrix, bring it under control.

It was done. Regis found himself kneeling on the flagstones, breathing heavily. Looking up, he saw the red light of dawn spread rapidly across the sky above the castle walls. Within the courtyard stood a large crowd. All of the cadets in the barracks must have come out, and not a few of the Comyn lords and heirs. A fading blue glow reflected off their faces.

Now, Regis thought dejectedly, it will be harder than ever to convince them to accept Stefan as the rightful king. Again, Regis looked at the awe-struck expressions, trying to think of a way to salvage the situation. But this time he noticed they were *not* looking directly at him, but to his right. Tilting his head

upward, he saw Stefan standing above him, holding
the rod, wrapping insulation around the matrix at its
end. The air around him still shimmered with a pale
blue light. Regis was still on his knees. Hearing the
sounds of movement, he turned to see the assembly
kneel by ones and twos, then as a group.

By the time Stefan had finished shielding the matrix, the glimmer had vanished. He turned to the assembly. "Lord Alton, take charge of your cadets."

He rose. "Yes, majesty." There was not a thimble-
ful of disrespect in his tones.

As the cadets filed out, Lord Elhalyn walked forward to cover a body with his cloak.

"I grieve for your loss, Lord Elhalyn," said Stefan.

He nodded. "If I'd known he'd had a wild matrix, I
would have told Denita to alert the Towers immediately."

While Elhalyn signaled his men to take the body
away, Stefan reached down. "Are you all right, *bredu*?"
he asked, hoisting Regis to his feet.

"Yes. Was that you? Thank you."

Stefan smiled. "Didn't think I had it in me, *bredu*?"

"On the contrary," said Regis. "But I didn't know
you were nearby."

Stefan shrugged. "I was drawn somehow. I don't
know how."

"Drawn through Regis' distress, perhaps," said
Gabriela. Regis turned to see her standing behind
him. She was dressed in a long red robe and covered
by a long red veil.

At that moment, Alastair walked up. Seeing Stefan,
he bowed. "Majesty."

Stefan nodded.

"I think, Majesty," said Alastair, "that you have
given a demonstration of the powers of a Hastur king
that few will forget."

"I hope so," said Stefan. "In the meantime, as

senior *tenerezu* of the towers of Comyn Castle, will you take charge of this weapon?"

"Gladly, Majesty," said Alastair. Regis caught the additional thought: *the king is indeed as strong as a tenerezu*.

Stefan smiled at Alastair, then glanced at Regis. Regis nodded; he know how it might look if Stefan handed the artifact to him. Alastair and Gabriela bowed and exited, leaving Stefan and Regis to themselves.

"Council is in session after breakfast," said Stefan. He took a long deep breath. "I'm weary, but I think I'll last the day without a nap." He touched the back of Regis' hand with a fingertip in farewell. "Long life to you, *bredu*." He walked back to the castle.

. . . *and to you*, thought Regis.

A King's Ransom

By Kay Morgan Douglas

About this story, Kay Morgan Douglas writes: "It makes the assumption that with the development of the Comyn as an all-powerful warrior caste, the contribution of a merchant class to Darkover is going to be disallowed and actively despised." Well, I don't think of the Comyn as a warrior caste, but as a ruling caste; rather than warriors, most of them are some form of gentleman farmer. But she goes on to make an excellent point: "I have made a further assumption that with every man's hand against them in a violent society, so few traders survive their perilous environment that differences in gender roles among them are of necessity minimal; they simply can't afford to waste a quick-witted mind . . . whether male or female. Consequently women are accepted among them as full members—"

This assumes, of course, that the traders of Darkover are more rational than the rest of mankind and make their decisions sensibly; for of course no group can afford to waste a quick-witted mind. But they do. . . .

Still, that's what science fiction is all about; behaving as if people could make their decisions on a rational basis, rather than on the basis of superstition and prejudice. Nobody does, of course; man is not a rational animal, but, as was quoted in my psychology class, a rationalizing animal.

But it's a good story. (MZB)

The chase ended as the sun blazed low in the sky across the Drylands. Mirrei's roan stumbled, exhausted by the speed she'd demanded of it, flinging her to the sandy ground. Bruised and shaken, she struggled hastily to her feet beside her uninjured mount and prepared to meet her pursuers.

"So, Traderwoman, why do you ride away from us in such haste?" the largest of the three men demanded, reining in his powerful gray. His glance raked Mirrei from her dusty boots of glove-soft *cralmac* leather and travel-stained breeches to her disheveled braids. "We only mean to do a little business with you." The innocent words were belied by the sneer with which they were spoken.

Mirrei faced him squarely, seeking to control her irritation. Thieves and outlaws were a common threat to every Trader. And every Trader worthy of membership in a guild knew how to handle them. *But why must I be plagued by these gre'zuin on this journey of all journeys?* It was imperative that she reach Temora before that city's fabled gates of copper and cast *argelium* were barred and bolted for the night.

"I am the Guildstra Mirrei of Carthon," she told him as coolly as if she stood in the Traders' Mart surrounded by all the City Guard of Carthon. "State your business, stranger." Handled properly, she would have little to fear from this one. Mere greed, she could tell at a glance, was his master.

"They breed strange men in Carthon, Meleng," the second of the three riders said and spat at Mirrei's feet. "They let their women run their business, vote in their council, and wear their breeches for them to boot." He was little more than an overgrown lad, carrying his poorly-crafted greatsword awkwardly, but the very real hatred in his eyes made him potentially more dangerous than Meleng.

"True words, Vardis. But they made a grave mistake this day." Meleng unsheathed a well-tempered *clevamore* as he spoke and pointed it at Mirrei's throat. "Now, Guildstra, we'll have the treasure you carry."

Oh, Meleng. No originality at all. Just you keep Vardis in line and I'll bring this matter to a tidy conclusion in no time. "Tr-treasure?" Feigning a somewhat overdone innocence, Mirrei glanced away from her enemies for an instant across the thornbush-dotted plain. The lowering sun was stretching the angular shadows of the spiny bushes ever longer across the sandy ground. *Take the bait, Meleng. Quickly.*

"Aye, treasure." So certain a lone woman would be too fearful to be clever, he failed to even notice her glance. "All the Domains know the Traders of Carthon are gathering a vast sum to free their precious King Danilo—the Comyn lord who grants money-grubbing Traders the same rights as honest men. But what *I* know is that a certain Guildstra of Carthon was chosen in secret council to carry the wealth of all Carthon to Temora to pay the ransom. And *you*"—the swordpoint pricked her throat—"are that Guildstra."

"You speak some truth," Mirrei agreed calmly, despite the shock that tightened her stomach into a knot and made breathing an effort. These were no outlaws whose trail randomly happened to cross hers while the sun was high; they knew who she was and knew what she carried. The ruse of a lone rider leaving Carthon in complete secrecy had seemed so simple, so foolproof. But it had one flaw; once divined, a single rider had no protection save her own wits.

"It's no secret the Traders' Guild of Carthon has agreed to pay a portion of the sum demanded by Doschadis of Temora. But the price he demands for our King's freedom is, as you say, a vast sum—ten wagons of copper. What do you see here? A lone Guildstra of Carthon. No wagons of copper, no treasure."

"No treasure! You lie!" Vardis snarled, his Hellers-bred accent thickening his words. "All you worm-tongued Traders carry fortunes about with you! Starstones, seapearls, or some such treasure—the sweat and toil of honest, hardworking men always has a way of ending up as the copper lining of a thieving Trader's pocket!" Beside himself with the rage and hatred of Traders that Mirrei had seen all too often, he wheeled his rawboned bay between Mirrei and Meleng. "We'll take whatever your pack yields, Trader bitch," he stormed, raising his sword high. "We'll take it and call it fair!"

"Kill me and you die in the same instant, Vardis of the Hellers!"

Startled by the sudden threat and dramatic change in her manner, the boy drew back, the bay squealing in protest against the sudden pressure of the reins.

"Beware, Vardis," Mirrei warned him, now committed by his threat of violence to a riskier course than she would otherwise have chosen. "We Traders have powers unguessed at even by Tower-trained *laranzu*. Have you never heard of the pact we made in the dawn of time with Zandru? How else do we survive despite every man's hand being turned against us save by the virtue of the *laran* Zandru himself granted us."

Vardis drew back again, the mere mention of *laran* invoking awe and superstitious fear.

Meleng wasn't so easily cowed. He gazed at her with narrowed, thoughtful eyes, but his heavy *clevamore* was steady in his hand and a faint smile played across his mouth. It would take more than just words to convince him she possessed the awesome power of *laran*.

Clever Syrtis, patron of all Traders, guide my words. "Your informant, Meleng, the one who told you I carried the wealth of the Guild of Carthon to Temora— she is Evandaline, the scribe of Blind Liam, is she not?" Meleng's clothing and accent proclaimed him to be Valeron-bred, like Evandaline. Perhaps he was a kinsman, perhaps her lover, perhaps the woman was completely blameless, but by Mirrei's quick reckoning Liam's blindness made his scribe the likeliest to have learned of her secret journey—and his scribe alone was not bound to the Guild of Carthon by ties of kinship.

The sword wavered a bit as Meleng's eyes widened— her guess was right.

"Never mind the treasure," Vardis urged, his bay sidling nervously away from Mirrei. "Best not to meddle with one bearing Zandru's powers—"

"Silence!"

The third rider, unheeded until now, rode forward in the very silence he demanded. The other two fell back, Vardis flinching away at his approach. Mirrei felt her blood freeze in her veins as she looked into his eyes of Comyn blue. A *laranzu*! A true possessor of *laran* powers! The same fear that governed Vardis now gripped her.

Since the dawn of time the Comyn lords of the Seven Domains had despised the Traders and used their *laran* powers against them whenever it suited their own ends. King Danilo was the sole Comyn lord to ever grant the Traders of his realm full protection under Comyn law. For that reason the Traders of Carthon had willingly yielded up their fortunes to save his life. And for that same reason there were many among the Comyn who called him "traitor" and would pay any price to destroy him. The death of a Guildstra of Carthon would be reckoned as no price at all in their eyes if it ensured Danilo's death.

Still in silence, the Comyn *laranzu* leaned down and touched her face with fingers oddly cold in this blazing land. "She speaks the truth," he murmured at last, blue eyes pale in the fiery glow of the westering sun.

"She names our informant in the tones of truth, and yet—and yet, she lies."

Her skin crawling, Mirrei could barely keep from flinching at his touch, but for all her fear she couldn't break away from his compelling gaze.

"Aye," he crooned softly, still stroking her cheek, "there's a riddle here. A mixture of truth and lies, a mixture, a compound, no clear boundary between: part foul mist, part pure air." Still his cold, clammy fingers stroked her face and forehead. "She's been clever in sly Trader fashion—I can hear it in her words, but she can't hope to keep a secret against *my* powers!"

Mirrei of Darkover was terrified by this man and the powers he possessed, rendered as helpless by his gaze as she would be by the scream of a banshee in the high Hellers, but the Guildstra of Carthon continued to weigh and assess every detail. To turn every situation, however bleak, to her advantage was the hallmark of a Trader and any detail at all might be the very one that would enable her to turn disaster into success.

And there were details here, the Guildstra of Carthon saw, that simply didn't fit. Was he truly a Tower-trained *laranzu*, this blue-eyed, red-haired descendant of Hastur? He wore a robe in the style of that most gifted class of Comyn, but it was frayed and filthy and clumsily stitched from plainweave, the coarse sacking used for clothing only by the very poor of the Domains. And he spoke with accents of a Valeron herdsman, this "*laranzu*." Was he the *nedestro* product of some Comyn lord's careless philandering, driven half-mad by his Gift, dreaming of currying favor with his arrogant kinsmen by being the instrument of King Danilo's death?

"Ask her about the ransom, Drago," Meleng demanded. A practical man, he was quite uninterested in any riddles Drago might sense. "Show us the worth of the *laran* you claim. Make her tell us the truth."

Eyes of Comyn blue bored into Mirrei's, seeming to divine every thought, every plan, every dream she'd ever had. Mirrei of Darkover knew there was no reason not to answer his questions.

"Do you carry the ransom with you?"

"Yes."

"That's a plain enough answer," Meleng exclaimed. "Turn out your saddlebags, Traderwoman. We'll solve Drago's 'riddle' quickly enough. Show us everything you carry with you. And none of your Trader lies either—Drago here can sniff 'em out like a hound on a rabbithorn's trail."

"You shall see all that I carry with me. If you see any treasure here, it shall be yours," she said measuring her words carefully. If what the Guildstra of Carthon suspected was true, she had a perilously slim chance of bearing the ransom in safety to Temora after all.

Speaking softly to the roan, Mirrei set to turning out her saddlebags as neatly as if she was unpacking for the night. It didn't take long. The last of her food, a nearly empty *boda* of water, several dozen scrolls of faun-hide used by Traders for inventories and such. The tunic of plainweave and the heavy wooden necklet all Traders were required to wear by law within the city walls of Temora, these all were soon spread on the dry sandy earth amid the deepening shadows of the thornbushes.

"There's nothing here worth taking!" Vardis exclaimed in disgust. "What about the fortune you promised!"

Meleng paid no attention to the boy's demand. He kept his eyes on Drago. "Ask her, Drago. Make her tell us the truth."

Once more the eyes of Comyn blue bored into

Mirrei's and she had no choice but to answer his questions.

"Is this all that you carry with you to Temora?"

"Yes." *I'll answer, but can you truly "see" the truth?*

"You lie!" Drago was more exultant than outraged. "You dare lie to *me*? I see the truth as clearly as you thieving Traders see a profit in the hardship of others. It has a tone that rings sweet and clean, the truth does, for all that you've done your best in your under-handed fashion to sully and mar it."

"Get on with questioning her! Ask her what else she carries."

Drago turned to glare at Meleng, his rambling ti-rade interrupted, but Meleng was too intent on his own goal to be cowed. "You carried something else," he demanded of Mirrei. "Where is it?"

"I buried it," she told him with a fair show of fear as once more the *clevamore* threatened to pierce her throat. "Among the bushes yonder before you rode up."

"Her treasure!" Vardis exclaimed. "I knew the tales were true—they all carry a chest of copper with them wherever they go."

"Is that true, Traderwoman?" Meleng demanded.

"No." *That's a true enough answer at any rate.*

"But this thing you buried before we caught up to you, it is worth a king's ransom?"

"It has immeasurable value." *Since it may be the means of saving my life, its value is certainly beyond measure to me.*

Drago hesitated as if sensing the double edge to her reply and Mirrei's breath caught in her throat. If she was right and he was just a Truthsifter whose *laran* was limited to seeing the truth in "yes" or "no," perhaps all would be well. But if she was wrong, if he had any trace of true telepathic power, all was lost.

"Make her show us, Drago," Meleng ordered, too

greedy to notice the other man's hesitation. "Where is it?"

The little chest she had buried lay only steps away, the marks of its hasty burial clearly imprinted in the coarse sand. With a yelp of delight, Meleng put up his sword, dismounted and fell on his knees flinging sand in all directions like an ill-bred hound.

"Watch her closely, Vardis," he ordered over his shoulder as the boy dismounted from his bay. "Keep your knife at her throat in case this is some trick."

"She spoke the truth," Drago told him, plainly affronted at this slur on his Gift, his earlier hesitation quite forgotten in his eagerness to be the agent of Danilo's death. Hitching the hem of his ragged robe away from the clutch of the thorns, he took up a stance at Meleng's shoulder. "I see the truth as clearly as lesser folk see the sun rise and set. No falsehood can escape my Sight. And it's Hastur's will that I should be responsible for destroying this traitor to his descendants, and the foul dross of usury shall be purified—"

"They'll divide the ransom between them, Vardis," Mirrei whispered. It was for exactly this moment that many Traders carried the "treasure chest" of the tales of Vardis' childhood. "See how they station themselves near it, leaving you here alone? Ask Drago to read Meleng's words about the promise to divide the ransom with you."

Vardis hesitated, his hatred of Mirrei in conflict with the suspicion natural to all thieves, even the rawest.

Meleng's cry of delight as he lifted up the chest of fragrant *vata*-pine studded with bright *faux-diamantine* and flawed seapearls was more than Vardis could bear.

"You promised equal shares!" he shouted, hurling Mirrei to the ground. "I stole the horses—for that I get half!" Sword drawn, he advanced on Meleng as the older man knelt fumbling with the lock of crude dross-copper. "Make him say it, Drago! Make him repeat the bargain and tell me if he lies or not!"

Startled by Vardis' sudden vehemence, Drago scuttled away, nearly tripping over Mirrei where she still sprawled breathless on the ground. Meleng's sword was back in his hands with practiced ease, the chest of *vata*-pine dropped to the sand and forgotten as he put Vardis on the defensive with a single stroke. Thrust and parry, it was age and skill against youth and raw strength, and Mirrei had no interest whatsoever in who was going to win.

One last obstacle: Drago. He loomed over her as she struggled to regain her feet, blue eyes locking with hers, seeking to control her again. She could feel the superstitious dread of the *laran*-gifted all Darkovans labored under close around her. Feeling her self-command ebbing, she clutched hard at reality; the feel of the coarse sand under her hands, the sound of sword on sword behind her. Before his compelling gaze could paralyze her utterly, she took the only action she could: she flung a handful of sand squarely into his face.

Squalling and clawing at his eyes, he staggered backward, crying out again as he stumbled into the needle-sharp spines of a thornbush.

Fully in command of herself again, Mirrei took full advantage of the situation. Scrambling to her feet, she cannoned into him with all her weight, knocking him headlong into the gnarled branches of a tall thornbush. His howls of pain and helpless fury faded quickly as she scooped up her belongings, reined in the three riderless horses and rode swiftly away into the blood-red sunset.

She looked back once as she rode; swift-rising Kyrrdis, herald of nightfall, was already visible above the distant mountains of the Seven Domains and soon the city gates of Temora would be bolted for the night. But as she looked back, she couldn't help but laugh aloud, despite the desperate race she was riding. Couldn't help but laugh at the memory of Drago sprawled nearly upside-down in the thornbush, his tattered robe hitched high on the thorns revealing what was surely the scrawniest, most bowlegged pair of legs on all Darkover.

"You display little concern, Guildstra." *Dom* Rael, King Danilo's spokesman in Temora, regarded Mirrei with obvious distaste as she stood disheveled and sweat-stained in the smallest of his audience chambers—the one set aside in all Temoran households for dealing with servants and Drytown slaves. "You arrive just as the gates are being closed, knowing full well Doschadis expects payment of ten wagons of copper by tomorrow's first light. *I* tell you we have but six wagons of copper and you smile as you inform me that Carthon sends its four wagons of copper with *you*—a lone woman who rides in with four horses and no wagons at all."

"I smile, *vai dom*, and display little concern because there is little to be concerned about. True enough, I bring no copper from the warehouses of Carthon with me, but I *do* bring you Carthon's share of our King's ransom. The full amount pledged by the Traders' Guild of Carthon for the freedom of our King is here in my hands." She couldn't resist smiling again as even this Tower-trained *laranzu*, a learned man among the Comyn, stared at the scrolls of faun-hide she held, as blind to the wealth they contained as the Drylands outlaws had been.

"These scraps? What wealth can be contained there?" His bewilderment deepened into the distrust that always lay between Traders and the Comyn lords. At his tone, the armed paxmen who flanked him stirred, weapons at the ready. "I have heard it said you Traders pride yourselves on greeting Death itself with a jest, but beware, Guildstra, if you dare jest at the death of your King—"

"No jest, *vai dom*, for all that I smile. Many of the Traders here in Temora owe amounts payable in copper to a Trader in Carthon. These sheafs of faun-hide, each signed by a Trader of Carthon and stamped with her or his seal, call upon the Traders of Temora to pay the debt, in copper, at once, to me. If I begin collecting these debts now, by dawn's light Doschadis' ten wagons of copper will be waiting for him as he demands. So you see, *Dom* Rael, I have good cause to smile—I do indeed bear a King's ransom."

Man of Impulse

By Marion Zimmer Bradley

When I wrote THE HERITAGE OF HASTUR and created Dyan Ardais as a villain, I had no idea that he would prove so popular; there were stories about Dyan second only to the many free Amazon stories. This variously complex man seems to have touched something both in men and women. I received at least four such stories for this anthology, but was rather reluctantly forced to reject them all—since I had already decided to print one of my own stories about Dyan.

Early in SHARRA'S EXILE, Dyan tells his foster-son Danilo that he has fathered a nedestro son by Marilla Lindir; making no excuse for his behavior except that he is, as he says, "a man of impulse."

Not that he needs an excuse; I freely admit that I never quite know what Dyan will do, and that his adventures are as much a surprise to me as they may be to my readers. (MZB)

"You keep good company, *chiyu*," Marilla Lindir blazed at her brother. "By all accounts you are just what he likes, the Lord Ardais—a boy not yet a man, old enough to be almost a companion, young enough that you will never contest his will, and pretty as a girl—has he yet made you his—"

Merryl heard the word in her mind, and colored

before she spoke it, but he said stubbornly, "You do not know Lord Dyan as I do, Marilla."

"No, and I thank all the Gods for it! Is it not enough that all our Aillard kin think you sandal-wearer because you shirked your term in the Cadets—"

"That is not fair, either," said Merryl quietly. "What ails you, 'Rilla? Are you angry because for once there is something we do not share? You have woman friends and I do not grudge them to you. You know why I could not go into the Cadets; after our brother Samael died, Mother thought always that I would melt in the winter rains or catch the fever in a summer heat, and truly I did not ask it—to be coddled and made a housepet, tied to her sash even when I was grown to be a man. Now for once there is a man of our kinfolk who accepts me for what I am; a man, a telepath . . . and does not mock me for what I cannot amend, that I grew to manhood without the company of my own kind. He *accepts* me," Merryl repeated, and Marilla, through her anger, felt the pain in her brother's voice, steadied though it was. She swallowed hard. Perhaps it was true, perhaps her anger was only jealousy . . . she and Merryl, twin-born, had not been separated as most brothers and sisters were when one moved into manhood and the other was confined to the narrow limits of a Comyn lady. Was she jealous, that now Merryl moved on where she could not follow, into the larger world? She reached for Merryl, and he hugged her close. She was still almost as tall as he; and though her hair was braided in a flaming rope down her back, while his clung in tendrils around his freckled face, her shoulders were nearly as broad as his own.

For years, our father said I was more the man of us two; I can ride as fast and as far as Merryl, my hawks are better trained than his, I even practiced with him at such weapons-training as he had . . . because Mother always felt that the rough lads around stable and bar-

*racks would contaminate her precious baby boy. But
Mother is gone now and there is none to keep Merryl
from becoming a man. And I* . . . Marilla shrank from
the relentless implications of that, *must I become no
more than a woman? Because I was allowed to share
what little Merryl had of manhood, have I been spoilt
for the only life that must be mine?*

She drew a long breath and said, "True it is that I
do not know Lord Dyan as you do. Yet I feel he is
using your—" she sought for a word that would not
offend him, considered and rejected *hero worship*, and
finally said hesitantly, "using your—your admiration
for him. I am not a fool, Merryl, I know that—that
young men, boys, care for one another this way, and I
would never have grudged you that—"

"Would you not?" he broke in angrily, but she
shook her head and gestured him to silence.

"Truly, had you had such a friend . . . companion-
ship I have given you and such friendship as you have
had—"

"Marilla, Marilla—" he held her tight again, "Do
you think I am censuring you because—"

"No, no—wait—that is not what I mean; I am your
sister, there are some things a friend, man or woman,
could give you that I, your sister and twin, could not,
and I—I would have tried not to grudge you that," she
said honestly. "The world will go as it will, not as you
or I would have it . . . a man is free to explore in this
way and a woman is not. . . ."

"That is not quite true, 'Rilla—"

She smiled at him a little and said, "Maybe not; I
should have said, a boy is something more free than a
woman, since they need not fear disgrace—"

"And I have no wish to disgrace any woman or
bring shame on her," Merryl said quietly, "but I have
had no *bredini* either."

"Till now?"

A flare of anger; the barriers were down between them, but she felt them slam shut. Merryl had never before shut her out of his mind. She said urgently, "Merryl, listen to me! For you, perhaps, this is right, this is the time for such things—but in the name of all the hells, in the name of Avarra the merciful—I can see why you love Dyan, perhaps, but what does he want with you? He is old enough to have outgrown such things before either of us were born, he could be our father's father—"

"He is not so old as that," Merryl interrupted. "If he had been grandsire, then would he have been wed full young—and what of that, anyhow? Would you judge a man by the years he has numbered, rather than by what he *is*?"

"Of what he is, I know only that he is a man past his first youth, at least, who seeks lovers among boys not yet grown to manhood," Marilla blazed. "What kind of a man is that? And I heard, if you did not, of the scandal in the Cadets six years ago, when he seduced a boy so young that he had to be sent home to his family because—"

"I might have known you would throw Octavien in my face," Merryl said, with an odd, smug smile. "Dyan told me before any other could rake it up against him. He took Octavien into his own quarters just *because* he was young and childish and the other lads who were more mature, bullied him—Dyan had been small and frail too, and knew what it was to be bullied, and he thought perhaps he could make a man of the lad by treating him as one . . . he taught him, supervised him, stood friend to him. But the truth of the matter was only this; Octavien was a whimpering child who should never have been sent into the Guards at all, and under the double strain he broke and his mind snapped . . . he got it into his head that the other lads were talking about him night and day because of Dyan's

friendship and attention, that they had nothing better
to do with their time than to taunt him and call him
weakling, sandal-wearer, catamite—and then he began
to weep night and day and could not stop himself,
and, like all such sicknesses of the mind, he turned on
the very one who had most befriended and helped
him, and accused Dyan of such unspeakable things
. . . and so they hurried him away, poor brain-sick
child, before he could grow worse."

"That, I suppose, is Dyan's version," said Marilla.

Merryl said, "I am enough of a telepath to know
when I am being lied to. Dyan spoke truth—nor would
he have stooped to lie about it. Had he known how
frail was Octavien's hold on reality, he would have
sent him home before—but he had grown to love the
boy, and Octavien did not want to be parted from him
then, he said Dyan was the only one who cared for
him and understood him, and Dyan felt that sending
him away would have been to hurt him worse." Merryl
was silent, but Marilla could read even what he did
not want to say aloud to her, *Dyan wept like a child
himself when he knew what had befallen Octavien; he
did not tell me this, but I saw it in his mind. . . .*

Marilla thought: *Dyan could have stood friend to the
boy without seducing him first to his bed; and it served
him right that he did not observe the proprieties.* One
of the strongest taboos in the Hellers was that which
prohibited such affairs between generations; it came
from the days when any kin of the mother's or father's
generation might have been the true mother or father,
since marriages were group affairs and true parentage
often unknown. "Could Dyan find no men of his own
age for his favorites and friends?"

"You are prejudiced, Marilla. Like all women, you
think a lover of men has insulted all your sex—"

"Not so," she said, "but he, too, is prejudiced,
then, like to a man who deserts his wife of thirty years

who has borne him many children, because of her wrinkles and gray hairs, and takes a younger and prettier maiden. Does he think, if all his lovers are young, that no one will see the lines in his face?"

Merryl flushed, but said stubbornly, "Nevertheless, he is my friend, and as long as you keep my house, you will be civil to him and receive him with courtesy."

"Oh, is it so?" she flared. "While I do your will at all times, we are as equals, but when our wills clash, you say only, *I am master of this house and you are no more than a woman?*"

He lowered his head. "I say not so, Marilla, Evanda forbid—but sister, will you not be kind to my friend for love of me?"

She said crossly, "It is for love of you that I would show him the door," but when her brother spoke in that tone, she could only grant him what he wished. She said, "I neither like nor approve of the man. But you must do as you will," and turned away from him.

Lord Dyan, she thought, was rather like a hawk: proudly poised head, lean to emaciation, high-bridged nose, and now and again, when he laughed, the far hint of wildness in the harsh sound. His manner to her was delicately punctilious; he called her, not *damisela*, but *Domna Marilla*, in recognition that she was chatelaine of Lindirsholme. In the evenings when they sat in the hall or danced to the sound of the house-minstrel, he was always first to ask her to dance, and even courteous to her lady-companion and the elderly chaperone who had been her governess and Merryl's. During the days he was out with Merryl, hunting or hawking, or simply riding across the broad lands; in the evenings, sometimes, he borrowed a harp from one of the singing-women and sang to them himself, strange sorrowful ballads older than the hills themselves, in a voice well-trained and musical, though without much tone. Once he said, with a faint, rueful shrug, "A boy's tragedy is always this—that no matter how beautiful his voice before it breaks, there is no way to tell whether his mature voice will be anything but another well-trained croaker."

"Yet the songs are beautiful," Marilla said, truthfully, and he nodded.

"I had them from my mother . . . she spent years studying under one of the great minstrels of the mountains; of course my father could not abide music, so she sang only to me. And I learned more in Nevarsin."

"Were you destined then for a monk, Lord Dyan?" she asked him. He laughed, that harsh bird-sound.

"Not I! I have no call to fasting and prayer, and less, perhaps, to the way of the ascetic . . . I like good food and warm beds and the company of those who can dance and sing . . . only the music kept me there; I would have endured more than that for such learning. No, I was apprenticed to be a healer, and now—" he shrugged, "I have scarce enough skill in these to set a broken bone for a dog." He stared at the long delicate fingers which moved so skillfully on the harp. They were still fine, but the joints showed lumps and knots and calluses from sword and reins. "For one of our kind, there is no task worthy of a man, they say, but the sword. Duty called me there, and I did what I was bound in honor to do. How lucky you are—" his eyes sought Merryl's, "that you escaped this destiny."

"At the cost of manhood," Merryl said bitterly.

"Faugh!" Dyan made a harsh, guttural exclamation, "If that is manhood, perhaps 'twould be a saner world if we all put skirts about our knees, lad!"

Marilla asked him, "Do you truly think women are better off than men?"

He shook his head. "Perhaps not, Lady Marilla—I am no judge; my grandmother Rohana ruled the Ardais lands better than any man could do, and my father—"

he shrugged. "I never saw him sober, or sane, after my thirteenth year. My sister was Keeper, *leronis* at Arilinn, and no man could be her master, yet she gave that up to die in trying thrice to bear a child to her Terran-reared lover. My mother endured my father's madness and folly till she died of it. My grandmother lived all her life subject to a man who was scarce her equal, yet she treated him always as her better. Can you blame me for saying I understand not women? Nor, for that matter, men . . . even you, lad—" his smile at Merryl was so frank, so warm and tender, that Marilla winced, "you have escaped the worst of what your clan demanded of you, yet you pine as if you had been forbidden something splendid! I would have given much for just such incapacity as yours, so that I might have had my own choice . . ." and he sighed. "No matter. The world goes as it will. . . ." And he bent his head to the harp and began to play a merry and not too decorous drinking-song about a most inept crew of raiders from the mountains.

> "We have to tell them again and again,
> Rape the *women*, and kill the *men*,
> I think sometimes they'll never learn,
> *First* you plunder and *then* you burn."

Not long afterward, Marilla rose, with chaperone and lady-companion, and withdrew; Merryl embraced his sister, and Dyan bent over her hand; for an instant she was shocked, wondering at herself, *Did I want an embrace from him, too?*

And late in the night she woke, shocked, from a dream such as had seldom come to her, she was held in someone's arms, caressed tenderly, mind and body touched in such depths that her whole body seemed to melt into a jelly of delight. . . . She woke in startled amazement, feeling arms still about her, the pleasuring touch still lingering in her body . . . but she was alone, and then, catching her breath in dismay, she slammed down a barrier; but it was Dyan's hands, Dyan's arms in the dream . . . or was it a dream? And slowly, shamingly, she knew what she had shared . . . she had guessed, of course, that Dyan shared her brother's bed, and the bond of the twin-born was stronger than any other telepathic bond. . . .

But I knew not that it was like this . . . Merryl has this and I, ah, merciful Evanda, I am virgin and I lie alone . . . till my family gives some man rights over my body without my will . . . and Dyan, Dyan wants no woman, he would turn from me in scorn, turn to my brother. . . .

The barrier was in place again. In her cold and lonely bed, Marilla wept herself to sleep. And in the morning she sent down word by her chaperone that she was ill in bed; she could not face Merryl, she could not face Dyan . . . certainly he had known that they had touched her. . . .

I never want to see him again. I will stay here in this bed until he has gone away, and damn him, he can take Merryl away with him, I never want to see either of them again! But she knew that she was lying. The next day, self-possession armoring her again, and chill irony, she managed to come down and be civil, to endure Merryl's and Dyan's kind inquiries about her illness, But she held herself tightly with dread, and watched, with something she now knew was envy, as Dyan and Merryl walked arm in arm. And once, when she sat among her women, sewing, she heard one of them giggling and speculating.

"What in hell's name can two men do with one another? It seems silly, doesn't it? And what a waste! I've hard that the Comhi'Letzii take one another to bed like lovers, but I've never been able to figure that out either . . . maybe they don't know what they're missing—"

"Maybe," Marilla said coldly, "they have more imagination than you do, Margalys," and left the room, hearing their curious chattering voices rise behind her.

It was that night, as they sat at music, that Merryl took the harp and began to sing, but broke off in a fit of coughing; and Marilla reached for his hand; it was hot as fire.

"You have fever," said she accusingly,

"Well, there is fever in the village, and I went to see how many of the farm-people would be away from the harvest," Merryl said, sighing. "True 'tis, that old saying, lie down with dogs and you will rise up with fleas. . . . I will be well enough, sister." He struck her hand away. "You are not our mother, to coddle me now!"

Dyan reached for Merryl's forehead, touching it expertly. "No, now, lad," he said. "Away to your bed; you have fever-bark? And if you are not well in the morning, we will ride another time, but you must not endanger yourself."

Merryl colored, but he rose and signaled to his body-servant, taking leave of Dyan with an embrace. He looked sick and flushed.

"I will see you, then, in the morning—it will be well enough," he said crossly. "Marilla is like all women, she likes having men sick and under her control."

"Only because men are too much fools to admit when they need care," said Marilla, just as crossly, and frowned. But as she climbed the stairs, to search out fever-bark from the stillroom and pour a dose into the protesting Merryl, she had already formed the plan in her mind.

She had still the riding-breeches of Merryl's which their mother, four years ago, had forbidden her to wear; and Merryl's tunics were only a little too broad

for her shoulders. She slipped into Merryl's room where
he lay restlessly tossing about with fever, and slid his
sword from the rack, belted it about her waist. She
had had enough training to walk without bumping it
on things; and she took his cloak and slid her feet into
his boots. They were too big for her; she pulled on
another pair of thick socks so she could walk in them
without blistering her heels. In the stable, Dyan was
already saddled and waiting.

"Well! You look well recovered," he said gaily.
"Did not that sister of yours jump at the chance to
keep you abed like a child?"

"Do you think I would let her?" Marilla blessed the
deep contralto of her voice; she could never have
carried this off if her voice had been high and light like
her companion's. She was glad to realize that she
could, in breeches and boots, jump into the saddle as
lightly as Merryl himself; only once had Dyan seen her
ride and then she had been cumbered with riding-
skirts and a lady's saddle which was, Marilla had always felt, an insult to a self-respecting horse.

"You said I might fly Skyclimber," Dyan said. "Have
you a hawk chosen?"

Marilla nodded. She said, wondering at her own
calm, "My sister told me that Wind Demon is not
being flown enough, and she is too busy to ride; she
asked me to handle her today."

*Bold as she was, she would not venture to handle
Merryl's hawk, Racer; Racer as a nervous haggard who
let no one but Merryl himself touch her.*

But with Wind Demon on her saddle, she felt competent to match Dyan himself at hawking. She rode in
the crimson sunrise, feeling the dawn wind in her face
with excitement, the delight of freedom; how long it
had been since she rode like this, forgetting the household duties which lay behind her! Surely she would be
missed, but what did that matter? There were plenty

to care for Merryl and for the household, and if she could not have one day of absolute freedom, what good was it that she was Lady of Lindirsholme?

The sun had begun to angle downward from the zenith, and noon was far past; Dyan began to loosen the hawk again from the saddle, then shrugged.

"We do not need any more birds," he said, "and the hawks, too, are full-fed; do we need to take more? You promised we should ride one day to the waterfall; is there time before sundown?"

"I think so," Marilla said, and beckoned to the hawkmaster who rode far enough behind them not to interfere, but close enough to take charge of the birds if he was needed. "Take them back to the castle, and the game too, Rannan."

"Certainly, *vai dom*," Rannan said, "but ye're not going to ride farther this day, are ye? Lord Ardais, ye wouldn't be takin' the boy all that way with fever just past and a storm comin' on?"

"Storm? I see no sign of storm," Dyan said, "but if Merryl wishes to return—"

Marilla sniffed the wind; it did not seem to her to smell like storm. Rannan had always pampered Merryl. She said coldly, "You are not now in my mother's pay, to keep me housebound. Take the birds and go."

The man ducked his head and rode away, and Dyan chuckled.

"When I was a lad, they used to have a saying for a boy growing up—*Well, lad, ye'll be a man before yer mother will,*" he said, imitating, with a droll twist of his mouth, the country accent of the man. "You may have been kept from manhood much of your life, but you make up for lost time now. But are you sure you are not wearied with riding? It is true we have come a long way, and no doubt the waterfall will wait on our pleasure."

Marilla was not accustomed to this much riding; she ached and was saddlesore. But she would not yield before this man! She hardly knew why she had come; *perhaps*, she thought, *I wished to know what Merryl sees in him. . . .*

And she knew; a charming companion, ready with jest and game, now and again tactfully suggesting a better way to handle the hawk . . . though, indeed, earlier he had said: "You grow better at this than you were; last time we went hawking, you did not handle Racer so well as this—"

Marilla had said lightly, "I have learned from your company and example, my lord."

Dyan smiled and leaned close and said, "I thought we agreed you were to call me only Dyan—or, if you will—*bredhyu*—" and she felt the questing touch of his mind, but she kept her barrier in place; she could not pretend to be her brother, not now . . . but still she could read Dyan, a little.

I like it that he is still shy, that he does not presume nor grow bold. . . .

"The waterfall lies beyond this ridge," she said, and set her teeth, racing ahead. How dared Merryl share this with Dyan? That had been their own private place, their rendezvous, the place where they went to share confidences from early childhood; and now Merryl would bring this man here? She felt simmering resentment; and yet . . .

I can see it now, she thought, *why Merryl loves him so well.*

The sky was darkening with cloud when they came in sight of the waterfall, and a few drops of rain had begun to fall. Yet the rushing cataract drowned out all thought, all sound, all speech; and Dyan, staring with delight at the great jagged cliffs with rushing water, was silent, too. He stood there without words, looking downward at the torrent, and after a time she could read his thoughts again.

Now do I know why you brought me here. There are not many who will own to their love of such beauty. Nor do I—much—when there are others near. It is the second—nay, the third most beautiful thing I have seen at Lindirsholme.

So close they were, so deeply sharing the silence, that for a moment Marilla was tempted to open her mind to him; she did not want to deceive him, let him show the tenderness he meant only for Merryl. But the thought of his rage and fury at being deceived, kept her barriered tightly, and after a little Dyan sighed and turned away, and again she could read his thoughts. *Still he defends himself against me, but perhaps tonight when we are together he will not barricade his thoughts from me. . . .*

In a wild confusion of feeling, dread and shame and some unidentifiable thing, she turned quickly away and hurried to her horse. Dyan turned in surprise and looked up, troubled, but she said swiftly, "Look, we cannot stay here . . . look at the sky, Rannan was right about the storm."

Within minutes, she knew, it would break and they would be drenched. Dyan threw himself into his saddle and was off after her, racing . . . he drew angrily abreast and said, "You are a child indeed. If you knew this storm would break, and if your clothes are soaked to the skin again, you will have fever worse than ever—are you always going to act like a child or a silly girl? This is such a trick as your sister might have played! Is there any place we can shelter from this, out of the rain for a little?"

"You are like my mother," Marilla snarled in Merryl's voice. "Think you I will melt in the rain?"

"Nay, but I hunted in these hills before you were more than a gleam in your father's eye," said Dyan, and again Marilla caught a picture in his mind, two lads racing over the hills breakneck on their horses . . . who was the other boy, younger than Merryl was now? She neither knew nor cared. Dyan said, "I know how quickly this rain can turn to sleet or ice at these latitudes . . . even now, feel that," and Marilla was aware of the sting of sleet against her cheeks. "We cannot reach Lindirsholme without freezing; must I seek a cave or ditch as we were taught to do at Nevarsin against bad weather?"

She said, shivering against her will, "There is a—a shepherd's hut." It had stood unused for years, since their father had sold his sheep and turned to breeding the black horses of the Leyniers. She and Merryl had kept childish treasures there, when they rode to the waterfall, and brought food and drink for out-of-door meals away from governess and tutors.

No doubt Merryl would have shared this too. He cares nothing for our old secrets now, only for Dyan. Well, let it be so.

Even Dyan was blue with cold by the time they forced the hut's stiff door open, and knelt at once to make a fire. When it was blazing up, he unsaddled the horses, brushing away Marilla's attempt to help.

"Stay by the fire, lad, you are chilled through, and I have not just risen from a fever-bed!" He laid the saddleblankets down beneath his outer cloak, pushed Marilla down on it. "Nor need we go supperless to bed, I kept the last bird, thinking we might cook our dinner out of doors."

She knelt upright on the blankets and said, "Let me then spit the bird for roasting while you deal with the horses."

Her hands were too cold and stiff still to do much at plucking it; she finally held it to the fire to singe the feathers away. He came when she had half finished, and took it away from her.

"Here could you use some of your sister's house-wifely skills," he said, laughing, "Plaster it in mud and ashes, lad, and the feathers will break away when 'tis baked. Did she learn your skills of riding and hawking without teaching you such things as this?"

Marilla flared at him, "Would you have me learn to cook and sew? Already I was womanly enough, was I not?" And as she spoke she knew she was speaking the very words Merryl would have spoken, the rage and resentment at never sharing a man's life . . . well enough it was to bring Marilla into a man's world, but if he had tried to enter hers, then would he have been ridiculed or worse. . . .

Dyan said, still laughing, "In the Cadets I learned to cook or go hungry, even if it was no more than grain-porridge and such field cookery as this; there are no cook-maids on the battlefield, lad. And my paxman darns my socks and mends my cloak—it is the price I pay for having no woman about me." As he talked, he was plastering mud and ashes on the bird; now he thrust it into the coals. "Leave it there to cook, and get out of your wet cloak, lad." He pulled it from her shoulders. His hand lingered at the nape of her neck. "Such fine hair—'tis pity you cannot let it grow long like your sister's. . . ."

Marilla bent her head. She would have to face that some day, too; and she thought with a sting of regret of the long braid of hair left on her floor. She forced herself not to shrink from Dyan's intimate touch. . . . *Yes, they have shared more than this, he has a right to expect it. . . .*

"I suppose you wonder why I would have no woman about me," said Dyan quietly. "I thought it not fair to marry as many of the Comyn do, to women with whom they have no more in common than horse or dog, to use a woman as a breeding-animal, no more. Once I dwelt with a woman for a year, and she bore my son; I had him legitimated, but he died, years ago. I have an heir by adoption—I think you may have seen him in Thendara; Hastur's paxman, young Syrtis. I do not dislike women as much as all that." He raised his eyes and looked at her directly.

"What do you want with me, Marilla?" he asked.

She bent her head. How long had he known?

"Since we stood together by the waterfall," Dyan said quietly. "I am no *laranzu;* yet telepath enough to know something of what you felt. Do you understand how much I love your brother, Marilla? I know you have hated me; yet I mean him no harm. He will leave me; a younger lad always does; I will have no choice but to find another. My—my friends seem somehow to grow to manhood, and I—well, perhaps it is something within me—" he shrugged. "Why am I explaining myself to you?"

She turned away and bent her head. Her voice was stifled. "You owe me nothing, my lord."

She wished he would not look at her; and as if yielding to her wish he got up and busied himself at the far end of the shelter where the horses were; he gave them grain from a bag, hauled some of the fodder stacked at the far end and spread it for them. She came and stood close, tearing apart the baled fodder so the horses could get at it to eat, and he smiled.

"What? Now I know you are a woman, you do not leave me to do the men's business here?"

"When I ride with Merryl, I am a boy with him; should I be less with you, *via dom?*"

"You are his equal, aye," Dyan said softly, "I would you were his twin brother, not his sister . . ." and she lowered her eyes before the sudden heat in his. He reached out and took her between his hard hands, holding her so that she faced him. "You have come here with me, Marilla—what do you want, truly?"

She turned aside, swearing that she would not cry.

How could she say, *I want what it is that you have shared with Merryl and never with me, what you can give to no woman—ah, fool that I am, caught in my own trap—*

He pulled her against him, stroking her hair, stroking the nape of her neck. After a time he lowered his lips against hers, and a little later he carried her to the bed of saddleblankets.

"But you are a child—" he said, after a time, hesitantly, "and, if I make no mistake, virgin—do I repay hospitality by violating the sister of my host?"

She half sat up, her arms still round his neck. She said fiercely, "You did not ask my leave to take my brother to your bed! What sort of ninny do you think me, that you must have permission from him to take me, when I myself have given you that leave? I am my own—my own woman, I belong not to my brother but to myself—nor to you, Lord Dyan! I give and withhold myself at my own will, not that of some man!"

He laughed softly, and for a moment she thought he was laughing at her, but it was a laugh of pure delight.

"One thing more you have learned of your brother's world, Marilla—if all women were like you, I doubt I should be such a man as I am today—" His lips sought hers again and he whispered softly, against them, "*Bredhya.*" Then he pulled her down again on the bed of saddleblankets.

"I must take care, then, if you are a maiden; I would not reward you for this with pain," he said, touching her more gently than she had believed was possible, and she sighed, letting her mind open before him as her lips opened under his, feeling his delight and surprise and wonder.

I thought you cared nothing for woman, Dyan. . . ."

I am a man of impulse . . . you know that of me, if nothing more. . . .

And then even thought was lost.

*   *   *

They rode home early in the daylight, holding hands. As they came within sight of Lindirsholme, Marilla halted, looking at Dyan with a certain dismay.

"Merryl will know . . . again I have stolen from him what he wanted; when we were little children, my father said always, I should have been the man, I was the stronger of the two . . . and always I bested him at riding and hawking . . . and now even at this I have stolen what he wanted most. . . ."

Dyan clasped her hand and held it hard.

"You have taken from Merryl nothing that is his," he said gently. "And I shall tell him, believe me, that it was for love of him. . . . I cherish you, *bredhya*, but without my love for Merryl, you would have been no more to me than any of the hundreds of women who would lure a Comyn lord into their bed . . . do you think women have not tried? Had you been older, more guileful, I would have thought it of you, and turned away from you, but my friend's sister was something else . . ." he lowered his eyes again and was silent. "Now he has shared with me what was the dearest of his possessions," he said at last, "his sister's love. Is it not so, Marilla?"

She clung to his hand. "It is so, Dyan."

Merryl met them at the gate, holding out his hands to each of them as they dismounted. "I was frightened, when I knew what you had done," he said. "The storm was so fierce—but you took him to our own old place, Marilla. . . . I am glad!" And, meeting his eyes, she knew that he was aware of what had befallen them, as she had wakened to share his delight in Dyan's arms. Dyan reached out and hugged them both together, turning his head from side to side to kiss them, Marilla's soft cheek, Merryl's downy one, and for a moment it seemed to Marilla, in an insight she never lost, that somehow Dyan was not a bearded, scarred, aging man, but somehow, inside, a laughing boy her own age or Merryl's. . . .

She took his hand and her brother's, and, walking between them, walked through the gates of Lindirsholme.

Dyan rode away ten days later, Merryl at his side.

"I wish I might come with you to Thendara," she said rebelliously, as she said farewell.

"So do I," Dyan said softly, "but you know why it cannot be." Already, with her *laran*, she knew that the night they had spent together had been fruitful; she bore Dyan's child, and already guessed that it was the son he needed and desired so much. He held her face between his hands again and said "You have given me the one thing Merryl could not, Marilla. No one else, ever, can take your place in that. I will marry you if you will—" he added, hesitating, but she quickly shook her head.

"If I held you in those bonds, I should desire of you what you cannot give . . . what the bonds of marriage demand," she said. "You would come to hate me . . ." and at his look of pain, she added quickly, "not to hate, perhaps; but you would resent me, that some one had put reins to your freedom . . . I have this." With a curious new gesture she held her hands, sheltering, across her body where the child lay cradled. "I am content with that . . ." and she raised her lips for his farewell kiss. And as he turned away, riding at Merryl's side, she whispered to herself:

Once you called me, bredhya. But I know, if you did not, that what you truly said was . . . bredhyu.

She turned before they were out of sight, and went inside the gates. There were those who would think that Dyan had taken from her what she had to give, and left her nothing; but she knew now that it was not true.

She was mother to the son of Lord Ardais; mother

to a Comyn Heir. Now no kinsman could force her, unwillingly, to marry some man for house and name; she had status enough of her own, wed or no. She was her own woman, now and forever; and Dyan had given her this, which was better than marriage.

Some day—perhaps—there might be another man; and perhaps not. Perhaps she was never meant for marriage. But some day, certainly, she would find someone to share her life who could accept her in freedom; and when she found that person, man or woman, she would know. Dyan had given her that.

Swarm Song

By Roxana Pierson

In the many Darkover stories I have to choose from every year, I try very hard to look for three things: a character I fall in love with, an unexpected use of laran, *or a plot which is* really *original—maybe there are no original plots, but I look for one which hasn't been used too often before. As I have indicated, there are a few I get over and over.*

(If I had a nickel for every story I have received about a woman escaping from the Dry Towns and just happening to encounter a group of Free Amazons, or a Free Amazon giving up her freedom, to name only two of the stories I receive every year, and most of them not well enough written for a fanzine—as I say, if I had a nickel for each of them I might be able to start my own publishing house.)

Maybe I am too hard on them, but still it seems to me that anyone who cannot think up anything original ought to choose another hobby. I try not to discourage them too much, but it's always a delight when I get a really original use of laran—*like this one. I don't know where she got her idea, but it's an original use of* laran, *and a not overused plot. (MZB)*

Julana pressed her ear against the rough bark of the crumbling log; inside, the bees hummed steadily. She buzzed back to them softly. It was wonderful in the hive. Dark, warm and safe, the fragrant golden comb was filled with honey and the sweet soft bodies of "those who are not yet" dreaming in their hexagonal cells, oblivious to the pulsing life that streamed around them. The hive was never quiet; there was always work to be done, and never enough mouths to do it. And now that the season of the swarm was upon them and two of "those who are not yet" were being fed the sacred Royal Jelly, the activity became even more frantic. From the strong-jawed workers to the fertile, fecund glory of the queen—each bee hurried about her duties with single-minded devotion. Workers, heavy-laden with pollen and nectar, flew from dawn to dusk in a steady stream and the honey dancers danced their sacred dances. Three turns to the right and a wiggle—good nectar to the East—taste me, smell me! Oh, there were many dances, almost as many as there were kinds of flowers.

The excitement was building to a fever pitch. Soon, soon, the new queen would emerge and the old queen, worn bald by the loving caresses of her attendants, would take her followers and seek a new hive.

Julana screamed as a hard hand closed on her wrist. The bees made an ominous buzzing and Julana's aunt, Shandra, swiped at them angrily. She gave Julana a vicious shake.

"Didn't you hear me calling? What's the matter with you? And look at you—you should be ashamed! I don't know what your mother is thinking, letting such a big girl run around like this."

Julana twisted away from the old woman. "Leave me alone, you have no right!"

Shandra grabbed Julana's arm with surprising strength. "I have every right, bold one! I'm your father's sister. Now, you come or you'll be sorry—they'll be here soon and I'll not have you shame us before guests.

How many times have I told you to keep yourself clean? You're too big to play in the mud. Wait till I tell your mother. . . ."

Still scolding, Shandra set off across the courtyard, dragging Julana after her. Julana went by stops and starts, dragging and scuffling her bare feet in the soft dust; she was in no hurry to see her father. He always fought with her mother, the Lady Allira, and lately it was worse—much worse—ever since she turned twelve and the subject of marriage arose. So far, her mother had managed to hold out against Lord Jharek's choice of suitors, but Julana knew that wouldn't last forever. Her father expected to be obeyed without question and in the end, she would have to do as he wished.

Her younger brothers, Nyal and Jemel came racing across the courtyard, screaming, "Nyah, nyah—dirtball! Dirtball! You're going to get a beating!"

"You shut up or I'll beat you!" Julana spat back. She swiped at the nearest boy and Shandra slapped her sharply.

Nyal took the opportunity to throw a stone at Julana and retreated quickly, teasing, "Zhalara's coming again—he wants you. . . !"

"Enough! All of you—into the bathhouse. They'll be here any moment. Hurry!" Shandra gave the reluctant boys a shove toward the door. So much rush and fluster, and all over old Zhalara!

Julana fidgeted nervously. Was it true what Nyal said, or was he only teasing? Surely her father wouldn't persist in trying to marry her off to fat old Zhalara. How could he possibly consider marrying her to a creature like that? Was money all he cared about?

"Sit still!" Shandra commanded. Hurriedly, she yanked a comb through the long auburn hair that was so different from the boys' sandy thatches. Julana stood out among the village children like a red poppy in a field of marigolds. It was easy to see she was no true child of the Dry Towns.

"OUCH!" Julana protested in startled outrage as Shandra hit her with the brush.

"Stand still—you'll never be ready in time. I don't know how your nurse put up with you. No wonder she left."

"Then leave me alone."

"And let you go looking like a wild woman?" Shandra gave the braid such a hard pull, tears sprang to Julana's eyes. "Now, stop daydreaming and get dressed. You have to look good tonight. We're going to have company."

"Not that horrible old man!"

"You should be glad your father cares enough to look for a good match for you. What if you were some poor orphan? You could be sold as a slave."

"I'd rather be a slave than marry someone like Zhalara. . . ." Her lower lip pushed out in a stubborn pout.

"That's enough. Now, here—put on the red dress. It's lovely and we've all worked hard on it."

"Then wear it yourself!"

"Do you want to anger your father? If he's not happy, you know what will happen." Shandra's eyes glowed. There was little love lost between her and the Lady Allira—and Jharek's fits of temper were famous. Although Shandra never dared to openly say it, she hated Allira. Who did she think she was anyway? Perhaps she was a noblewoman in the Domains, but here in Carthon, she was nothing. Shandra still remembered the day Jharek came home with Allira flung over the back of a pack animal—his share of the booty, he said. Well, that was a long time ago and most people had short memories. Jharek's days of banditry and his means of acquiring a wife and lands were both long forgotten—except by Shandra. She knew as soon as she laid eyes on the fiery redheaded beauty that she wouldn't last long in Jharek's house. No other woman ever dared defy him—but within a year, Allira had provided Jharek with a living son, something no other woman had done. He had married her. Even then, Shandra had insisted that the children should be removed from Allira's influence, but Allira insisted the children were delicate, and remembering his dead children, Jharek consented. *A mistake, all around,* Shandra thought, *and now we see the result.* Allira was forever telling the children long-winded tales of faraway places. To hear her tell it, her homeland was paradise compared to Carthon. The boys paid little heed, they were mirror images of Jharek at their age, but the girl was like Allira. Strange and difficult to manage. Shandra shrugged to herself. Well, it didn't matter. She was only a female anyway, and Jharek would have her married off soon, hopefully to someone willing to pay a sum for the privilege. Julana's flame-red hair was unusual enough that he would have no problem getting rid of her, even with her odd ways.

Shandra stood back, hands on hips, to survey her work. "There. Now you look a proper woman. Even your hem is straight for a change. Now we can go, and not a minute too soon either."

They were crossing the courtyard when there was a blare of horns, and Jharek galloped in, followed by guards in red tunics and the usual contingent of *cralmacs* mounted on shaggy *oudhraki.* Beside him rode a fat, red-faced old man in a purple tunic stiff with gold embroidery. Zhalara.

Julana quickly looked away as Zhalara turned cold, reptilian eyes on her. Him again! But what could she do? Julana stared in dismay from Zhalara, who was clumsily dismounting with the help of servants, to her father. At forty, he still retained the graceful power of his youth and a full head of pale hair. When she was younger, Julana had thought him handsome and dashing; now, she saw only the hard line of his jaw, the anger waiting to spring forth like a coiled serpeant.

Allira, tugging the two youngest boys along behind her, arrived just as Jharek dismounted in a flurry of dust. She bowed low, touching her head to Jharek's sandaled feet in Dry Town fashion. "Welcome home, my lord," she murmured softly. "And Lord Zhalara. Grace be with you."

Jharek grunted in reply. Slapping his riding whip against his thigh, he paced past her to halt before Julana. Under his scrutiny, she flushed and lowered her eyes. There had been a time when she had been welcome to climb on his lap and beg for sweets. No more. Now, he was so stern and unapproachable she dared not even speak unbidden.

Jharek twitched at the richly embroidered sleeve, "So, my daughter," he said gruffly. "I see your mother has finally come to her senses and clothed you as befits a maid." He chucked Jemel under the chin. "And you my boy—have you been a good boy?"

"Yes, Father, except for . . ." Jemel stared at his feet.

"Yes?"

"I pulled the cat's tail and frightened the cattle."

Jharek chuckled. "Well, if that's all . . . boys will be boys. What about you, Nyal? "Have you learned your studies?"

"Yes, Father. Even the new book you gave me."

"Good. Good. I see all is in order then."

"Father?" Jemel asked shyly, "Have you brought us gifts?"

Jharek's face clouded, "Not this time, boys. I had other things to buy."

"But you promised," Nyal whined.

"Eh—don't beg. If you complain, I won't bring them

at all. Now," he took Allira's arm in an iron grip, "let's go in. I hope you have prepared a dinner fit for our guest."

Lady Allira took up a small bit of meat and chewed delicately. Cautiously, her voice cool and polite, she asked, "I trust you had a profitable journey, my lord?"

"Good enough. That scoundrel, Eldryn, took the lion's share, as usual. But," he exchanged a knowing look with Zhalara, "things may work out after all. . . ." Jharak regarded Julana speculatively. "I trust you're pleased, Lord Zhalara?"

Julana cringed as the old man's eyes traveled over her, mentally stripping her. She swallowed hard and closed her eyes. They must have reached some sort of an agreement or he would never have dared look at her so boldly. If the bride price was agreed upon, soon, all too soon, the pudgy bejeweled hands would be stripping her for real. She shuddered. Shandra had delighted in regaling her with the horrors of the wedding night. And with a creature like this! It was simply impossible to consider marrying this hideous old man with his baggy eyes and spider-veined nose. Not those clammy hands. Never!

Allira was staring at Zhalara with open hatred. Julana could almost hear her thoughts. *If I have to kill him myself, I will. . . .*

Zhalara cleared his throat and picked at a back tooth with a long, black nail. "Yes," he lisped, "yes, of course. I'd like to make the final arrangements as soon as possible."

"At your discretion, my lord," Jharek bowed slightly. Zhalara was a powerful neighbor, if he could cement an alliance by pawning off Julana on the old man—so much the better!

Julana studied her plate. Surely it wasn't true. The servants claimed Zhalara beat his last two wives to death. Servants' talk, Shandra had said. Still . . . Julana couldn't believe that even Jharek could do such a thing.

"Has a price been agreed on, then?" Allira's clear voice cut through the silence like a knife.

Zhalara cleared his throat. Without taking his eyes from Julana's breasts he said, "There are still a few details, but . . . I'm sure. . . ." He gave a dry little laugh.

"How could you?" Allira hissed at Jharek.

"Silence, woman!" Jharek's voice was low and dangerous. "How dare you. . . ?" He half rose, towering over Allira, who stared back, stony-eyed.

Zhalara politely busied himself picking his teeth. A bee paused to examine the honey cakes and Jharek shooed it away. "Can't you even keep this place clean?" Jharek accused. He motioned to a servant, "Bring desert."

The cake arrived, followed by an angry cloud of bees. The servants clucked and swatted at them while Jhared glared at Allira in self-righteous rage.

Glad for a diversion, Julana reached out to the bees, tentatively at first, then slid into the familiar empathic state that was more real than her own life. Had the swarming begun? *Yes,* they buzzed, *"Those who were not yet" have become and we are one,* they sang. Unconsciously, Julana hummed with them. She stopped suddenly, aware that every eye was fixed on her. Shandra poked her and hissed, "Stop that noise, what's wrong with you?"

"You should teach that girl some manners. She's old enough to know how to behave," Jharek said.

"She will learn, she will learn," Zhalara crooned. "Come my girl—sit beside me." He patted the floor at his side.

Panicked, Julana looked to her mother with a silent plea for help. Almost, it seemed she heard her mother's voice speak out loud. *Save yourself, my daughter.*

You know what to do. A grim smile played about Allira's lips, and sharing her vision, suddenly Julana understood. Yes, that was just the thing! Why didn't she think of it before?

She bowed to Zhalara and replied, "Certainly, my lord. It's a pleasure to share your company." Reluctantly, Julana joined him. Under the table, Zhalara slid an exploring hand under the hem of her dress.

"There, my girl," he whispered, "that's not so bad is it?" He looked both astonished and delighted when she boldly returned the gesture. *Here*, she guided the searching bees under Zhalara's robe. *Here, sisters, a nice, dark spot . . . you'll like this place.* Julana shared their journey as they crawled blindly through a forest of moist curling hair, searching for the promised nest.

Zhalara grunted and scratched with a surprised look, shook one leg, then the other.

"My Lord?" Allira inquired politely.

"Only an ant, or something." He slapped at the offending itch and sat bolt upright with a howl. "ZANDRU'S HELLS AFIRE!"

"Oh, my lord." Allira leapt to her feet, calling for servants. "Hurry—Lord Zhalara's ill." Zhalara turned beet red and spluttered so hard Julana thought he would have a seizure. His eyes rolled and gasping, he finally stuttered, "A bee, just . . . a . . . bee. . . . I think. Here, help me up," he commanded the servants.

"Are you all right?" Jharak demanded.

"I'll send for some herbs." Allira suggested.

"No. No. Forgive me . . . I . . . must visit the outhouse a moment . . . I'll be all right . . . only a bee. . . ." He hitched gingerly at his robes, and bent double, shuffled out on the arm of a servant.

Julana stifled a giggle and kept her eyes steadfastly lowered as Jharek said, "I can't understand it. Last week when Loman was here, it was ants everywhere. What's wrong with this house? Don't you ever clean?"

Allira shot daggers at Jharek and hissed, "Can I help it if an insect flies in the window? I'd have stung him myself if I could. How could you? That . . . that thing!" she exploded.

"I've given my word—would you have me break it? He'll marry her and that's that."

"Over my dead body!"

"That can be arranged," Jharek threatened. "Here, you—do something about this!" Jharek called to a servant to fan away the bees that suddenly seemed to be everywhere. He slapped at a bee circling his head, then cursed loudly as he connected and got stung. Julana could hardly restrain herself as she directed another bee to the tip of his nose. Yes, this was the way. And if Zhalara returned—well, there were always the red ants. Julana shared a look of secret mirth with Allira as Jharek howled and the servants flapped wet towels at the bees which only urged them to greater fury. And then she was in the hive, dancing, singing the swarm song, *We are one, we are one, we come, we come.* The song buzzed in a thousand golden breasts and quivering abdomens until the excitement exploded and burst forth in the wake of the old queen. Merged in the ecstatic union of the swarm, they swooped through the hot afternoon air, one mind, one desire: the new hive must be found, the precious queen made safe.

They came in a dark, roaring wave, and Julana called to them, *Here—this one. He is not of the hive. He is danger!* The bees took up the cry, *He is not, he is not!*

From outside came a terrible screaming and a crash of splintering wood as Zhalara emerged from the swarming outhouse at a dead run, tripping and stumbling over his flapping robes. The bees followed as he galloped away.

Julana, smiling blissfully, buzzed, *We are one, we are one, I am you and you are me and we are we. . . .* And then she laughed out loud.

Out of Ashes

By Pat Cirone

Every now and then I get a story which, though written elsewhere, seems to fit right into Darkover. Pat Mathews wrote one last year, and now this story was written about fire-fighting and laran, *though by another name. I wanted to bring it to you, although it did not have anything else about fantasy in it, and thus did not fit into SWORD AND SORCERESS. So when Pat Cirone submitted "Out of Ashes," I felt it was so much in the Darkovan manner that, although she had written it for SWORD AND SORCERESS, to which she had made her first sale ("S.A.R." in SWORD AND SORCERESS III), I felt it more rightly belonged here. Although not about Renunciates, or about Towers, it seemed somehow to belong to their mythology.*

I could be mistaken—what do you think? (MZB)

A sleepyheaded baker's apprentice had dragged himself off his pallet, stoked his master's oven and yawned his way into the preparation room to start the usual pre-dawn routine of making the dough for bread. Lazily, he had only snicked down one of the latches on the heavy iron oven door, and that not well enough. The weight of the oven door, the slant of the old flooring in the baking room and the quirks of fate had brought about the rest. The city of Liridium was on fire.

97

The woody scent filled Shilla's nostrils and brought painfully incongruous images of cozy fireplaces to her mind. Wearily she shoved a gray-edged wisp of brown hair out of her eyes and watched as the road she and the other pathmasters had struggled to keep open burst into an arch of flame. The fire had taken less than an hour to overcome their efforts to hold it at bay. Sudden screams from a panicky horse jerked her attention down the street. A woman, caught beneath the roaring flames, hacked the horse loose from the cart bearing her goods and frantically tugged him toward the safety at the end of the street, protecting her face with her sleeve as she ran. Shilla wondered if there were any others trapped behind the cart which quickly became one with the orange around it. She did not reach with her mind to find out. She had felt death too often recently to knowingly seek more. Her dry eyes no longer had tears to shed; they ached with the grit of the windborne ashes and the heat of the flames. And the inside of her head ached with the use of her pathways; it was as if fire traced along them, too.

"What now?" Terel asked hoarsely.

"The next main avenue is Buryrow. We'll try to keep that open as long as we can," Shilla replied. She turned and hurried up the river. Her boots squelched in the layer of mud that lay on the cobblestone path. The bucket brigades had moved farther upriver already, but the signs of their futile efforts still marked the riverside path that blessedly remained free of the fire. Stone warehouses, built to withstand the damp and tides of the river, also withstood fire.

Not so the wharves at the mouth of the river. On them barrels of pitch and lamp oil sent beacons of light flaring into the sky. It wasn't difficult to see where you were going even though it was the middle of the night. The city made quite a splendid, if expensive, taper. The corner of Shilla's mouth crooked a little at the thought. Humor did not come easily to her these days, and when it did, it was usually black.

She was so tired. She had been up the night before, again, trying to save the life of a child stricken with the fever that had been plaguing the drought-stricken city. It seemed as if she had not had a night of unbroken sleep in months. Near dawn she had finally eased the child into a natural sleep and left with but one thought on her mind: to crawl into bed and dream of a life free of fevers and drought and loss. But when she had slipped out into the narrow roadway under the garrets of the house she had attended, she had been greeted with a sky lit with more than dawn. And now, eighteen hours later, the fire was still raging.

When they reached the end of Buryrow, the five pathmasters quickly moved into the loose pattern they had fallen into over the last few hours of working together. Shilla took a deep breath to steady herself. She knew. As she opened her mind, pain lanced through her head and sank claws into the pathways she had once used with brilliant ease. Shilla steadied her breath against the pain and forced her reluctant pathways to let her use them. Carefully she melded her mind with the others in the light contact that was possible, with experience, between non-linked pathmasters. Together they focused their powers and reached out along Buryrow, seeking the fire with their extra senses. The houses there, as throughout most of the city of Liridium, were built back to back, side leaning cozily against neighbor's side. And the fire crept from one to the other without pausing. It did not need the wind that whipped burning brands onto roofs; the fire was at home in a city whose narrow roads were often roofed by the overhanging upper stories of the homes that lined them.

Now the fire was reaching into the houses that backed onto Buryrow's stores and homes. The pathmasters imaged a wall of cold in their minds and slid it protectively down the backs of Buryrow's houses. Shilla felt the ache in her head deepen; it was hard to work with purely imaginary constructions, much harder than moving physical objects. She concentrated as they strengthened the wall of resistance, extended it as far as they could and then pulled it down the other side of the street to complete the circle. Shilla relaxed a bit. A circle was easier to maintain than an open-ended wall. Now it was just a matter of endurance, of willing the wood not to burn despite the flames lapping at its sides. It would be temporary; there were not enough of them to put out the fire, just contain it where they could. But for now there was a path to the river. A path for the fleeing to use, carrying their children and belongings on their backs or in precious carts. A path for those fighting the raging fire with pitiful buckets of water drawn from the river and thrown on the guildhalls, the churches and whatever else they thought they could save.

Save. Sometimes Shilla wondered if there was anything left to save. First there had been the drought that had dried the crops in the field and baked Liridium into tinder. Then fever had crept among them, claiming first one victim, then another. Brigid had been one of them. Her pathmate of thirty years, gone in a week. They had been nine when they had discovered, with delicious surprise, that the tentative mind touches they were feeling came from each other and not from some stranger across the city or even across the land. Pathmates, linked one on one, mind to mind for life. The aching void she left behind was only partly due to her loss as a friend; her absence as pathmate crippled Shilla. Only beginners worked alone, their powers feeble, their pathways little more than the itch that identified those who would become pathmasters. But by stretching and using the pathways they became stronger until, one day, there was linkage. Another mind opened to yours, its pathways filling the voids that paralleled your own in a head suddenly filled, completed, and able to do what you had only dreamed of before. Death ended those abilities. Shilla had felt Brigid torn from her mind when she had died. Her mind still felt tattered from the loss. Pathmasters didn't work after their pathmates died. They weren't able to.

But Shilla had sat and watched her daughter Kayeta weaken when the same fever that had taken Brigid gripped her. There were so few pathmasters available; she had waited in vain for one to come help her daughter. At last, in desperation, she had tried herself. The pain had been excruciating—but it was her daughter that was dying. She had kept reaching into her daughter's body, reaching for the fever with a sense she no longer felt, catching glimpses of success through the veil of pain. She had driven the fever out of Kayeta, stumbling, faltering, shaking with pain and fatigue. But she had done it. And that knowledge had made it seem selfish to deny that hope to others. So she had resumed working, a crippled pathmaster, measuring her pain against the needs of others and deciding each time she could endure.

A touch jerked Shilla out of her introspection. Dazed, she focused on the street before her and the protective circle her pathways had helped hold steady as her mind had wandered. One of the refugees fleeing down Buryrow toward the river was hanging on to her arm.

"St. Katrina's has fallen," he sobbed. "The stone itself cracked and fell!" He gulped and staggered on to grab and tell the next person in his path. Shilla heard him repeating the same words over and over again before he boarded one of the barges ferrying people up the river to the fields east of the city. *St. Katrina's. My God! The fire was hot enough to crack stone?* Shilla cast an anxious look at the stone warehouses whose protection they had been taking for granted. She wiped a sooty hand across her brow and thought wistfully of the soaring beauty of St. Katrina's. Its set of bells, installed just a few years ago, had been so expensive the people were still paying an extra tax for them. But they had been the pride of the city; people had come from miles just to hear them ring. *Would anything of beauty be left?* Shilla cried to herself.

Her mind wandered back again to all that had been torn from the city during the last few months: the people, the food in the drying fields, now the shelter of the city itself. Her thoughts jumbled. Her head itched. She lost her focus on the group. Her pathways seemed muddy and the itch grew worse, spread to inside her head. With a cry Shilla dug her fingers against her scalp. Abruptly she was severed from the group. She staggered, almost falling. Someone passing grabbed her arm and steadied her. The itching left and pain and exhaustion rushed in, hitting her like a wall. She moaned and put her hands up in front of her face.

She felt like a child, nine years old again, with the itch of the pathways forming in her head, the itch that was the first sign that a child would become a pathmaster. It came long before the pathways could be used. What could it mean in someone who had used the pathways for thirty years? Did it mean the end of their use? Had she injured herself, forcing herself to use the pathways after Brigid had died?

She lowered her hands slowly, trying to gain time, trying to rub some of the tension out of her face. The others of her group were looking at her, worry plain in their eyes.

"Are you all right?" Steven asked.

"Yes." Shilla's voice wavered, to her dismay. She took a deep breath, ready to try and join in again.

"No!" Terel almost shouted it. "You need to rest," he added more softly.

"I'm strong. I can rejoin," Shilla argued.

"Shilla, you almost broke the concentration of the whole group. We can hold Buryrow another hour maybe. Hopefully. But not if you break like that again and cause us all to scramble and readjust. We're better off without you right now," Terel said bluntly. "Rest. Get something to eat. Then rejoin us."

Shilla's shoulders settled; it wasn't enough to call it a slump. She knew they were right. She nodded, not trusting her voice to speak. Turning, she walked across the cobblestones to the river bank.

She hitched a ride on one of the barges, one foot on the deck, hands gripping the rail. The ripples in the water danced in red and orange. Gradually, as they left the fire behind them, the water faded into its usual night black. As the bargeman poled around Wheel Point, she jumped off. The itch in her head had returned. She dodged up narrow streets and ducked into one of the public eateries. There she could grab a meat roll, sit and think. And itch.

She tried not thinking. She still itched. She wiggled her shoulders, stretched, rubbed the back of her head. It eased it a bit, or maybe that was just her imagination. What was happening to her? She finished her meat roll, downed a glass of ale and left.

She couldn't rejoin the group she had been with. Working with four was tricky and she couldn't risk throwing them all out of balance again. Terel had been right. They were better off without her. But she couldn't sit and do nothing. Shilla struck off north through the city, gradually angling back west, toward the fire. There had to be something a single pathmaster could do. Even if it was just help load carts with the sick and injured.

When she reached Wick Street, one of the widest in the city, her way was blocked. Crews armed with poles, hooks and ropes were pulling down the houses, trying to create a break wide enough to stop the fire. A young girl was helping one of the crews. A pale blue cheek tattoo, its circle still open, marked her as a fledgling pathmaster, not yet linked to a pathmate. But still she was working, using what little skills she had to help others.

Shilla watched as the young girl used beginner's exercises to guide the hooks the men were hurling toward the roofs. She bit her lip in concentration as she nudged them into niches where they caught and held. With swift pulls the men could then bring down the wooden structures, finishing off with the poles to knock down the lower walls. They worked swiftly. Teams with carts labored to remove the splintered remains from the street. It wouldn't be enough to have the houses down if the debris left a path for the fire to walk across the street. Shilla felt her spirits rise. Here was work she could do, too.

She walked forward and laid a hand on the young girl's shoulder. Startled, she looked up. Her eyes widened as she noticed how heavily Shilla's small tattoo was filled in with marks of achievement.

"May I be of assistance, chargemaster?" Shilla requested, extending to the girl the professional courtesy of recognizing her status as the pathmaster in charge of this effort, regardless of her age or lack of experience. The girl's shoulders straightened further.

"Of course. I'd be honored to work with you."

Shilla nodded. "I'll work with that crew there," she said, pointing toward the crew on the opposite side of the street.

"It would help," the girl replied, losing a little of the mask of professionalism she had carefully tried to adopt. The fear and desperation that was in all of them glimmered through. Shilla smiled, a genuine smile that lifted the girl's spirits as well as her own. Then she turned to the task at hand.

God, the child was so young . . . just beginning,
Shilla thought to herself as she worked. She thought
back to when she and Brigid had explored and ex-
panded their powers. There was such a rush to learn
every skill as if it would vanish if you didn't acquire it
the first time you tried. And such a shaky pride in
your newfound status. And then the shock when you
linked with another and found out what it was like to
truly share. *And then the second shock,* thought Shilla
with a wry smile, *when you found out that insecurity
did not disappear the minute you became an adult. If
that child knew I don't trust myself to group with other
pathmasters, that I itch unbearably and am having difficulty doing this child's play of guiding hooks and poles,
that fear of this fire gnaws at me the same way it does
her, she wouldn't look at me as if I were Selina
reincarnated.*

As fast as they worked, the fire moved faster. Shilla
heard its distant confusion turn into a steady murmur.
The hot woody smell of burning grew stronger and
occasional puffs of smoke came down from the sky to
eddy about their feet. Frantic people and their carts
shoved around the crews trying to clear the timber
from the street. It became difficult to work.

The three demolition crews working without the aid
of a pathmaster had to cast and recast their lines
before they caught. Sometimes one of them would
have to shinny up and fasten the hooks by hand,
delaying them further. *We need more time,* Shilla muttered to herself. *And more pathmasters.*

As if in answer to her thought, Shilla spotted the
blue circle tattoo on a woman pulling a small cart
down Wick Street toward them. Shilla motioned for
the men she had been aiding to go on working and
darted toward the pathmaster.

"Can you spare the time to help us here? If we can

stop the fire here, there'd be a good chance of saving the rest of the city," Shilla said breathlessly.

The woman stared at her blankly, then lowered the shafts of the cart. "I can't help," she muttered hoarsely.

"Are you on an assignment?" Shilla paused.

"My pathmate was killed by the fire an hour ago." The woman bent to lift the shafts and started moving down the street again. Shilla paced sideways beside her.

"I feel for your loss, but we need you. Please help! Think of all the other lives you may save; it won't bring back your pathmate, but it might prevent someone else losing their's."

The woman stared at Shilla in disbelief. "I said I lost my pathmate. He's dead. I felt him die. I can't work anymore." She kept on plodding.

Shilla darted around one of the crews clearing the debris and attacked the woman again: "But you *can* work! It's painful and you can't achieve near what you could before, but you can do it. I know. I lost my pathmate two months ago and I'm still working, using the pathways. What we're doing here is simple. Child's games. Your help could mean the difference between stopping the fire here and having it eat through the rest of the city!"

"I can't help. I've lost my pathmate. The pathways are closed to me now."

"Damn it, woman!" Shilla screamed. "I've just been telling you you can go on working after your pathmate dies! You have to! I did! We're needed!" She grabbed the woman's arms and shook her.

The woman shrugged free, set her lips and pushed away from Shilla. She plodded on, pulling her cart, ignoring the others around her. Shilla bit her lip and felt tears of frustration rise in her eyes. Her fists clenched and unclenched. How could a pathmaster ignore others in such desperate need?

"Is it true? You've lost your pathmate?" a soft voice asked at her elbow. It was the novice pathmaster.

"Yes." Shilla's answer was clipped. "She died of the fever two months ago."

"I'm sorry."

Shilla shrugged slightly, not knowing what to say.

"And you've gone on working?" the girl asked, amazed. "I was taught a pathmaster couldn't."

"So was I. But you can work. A little. It's painful, but possible."

"Why do you do it?"

"I'm needed," Shilla answered simply. The girl nodded, half to herself, affirming the creed of those given the gifts to be pathmasters.

"I'm Toria," the girl said.

"Shilla," Shilla answered. They smiled at each other and went back to work.

Rage at the woman who refused to even try to use her skills lent strength to Shilla. It pushed away exhaustion and even lessened the fury of the itching along her pathways. The clanking of the hooks as they landed on the roofs were arguments she could have used to persuade the woman. The poles pushing against the walls were Shilla forcing the woman to work with them. She pushed herself harder and harder, using the rage as a weapon. She started slipping into the tinny state of overexertion where she could hear the thoughts of the others around her chatter in the back of her head. She recognized the state as dangerous, but above the voices and fears that floated in her mind she heard the crackle and roar of the fire. That was a danger more immediate than injuring an already injured mind.

Shilla worked like a demon, shouting at the men to work faster, grabbing some of the hooks off the ground and settling them in by herself. They were so near the point where Wick Street opened into the central market square. Shilla prayed they'd have enough time to clear the houses to that point. Fire would never be able to jump the square's open spaces except by circling around it. Which meant if they cleared Wick Street, the fire would be denied any passage to the south of the square. And there were enough workers to hold it to the north once they were able to concentrate their efforts instead of being dribbled all over the city.

One of the crews clearing the debris looked fearfully over their shoulders and started to edge away. In a flash Shilla was over by them, throwing scraps into the cart, glaring at them with eyes fierce from the determination to keep them working. They worked. Shilla was so extended she could hear what they thought of her. She turned her short laugh into a cough; no sense confirming their belief she was crazy.

Shilla felt fear rising in Toria's mind. She glanced over at the young pathmaster, but the girl was working with a calm expression on her face. *She will become a good servant of the people,* Shilla thought with pride.

Out of the corner of her eye Shilla caught a flicker of light. She whipped around. A lick of flame was eating through the sagging back of one of the houses exposed by the tearing down of the houses on Wick Street. Shilla's eye swept down the length they had cleared for more signs of fire. Smoke broiled up from just behind Wick Street but, for as far as she could see, the flames were not yet testing their work. She wished she dared extend her senses the length of the street to know for sure, but she was too near the edge of total shutdown. She glanced up the street. Three houses to go. But they couldn't risk it. For all they knew the backs of them could already be on fire. Hurriedly she waved the men back from them and turned to Toria.

"Let's pull as much of the wood to your side of the street as we can," she shouted above the roar of the fire. Toria nodded and they began sweeping the debris across the street with their minds. The men saw what they were attempting and began grabbing the bigger pieces and hurling them to the far side. Shilla paused, eyeing those three houses. She pushed her senses, straining beyond her limits, feeling for fire.

"I think we have time," she shouted to Toria. "Imagine the men throwing the hooks. Carry the hook through the arc as if one of them were throwing it and settle it in place as you have been doing. I'll pull."

Toria looked worried. Shilla could hear her uncertainty in her mind just as she could feel the men wondering what they were doing. And the fear of people shoving down the street. And the fire greedily moving closer.

Toria took a breath and concentrated, slowly building her still forming powers. A hook arced through the air gracefully and caught. Shilla pulled as if she were at the end of the line, added a pull to the second hook as Toria locked it into place, watched with eyes hazy as the building collapsed. "Next," she shouted to Toria. Obediently Toria started hooks arcing toward the second even as Shilla heard her worry that they would defeat all the work they had done by giving the fire a pathway across the shattered wood left lying in the street. The second and the third building fell as rapidly as the first. Shilla's head rang with pain and noise and she could no longer tell pain from the itching. She half-pushed, half-motioned Toria away. She forced her aching, confused pathways to her will one more time and with a whirlwind of thought blew the debris from all three houses across the street and farther, packing them as tightly as she could against the houses that nestled against the far side of the square.

The world went silent and still. She saw the backs of the houses she had just exposed ripple into a wall of flame. But she couldn't hear it. Nor could she feel

anything in her mind: no itching, no tinny thoughts
from other people . . . and no sense of any pathways.
She felt a tug on her sleeve. It was Toria, pulling her
back. The two of them ran from the suffocating heat
and joined the rest of the crews across the square.
Shilla sensed crews on the north side of the square,
working as they had. But all her attention was on the
wall of flame fronting Wick Street. Burning pieces of
wood flew loose and landed in the street. The wind
gusted and a few blew farther. Shilla clenched her fist
and realized she was still holding Toria's hand. The
two of them gripped each other and watched as the
fire fell short, again and again, of igniting the east
side. They angled north around the square, to see
down the length of the street. It looked like Wick
Street was holding the fire. Shilla felt tears of relief
shake loose and run down skin tender from the heat of
the fire she had stood so close to for those few moments. *Oh, God, let it hold, let it hold,* she kept
murmuring to herself. Gradually her hearing crept
back and she realized she was murmuring her prayer
out loud. But it didn't matter. Everyone was praying
the same prayer. She glanced behind her and saw that
High Street had been cleared as they had done Wick.
The hope that the day and night of horror might be
coming to an end rose.

They watched for two hours as the fire consumed
everything west of the barrier, turned the houses and
halls to embers and ashes but left the eastern side
untouched. The few times burning debris had blown
far enough to land on wood and ignite it the bucket
crews had quickly doused it. The fire was done.

Shakily Shilla brushed the hair out of her eyes and
assessed what condition her mind might be in. As
gradually as her hearing had returned, so too had the
itching beneath her skull. But it was much lighter,
bearable. Gone were the stretched, overstrained senses

that had picked up the thoughts of others not linked to her. Maybe she hadn't damaged herself irreparably.

A tendril of thought not her own slipped into her mind. Its passage coursed along her abused pathways and soothed them as balm. Shilla reached out eagerly, pulling the thought and the mind behind it, thinking for one joyous moment that Brigid was alive again. She saw Toria jerk rigid with shock, her eyes widen. Shilla sent out a delicate question, wondering.

Toria turned to her, her eyes alive with amazement and discovery. "It's you!" she whispered.

"Yes," Shilla replied, as mystified as the young girl. Without volition on either part, their pathways had met and flowed beside each other, twined in support in each mind. The itching had been a new pattern of linkage etching itself into her mind!

"But you should have someone nearer your own age!" Shilla whispered in dismay. She felt Toria's rejection of the thought and her joy in linking with someone whose years of experience could aid and instruct her. She was glad to be linked with Shilla, who had worked with her when others had passed by, whom she could admire for working through pain and defeat. And Shilla felt humbled by the confident joy that flowed from Toria. So be it. They were pathmates. Not that either had any choice. It couldn't be willed and it couldn't be undone. The pathways chose and you worked with the one you were given. Shilla let go of the dismay and the worry and let the winging joy and blessed peace of being linked once more fill her and wash away the pain and tiredness. It was a joy she had never hoped to experience again, and it was just as precious as the first time. Once more, by being a part of a whole, she was completed.

Toria and Shilla smiled at each other, linked hands and looked out over the blackened smoldering remains of the city. You could see for miles where once your gaze would have been halted again and again by rows of houses. Gouts of flame still issued from some basements. Smoke billowed in lazy cones that eddied as the incessant wind, finally, began to die. The taste of burning lingered in Shilla's mouth and nostrils, but she was thinking of the future. There would be a lot of work to do. But she would be part of it. With Toria as a pathmate she would be strong again; her own formidable powers enhanced and supported by one who showed every sign of becoming as adept, and as caring, as herself. With Toria by her side, she would be able to help rebuild her beloved city.

My Father's Son

By Meg Mac Donald

It's one of my greatest pleasures when someone whose first works are unacceptable finally makes it into a lineup. I think Meg Mac Donald has sent me something since the first of these anthologies, and I find the hardest thing I had to do is to reject work without overly discouraging a young talent. (Of course, anyone who can be discouraged, says the conventional wisdom, shouldn't be writing at all; but if that were true, I wouldn't ever have made it into print; for I can, and often do—yes, even now—get discouraged with this field I've chosen.)

It's one of the greatest paradoxes of writing that would-be writers must be sensitive, or they couldn't be empathic enough to write; yet, conversely, they must develop something like rhinoceros hide, since rejection is always the first experience of a writer. How do you resolve this problem, then?

If I knew the answer to that, I would be not only a successful writer and editor but a saint, too. It's the question we are all looking for the answer to—how to reject the work that simply doesn't come up to standard, meanwhile not unduly encouraging the talentless. Some editors get so discouraged by the flood of manuscripts that they forget this all-important business, and buy only from guaranteed best-sellers. (And who can blame them?)

But it's fun to encourage young talent—and sometimes, as in this case, it pays off a jackpot. I think all of you will enjoy the result.

What, then, is the criterion for kinship? Or for Comyn? Is it blood, or laran? Or even humanity? (MZB)

It was a battle of the heart.

From the beginning of time—at least from the beginning of time that Maol could remember, it had been a battle of the heart between him and Caelly Muir. When Caelly married, the battle would end. Forever.

Leaving the stone and mortar walls of the manor behind, Maol was free, if just for the short time before his duties would begin. Outside the Muir estate the blushed sky was wide and clear, pink and purple rays streaking out over the watery horizon so early in the morning. Maol relaxed to see the new day, wishing one new morning would change him or at least allow him to forget who he was, and who he was not.

Walking alone along the ridge helped still the bitter flow of emotions. Emotions he was told he could not feel—for what can a nonhuman feel? But what did *they* know; how could they feel his feelings? How indeed!

After the marriage feast on the morrow, Maol would beg his lord the freedom to leave the estate. He feared the unknown lands less than the power of the red-haired *laranzu'in* from the north. And if Caelly refused . . . perhaps he would leave sooner, tonight, saving them both the sorrow his remaining might bring.

Fishing boats dotted the seascape before him. Peering down the steep mountain ledge, Maol sighted men and women coming and going already in the wee hours of morning; perhaps they, too, prepared to leave the

Ridge for the freedom of the south. They were bundled warmly in woolen trews and cloaks; even summer's warmest days had grown increasing colder, it seemed, as if the Ice King—was he the same as the northerners' Zandru?—crept down from the winter regions a lifetime away in the mountains of the Hellers, seeking to choke the life from the Ridge. Did he come with the northerners who came smiling under false eyes, bringing new ways, strange customs to plant in the heart of simple folk from Finn clear south to Marcone?

Marcone . . . the place from which the Muirs had come. His kin. . . .

No!

The thoughts were forbidden. Of the seed of a clan lord he was, but not born. Nay, not *born* as a babe was born of a woman, of a loving mother. Maol drew his undyed wool cloak closer around his shoulders, tasting the cursed word used on him since the new lord's coming four years before. His lips drew up in a sneer as he whispered it. *Ri'chiyu* . . . how he loathed the very thought. A great *laranzu* had promised the then Lord of Finn, Rabharty Muir, a fine servant to be raised along with a hoped-for son. But he had failed miserably and had given Rabharty another son, one he could not acknowledge.

Maol smiled, flexing the muscles his arms should not have had. When the Comyn lords and kings came to Finn, they were appalled to see him so obviously human. Caelly's future in-laws nearly broke off the marriage thinking Maol was Caelly and learning of his origins. Squabbling land grabbers deserved the shock, he thought, having tampered with nature to get it. But what of him? Caelly's father was dead these four years and an uncle governed. Raghall Muir-Aonghus spared few feelings for his appointed heir, let alone his heir's specially-bred "pet."

"Maol? Maol, I been lookin' up and down the house for ye."

Maol lurched, hearing his young master's voice, the motion nearly throwing him over the edge of the mountain. He turned slowly to look into Caelly Muir's handsome face, to trace the slightly curling dark hair that framed the highboned cheeks and slightly upturned nose. He had nicked his face shaving; as if whiskers would make an appearance on such a youth's face yet! Like looking into a mirror it was, and why not? Were they not born of the same seed almost to the day? But Caelly was nurtured at the breast of the Lady Alaine and he at the nipple of one or another nursemaid after being "born" of some *laranzu*'s unholy excuse for a female creature that had little to do with Maol was. And what Maol was was not what he had been intended to be at all.

"Sorry, milord." Maol ducked his head the way his uncle expected, seeking to slip by this, his half brother, his master in a short time. Once, as little children, they had laughed and played together. Then Caelly's uncle became regent and taught the boy to be a prince, a young lord, and gave him playthings more fitting, like a hawk and a stag pony and the fine *skean dhu* he wore along his right calf.

"Wait."

The command stopped Maol dead in his tracks. Another cool wind rose off the ocean below and he shivered. Caelly, too, felt the breeze and drew his own fine cloak of fur and woven cloth closer around his linen shirt.

"Ye're pale as spooks," the youth remarked, arms crossing over a chest that would never be expansive, yet still had the promise of a masculinity Maol was supposed to have been denied. Maol ducked his head lower, knowing that were he to cross his arms and stand tall they would be equal . . . equal. Not at all what that northern wizard had intended, no, not at all, and not what Caelly's uncle would ever stand for.

"Ye been seein' ghoulies and ghosties, Maol?" The lad smiled broadly, flashing pale eyes that matched Maol's. "Ye'll 'ave me thinkin' *ye* be the nervous bridegroom. Is Uncle worryin' ye, Maol? Listen," he said, casting a quick glance over his shoulder before drawing nearer. He continued in a whisper, tugging Maol's sleeve to get him closer. "After the feast and the beddin' I'll be Lord here, and I ain't sendin' ye on no matter what 'e says. Aren't ye pleased, Maol? We played together as laddies . . . I've told me lady o' ye. Her mama comes from up north, but her papa is Clan Cinneididh right down to his heart. She'll love ya, Maol, like a wife should love her husband's brother. We'll find ye a bride, too—ye can 'ave one, ye're made for it, not what Uncle thinks."

"Thank ye, lord," Maol answered softly, quickly, uncertain how to take the compliments by reasoning that a polite response would give him the least worry later. He glanced about, fearful Caelly's uncle would hear.

"Ye don't sound very thankful, Maol. I need ye to 'elp me now, a'right? Say, me uncle's lettin' ye come to the weddin' feast even; ye've nae cause to be sae black."

"Me Lord Raghall's most kind. . . ."

Most kind . . . the words echoed in Maol's head as he trotted behind Caelly and back up to the manor. At the wedding feast Maol would be dressed up in bright gold and red trews and a full, pleated plaid of the Muir House—though not so fine as to be mistaken for someone of importance. Most kind . . no, he knew, it was not kind, it was cruel. Caelly's cousins—*his* kind, too, by the mighty God, Lord, and Spirit!—always whispered and pointed at him. And guests would stare and hide their smiles. A bastard at least would have a name, but him . . . *him,* they only scorned. Even his sire who had shown him love had given him but half a name.

It would be worse with northern Comyn there. They knew he was a failure, because they knew what *ri'chiyu* were supposed to be. Sexless, for the most part. Hairless bodies like little boys despite age. Made as servants; made for other things. Sterile. Horrible anomalies. They were bred that way . . . and Maol, Maol was better than Caelly's father had planned when he inquired about a playmate and companion for his son, knowing his wife might have no other children. A joy once, being better was Maol's sorrow now.

The warmth of the fire in the main hall did nothing to comfort Maol as he walked by. Within him, ice flowed freely in his soul. *Were I human,* he thought to himself, *I would cry . . . I would cry and leave this place before those* Comyn *magic-crystal wearers get here. . . .*

"Maol, pay attention!"

The voice cracked into his thoughts and Maol blinked, embarrassed. Caelly stood before him, hands on hips, lips curled into a deep frown.

"If ye nae wanna come, have it out, but I've a night to spend in the forest by clan custom, and I'll 'ave me stag as well, with or without ye."

"Wha . . ." Maol stared at him. Go with Caelly? That was the place of his groomsman, a brother, a . . . The ice shifted in his soul. Caelly was smiling, looking pleased with himself, but Maol shivered at the thought. Caelly raised him up. Caelly would make them equal in the eyes of his clan. Maol swallowed. Raghall Muir-Aonghus would kill him, not to mention Caelly's new Comyn in-laws. Better for Maol to go off alone, head south, live like a hermit. . . .

"Maol, close yer mouth before ye drool. Say aye and 'ave done with it."

"I'll g'with ye, surely . . ." Maol told him, plotting

his escape. He'd fake a runaway pony, fall off, hide
and make Caelly think him lost in a river. The be-
trayal stung him. Caelly honored him—against all of
the adopted customs of the north. Maol wanted to
apologize, but Caelly had already turned away, in-
structing the aged household steward to have his bow
and arrows readied. "Saddle a steed for Maol. Nay,
say nothing to Uncle. . . ."

The forest yawned before them, trees rising high
into the darkening plum-red sky. Clouds hung low,
heavy with rain that threatened to pour down upon
them before nightfall. The dark woodlands gave no
hint of relief from what had turned into a dismal
evening.

"Queer weather for summer," Caelly commented,
reining his tall bay pony to a halt. The colt stamped
the moist ground, snorting his impatience.

Beside him Maol drew a ragged breath, exhaling a
wispy mist the color of the aged dirt-splattered white
pony under him.

"Nary a good omen before a man's weddin' day,"
Caelly said, swiveling in the saddle to look at Maol.
He grinned. "Grandmother swears on her crystal we'll
'ave our stag. I know enough not to go arguin' wi'
her."

Maol smiled and nodded. A "man's weddin' day"
Caelly had said. His fifteenth birthday was not for
another month, two weeks before Maol's own. But,
Maol knew, in the north a boy was considered a man
at fifteen, and Raghall Muir-Aonghus was struggling
to bring Finn into alliance with one of the northern
clans. Thus the marriage to a half-Clan, half-Comyn
daughter. Caelly's kinsman, Seanon, had spoken of
northern customs during his last visit. Thoughts of
Seanon warmed Maol for the fist time that day. He
was a man of great importance in one of the cities far

up the coast, a crystal-holder, *bredu* to one of the most powerful princes opposed to the dangerous and mysterious work of some *laranzu'in*.

A splash of icy rain on his face alerted Maol to the beginning of the storm. He exchanged looks with Caelly, smirking at the adopted adult curses. They urged their mounts into the darkening wood.

Maol spotted the first stag, holding his words in hope that the young lord riding beside him would take pleasure in the first sighting. When he did not, Maol resolved to tell him next time.

"It'll be dark soon," Caelly complained, shaking his damp brown hair out of his face. The forest roof was thick and shielding, but after several hours they were both drenched.

"Yer teeth be chatterin'," Maol said after a moment of listening to the clatter. He smiled at Caelly; the two of them were as alike as twins could be. Why couldn't Maol have been born of his father's wife's womb and not that . . . that *thing* in the north. "Ye don't wish to take sneezes wi' ye to yer bed on the morrow, do ye?"

"Nay," Caelly laughed. "Let's find us a dry spot for our fire and get settled for the night. Think we'll be seein' the wild men? Or maybe wood spirits? Ah, we'll 'ave to nab a stag early come mornin' else we'll be late for the feasting."

Maol had long thought his half brother nearsighted. Even as Caelly spoke, another stag, a tall, graceful one with a large rack, stepped neatly from the woods ahead of them in the rising mist. Maol cleared his throat. He did it again; finally, he spoke.

"My prince, Caelly, is that a stag before us?"

"Thunder! Aye, indeed," the other youth whispered, smoothly drawing an arrow. It flew from his bow an instant later, jabbing the stag in the shoulder. The animal let out a snort of surprise and pain, leaping from the path and into the forest. Maol and Caelly were on its trail in moments, cursing when the forest became too thick. Maol regretted having sighted their prey. Leaving the forest path was dangerous so close to dusk.

"Leave the ponies," Caelly insisted, dropping down to the wet ground. His boots squished and slipped in the mud. "We'll go on foot and flush 'im out. Come on Maol, hurry, we've got to git 'im before dark."

They tracked the stag to a small clearing, finding it already downed and panting heavily. Blood pumped from the wound it had given itself when the arrow lodged in its shoulder had rubbed trees in passing and torn up into the fine, sleek, golden neck. Bubbling red froth dripped from the flaring nostrils as the beast stared at their approach.

"Careful 'o the horns," Maol warned, slipping his borrowed dagger from the sheath. Beside him, Caelly dropped his quiver of arrows, moving in from the finishing stroke with his jeweled *skean dhu*.

The stag swiveled its head to watch, powerful legs struggling to raise it up for a final battle. The large head dropped, the rack of points daring Caelly to approach. It would be better to put another arrow into it from a short distance, Maol thought, than to risk injury getting so close. Those horns could tear a man's guts out.

A piercing cry interrupted the hunt. Maol looked up to see a tall figure standing at the edge of the wood, shrouded in mist. It was narrow and hawklike, fiercer than anything he could ever recall seeing or hearing about in any hearth-tale. The creature rushed toward them, screaming again, arms flailing.

Frightened by both Caelly and the raking figure stalking them, the stag lurched up, horns swinging. Maol scrambled to where Caelly had dropped his quiver of arrows, grabbing his half brother's bow. With

little time to consider the best course of action, Maol
let the first arrow fly at the rampaging stag. The second one he aimed at the monster as its wild, beaked
face spun to face him. A third arrow was nocked, but
he could not remember loosing it before he heard the
stag's death bellow, then screams he could not place,
then nothing.

The constellation of the Dancing Warrior flickered
down at Maol when he woke; from just above the
horizon of the trees he saw two of the four moons
already in the sky.

"Caelly?" he asked, sitting up too quickly. The dark
world swam in and out of focus. "Caelly?" he asked
again, glancing around.

The stag was gone, dragged away, it seemed from
the bent grasses. In its place lay a familiar crumpled
kilt. Maol crawled over to where the young prince lay,
catching his breath to find no body. He picked up
Caelly's *skean dhu*, noticing the blood on it and what
was left of the dark kilt. Staggering up, he searched
the darkness fitfully for any sight of their ponies. Seeing
nothing and no one, he palmed the knife and stumbled
off along the path of crushed weeds.

Moving through the forest, Maol thought of Caelly's
chiding him about ghoulies and ghosties. If any truly
did exist, they would be haunting this misty wood; that
knowledge did nothing to comfort him. He hadn't
gone far when he heard a soft moaning. Maol shuffled
to a stop, pressing his back against a tree. It was cold
and damp and helped to keep him alert.

Again the sound; Maol swallowed deeply. The wild
man might still be around . . . looking for more meat,
possibly. If Zandru and the Ice King were one, then
so, too, were the wild men and the summer-maddened
Ya-men.

When the moan came again, Maol stepped forward,

searching for the source. Caelly, he thought, it could be Caelly if the mad thing hasn't stripped his bones already. *Skean dhu* before him, Maol followed the low groans until he saw a glimmer of white against the grayish mist.

"Caelly? Caelly!" he whispered hoarsely, recognizing the tattered linen shirt. He nearly dropped his knife in his haste, then did drop it when he saw the arrow lodged in his friend's chest.

Afraid to touch the still figure, Maol only stared in disbelief at the bleeding wound. No . . . NO! He had aimed for the stag, and then for the monster. Fear made him scramble to his feet now, knife ready, sure the beast man was nearby. He looked back in the direction he had come. He had to get help before Caelly bled to death, and . . . and then what? Lord Raghall would never stand for the knowledge that one of his servants, an inhuman *ri'chiyu*, had nearly killed his nephew and his brother's only son!

"Maol . . . Maol, are ye there?"

"Oh, Caelly . . . oh, aye, aye, I'm here. Caelly, lord . . . Caelly I nary aimed for ye, I nary . . ."

"Shhh." A trembling pale hand reached up toward him and Maol clutched it, praying he could squeeze the life back into this, his half brother. The tears he had wanted to cry earlier began to fall.

"Shhh. Maol, come closer. I'm cold."

"Caelly . . . I canna stay and git ye 'elp, too," Maol told him, draping his cloak over Caelly before lifting him gently. "Am I hurtin' ye? Nay? Easy then while I git ye back where I can get a fire burnin', I'll . . . Caelly? Caelly, don't look like that . . . Caelly, you look like Death's a knockin' on the door."

The young prince's eyes fluttered as Maol struggled with as much weight as his own frame carried. "Aye, Death's a comin', Maol. I'm so cold."

The branches Maol found were too wet for a decent

fire and he cursed the smoke. Someone would come
looking in the morning, he realized; Caelly's wedding
feast was on the morrow! But tonight . . . tonight the
boy was to become a man by braving the dangers of a
dark world, not the dangers of a friend! When Caelly
complained of the cold again, Maol lay down beside
him, wondering if removing the arrow would cause
further damage. The blood was drying and it didn't
look deep, yet Caelly was the color of undyed wax and
his skin was smooth and clammy.

"Maol? Maol, where are ye?"

"Here—oh, Caelly, I'm here beside ye. The blankets are wi' the ponies."

" 'Tis all right. Ye feel warm, Maol," his eyes fluttered closed.

"Caelly!"

The pale eyes, mirrors of his own, snapped open.
"What was that thing, Maol? I was caught in the stag's
horns and it dragged me away. Ah, Maol, ye were sae
brave, I saw ye struck it with an arrow. Should be you
havin' a test o' manhood, not me."

Maol's heart twisted. He had loosed two arrows,
had nocked a third. He shook his head. "I heard o'
wild men, but that's the first I e'er seen. Caelly?
Caelly, I've got to get help for ye. Do ye hear me? I
haveta find the ponies before that thing comes back."

"No . . . see?" Caelly asked, smiling up into the
dark sky. "See the Warrior's dance above us. I kicked
the sword, Maol."

"Don't be sayin' such," Maol told him. "Ye've a
weddin' on the morrow, remember? Ye're a lord, a
prince that wants to keep the clans together."

"Me cousin nary would. Maol, Maol, Seanon's
countin' on me, and Dorian Hastur-Elhalyn. They'll
be comin' for the feast, Maol."

Maol smoothed his friend's dark hair against the
moist brow, scanning the field, listening for the sound

of a pony in the darkness or the crunching of bones as the beaked man chewed on Caelly's stag. "Hush. Ye'll be fine. I'll carry ye all the way back if I 'ave to."

"Nay! Maol, don't ye see? Ah, ye can't, ye're only a . . . a . . ." The pain those words caused must have reflected back in the smoky night because Caelly suddenly apologized. "Nay, nay, Maol, I nary mean to say such an evil thing to my father's son. I . . . I'm sorry . . . the pain . . ." His eyes closed again. A weak hand edged toward the arrow, fell away with a new, bright redness on the fingertips.

"Ye're right," Maol told him, gripping the bloody hand. "I don't understand. I . . ." He hated to lie to his friend, but perhaps it was better Caelly think him an animal in a man's form, just like everyone else did. Better Caelly never know the bitterness, the love and the jealousy in his heart.

"But ye could . . I know ye could." Caelly looked directly at Maol, a weak hand touching the other youth's cheek. "Papa once told me that we looked like twins, that mama and he sometimes couldn't tell. We played a game of that when we were lads, we . . ."

"Nay. Oh, Caelly, don't be wishin' such on me," Maol told him, sitting up. He added kindling to the smoldering fire, shivering in the damp, dark chill around them. "I'm not yer mama's baby; I'm not like you, I'm . . ."

"Ye're my half brother? Aye, aye, and better to have me place than any o' me other kin. I picked ye for comin' wi' me tonight, didn' I? Before Uncle came we used the northern word—not the one Raghall calls you, but the one Seanon taught us—*bredu*. Maol, ye used to love me, didn't ye? Uncle didn't make ye stop, did 'e? Maol?" Caelly gripped his hand with only the strength of a babe. "Ah, Maol, don't ye love me no more?"

Maol looked away, the fingers of his free hand digging into his kilt. Where had the love gone, the love of boys, of little brothers? Did Caelly not realize that it *had* been taken away in the few days after Rabharty Muir died and his own half brother had come to the estate with a flame-haired Comyn wife and chubby, freckled sons?

"Maol—ye once called me brother, even if it were in secret. Please, if ye meant it, ye'll do this thing fer me. Don't make me say . . . a'right," he gripped his friend's hand and Maol looked back, frightened by the glinting purpose in Caelly's pale eyes. "If I'm yer master," he said firmly, and Maol could tell he hated the words, "ye'll do what I say."

The sudden prospect of having everything his blood deserved and had always been denied made Maol's head throb.

"When I die, take me clothes and go back—tell 'em Maol lost 'is life protectin' me . . . go back for me, brother. Get me another stag, a fine, tall stag, and go back. Ye been by me all me life. Ye know me best of all, Maol, enough to do what I want to do as lord. If ye love me, brother . . ."

"Don't call me that!" Maol cried, burying his face in his updrawn knees. He could see the hall lit and filled with flowers and food; he could see Seanon MacDomhnall coming across the hall, imagined himself running outside, taking a pony, riding away to the south, far away, never to look back. "Don't! They'll know, they'll know!"

A moment of silence followed.

"Caelly?" Maol asked, looking up. Two ponies ambled toward the smoky fire, nostrils flaring. Beside him Caelly Muir's pale eyes stared at the fine *skean dhu* touched by motionless fingers, and Maol's sobbing began anew.

*   *   *

" 'e's here! 'e's here!"

The throng of worried guests parted when Maol was ushered by cousins and kinsmen into the hall in the middle of the afternoon, the two ponies and his provisions left outside. His uncle, aye, *his* uncle, came forward, smiling through a tight set jaw, dark eyes so unforgiving Maol might have believed he'd sent the wild beast-man after them to kill them both.

"We worried, milad, that ye'd met with injury."

Maol shook his head, looking down at the floor instead of the swarthy, dark-bearded face. The charade would only go so far, he knew. Someone would know, someone would discover, call him murderer and then he would have to run, run for his life.

"Caelly? Caelly!"

Maol struggled to look up when he heard his half brother's name called. His name now. His . . . mother . . . Alaine came forward, embracing him.

"Raghall, git ye outside," she told her kinsman. "Caelly's little friend, the little *ri'chiyu* 'is papa gave 'im is hurt."

"Dead," Maol whispered, suddenly glad to be hidden against the woman's soft breast. The light musk of her perfumes was sweet and her long, auburn hair draped around him, shielding him. "Accident," he stammered.

"Aye, lad, aye. Oh, but ye be pale, Caelly."

The crowd in wedding finery parted and soon Maol was seated on a low bench near the hearth. The smell of the feast's sweetmeats and cakes reached him from the other end of the room. His eyes locked with Seanon's. Beside his tall, bearded clansman stood a slight, pale-haired man dressed in blue and silver. The Comyn lord, he realized. His heart raced.

"Caelly?"

Grateful for a new voice, Maol turned. The girl was not as tall as he, her hair the color of honey, her eyes deep and blue. His bride. He had never met her and struggled to remember her name as the woman, his mother, moved away to get him a glass of warm cider.

"Ghleanna," she supplied the name. He rose slowly, taking a long look at her, longer than he knew was polite. Her lovely gown swept the floor and the flowers in her hair were twisted into the braids. She tilted her head, reaching out to touch his cheek. "You look different . . ." She smiled. Her accent was odd, flavored with the language of her mother's people. "I'm so sorry. How careless of me. I'm sorry about the . . . Maol, aye? I would have loved your *bredu,* too, Caelly, even . . . well, you know."

He smiled. She meant it, and the words gave him back some of the warmth he had been robbed of early that morning when Caelly lay dead beside him and he took the fine *skean dhu* in the northern fashion of a pledge.

"Lass, don't ye know 'tis ill for a man to see his promised bride before the weddin'?" Seanon asked as he came forward, taking her hand and placing it on the arm of the handsome, gray-eyed man beside him. "Milord Dori, will you take Ghleanna back to *Domna* Chiara and her maids?"

Maol watched her go, fearing he'd never stand beside her again. His eyes went to Seanon's, then dropped to rest on the thistle pendant at the man's neck. The blue stone winked at him knowingly.

"Kinsman, yer loss is great on yer weddin' day," Seanon said slowly. When Maol could not reply for fear of giving his promised act away, Seanon nodded. Maol glimpsed his . . . uncle . . . come into the hall again. Seanon followed his eyes, then put an arm over Maol's shoulder and moved him in the other direction, accepting the cup of warm cider from Alaine in passing. "Aye, aye, ye've had enough a shock, laddie. Raghall, Lady, I'll take the lad to 'is rooms."

"The guests are 'ere for a weddin.' "

"Aye, man, well, a few hours, eh? Pour more wine, Raghall."

At the top of the steps Maol slowed, turning to look up at Seanon's gentle compassionate face. He swallowed deeply, knowing he should have run. By the time anyone had found Caelly's body, Maol could have been far away, beginning a new life, a life he had the right to live.

"I'm not—"

"Feelin' well, aye, lad, I know," Seanon put in, steering Maol down the hall. From the corner of his eye Maol saw that Raghall had followed them to the bottom of the stairs; he felt a tremor in his legs.

"Seanon . . ." Maol tried again once they were behind the door of Caelly's chambers. He dropped onto the bed, tears spilling down his cheeks. The quilt and air smelled fresh, the chamber dressed for a wedding night.

"Here, now. I know ye grieve for Caelly, Maol. Cry, lad, cry."

Maol looked up, brushing the tears away with the back of a soiled sleeve. "I didn't kill 'im, Seanon—I didn't try to, I mean."

Seanon nodded. "I know, laddie, but Raghall's no reason to believe ye. Caelly asked ye to do this, didn't 'e? It'll be hard," Seanon said, sitting beside Maol on the bed, squeezing his shoulder. "Ye'll need help."

"First, ye best git washed and rested. Dori and I can make sure no one ever knows, M—Caelly." He smoothed Maol's hair back from a hot brow. "Do ye understand? Nary a one, not even another *laranzu* will ever know—but," he tipped Maol's chin up, forcing their eyes to meet, "ye may forget what's real yerself."

Ye may forget . . . echoed in Maol's head and he felt the blood drain from his face. He could not answer except with more tears as he rose, stumbling to the window. The tears felt good, cleansing, melting the ice Raghall had put in his heart. To forget he was something other than human . . . no, to forget that he had ever been called anything else. The thought made his heart beat faster, then he saw the stag ponies being led across the courtyard. A dark head bobbed stiffly along one pony's flank.

"Nay . . . nay, I—I nary want to forget, Seanon, please, don't make me forget. I—I 'ave to do this thing for C—*him*. I promised, but not if'n I 'ave to forget. Please." Maol pressed the word, gripping Seanon's hand when it touched his shoulder. He looked up at his kinsman. "Please."

Seanon nodded, leaving Maol beside the window when Lord Hastur-Elhalyn slipped into the room. Without a word the pale-haired, pale-eyed man nodded, smiling gently at Maol. He watched them bolt the door, saw Seanon take the pendant from his neck and extend it toward Dori.

"Careful, *bredu,* unlike you I *need* one o' these. He can wear it the rest o' the day; we'll 'ave to git somethin' else for 'im then. Hmm? Nay, he wants not to forget. I know, 'tis as it should be. . . ."

Maol hardly heard the words as he stared out the window. His stag lay on the cobblestone below, tall and golden, finer than the first. Beside it was placed a thin, bloodied form dressed in simple kilt and moggins. His father's other son.

House Rules

By Marion Zimmer Bradley

Nothing I have written about the Free Amazons has caused so much controversy as the rule in Thendara Guild House that they may not keep boys over five years old in the house. I modeled this after a woman's residence in Berkeley which had such a rule (some women felt very strongly that women should not be forced to confront males, even infants). The house has since broken up, but it has forced many women to confront their own feelings, political and otherwise, about child-rearing and male children. I even read a book in which one writer contends that that mythical business, the male establishment (to which I have supposedly sold out) already has the technology which would enable women to have daughters without male intervention (how dull) and is deliberately withholding it from women.

I think this is about as likely as the many other conspiracy theories I have heard about; I know something of biology, and I understand the technology in question has not yet been successful on anything more complicated than a frog—or maybe a rabbit. Doubtless, as we have seen in the case of surrogate motherhood, it will come; once the bottle has been opened, nothing will trick the genie back into it. To some women for some reason or other, their "right" to have children outside the male establishment is terribly important; just as mothers without children feel differently about surrogate motherhood than the mothers who must bear, and give up, such children. Such technology would, of course, open many cans of worms even more complicated than the house rules of any Amazon Guild House.

I had hoped to get through one anthology at least, having devoted one whole anthology to them, without a story dealing with Free Amazons; but as you will see elsewhere in this anthology, this was too popular a theme to let drop. So, forced to choose among many stories, what did I do? I wrote one of my own. (MZB)

"Here is my book Mama," Loren said. "Will you hear me read?"

"Certainly." Lora felt the skinny little boy leaning against her knee and felt the tears welling up again inside her. Two more months and then Loren must be sent to his father. *To be made into the kind of man I despise, the kind of man who fills Amazon Guild Houses.* Because of the rules of the Guild House that a boy child may not live among women, and Loren was no longer a baby.

Janna came bursting in, her hair long and messy around her shoulders. "Mama, what's for dinner?"

"I haven't thought about it yet, Janni," Lora said. "Why don't you go out in the kitchen and see if there are any potatoes left; I'll fry them in goose fat."

"I'm tired of potatoes," Janna said, "when will we have meat again?"

"When we can afford it." Lora said. "Janna, why are you wearing your holiday smock?"

"Because it's the only decent dress I have," Janna whined. "Am I supposed to go around in breeches all the time like you and Marji?"

"Why not? What is wrong with them? You can

work properly in them," Lora said, but she might as well have spoken to the wind.

It is Cara's doing. We should never have taken her into the House; she was very bad for Janni, Lora thought. She hardly knew her nice obedient child in this sullen brat who seemed to spend all her day arranging her hair and painting her nails, who would not work in the barn or the fowl house because she hated to get her hands dirty, and last week she had caught Janni, hardly ten years old, lingering at the gate, twisting her curls and simpering as she talked to young Raul of King's Head Farm. Ten, and already making eyes at the lads. What did we do wrong, Marji and I? Janna was one of the reasons I fled from Darren, a few days after Loren was born . . . so Janna would not be pushed into being a stick in a pretty frock, good for nothing but to dress up, simper at boys, and giggle and talk about boys.

Marji called from the back door, "Lora? Are you home?" and Lora pushed her unwilling daughter into the kitchen.

"Take the skins from the potatoes and slice them," she ordered, and Janna sulked.

"I spend all my time in kitchen work. If I lived with Papa at least there would be kitchen-women to do the work for me. I am a kitchen slave, that's all. And I have to be one because you and Marji—"

"That's enough," Lora commanded. "There are no kitchen slaves in the Guild; but you know no other work as yet. Marji and I do our share of the kitchen work, but I have other work to do. I have to bathe the baby before supper and you are not yet big enough to do that. And Marji is working this week getting in Farmer Coll's hay."

"The women said she could have married Farmer Coll," Janna grumbled, "and she wouldn't have to slave in the fields all the time."

And that, Lora thought, would have been a good trade? Coll was forty-nine, and had buried three wives already.

"I'll run away, like Cara," Janna grumbled. "I saw her today; she said when she and Ruyval are married I can come and live with her. At least she's a woman, a natural woman."

"That's *enough*, Janna," Lora commanded and went through to the front hall, where Marja n'ha Carisse was taking off her boots. They hugged each other, and Marji asked, "Nice day?"

"No, Janna's at it again. Spent the whole day playing about with her hair and down at the gate simpering to talk with that wretched Raul from the farm. Cara's simply ruined her. All she thinks of is clothes and boys."

"We should have sent Cara away a year ago," Marji agreed. "I did not realize how much harm she was doing Janna. I was like that at her age, thinking of nothing but clothes and boys; she'll get over it. We did."

"But not in time," Lora wailed. "Now she wants to go and live with her father, and keeps threatening it. It's bad enough that I have to send Loren—how can I bear to give up my baby girl, too!"

"There, there," Marji said comfortingly. "You are protected by the Oath, and the magistrate said Janna could live with you. But if she wants to go, it will do her no good to stay here. Next time she threatens to go to her father, don't just let her go, *make* her go. She'll learn. How is my baby?"

"I haven't bathed her yet," Lora said submissively, and Marji held her. "It won't hurt her to go without a bath for a night. You look so tired, Lori. It's too hard on you, being saddled with all the children while I get out among human beings all day. When haying is over I will stay home for a while and you can find work; it's not fair you should have Callie as well as your two all day, all year."

"Callie is giving me no trouble, at least. At that size, as long as I keep her dry and fed, she makes no other demands." Lori said. "And speaking of Callie, I hear her. . . ."

She ran into the next room, returning after a moment with a tousled, sleepy two year old. Marji kissed her daughter, and, carrying her over her arm, went through into the kitchen where Janna was sullenly peeling cold boiled potatoes. "Here, Janni, give those to me, I'll make a cream sauce for them, and the farm wife gave me some bacon; I'll cook it for supper." She set about preparing the meal. "No, sit down, Lori, you're worn out. Where is Lynifred?"

"A messenger came from Arilinn; a man there has a sick horse and she went to doctor it; she will not be back till tomorrow," said Lora.

"Did you remind her that we need leather for boots for the children?"

"Yes; she said she would bring some, and then I can make boots for Janna and Callie as well as the ones Loren will need," said Lora, and began to cry again. Marji patted her shoulder, dished up the potatoes and fried bacon, then sat down with Callie on her knee and began to feed her daughter.

When the smaller children were in bed, and Marji and Lora were tidying the kitchen, Marji said "I saw Cara in the market. She and that boy were married. . . ."

"Goddess protect her," Lora said, "Cara is not sixteen!"

"Not before time, though," said Marji. "She is beginning to show."

"Well, she had nowhere else to go, after we threw her out," said Lora, "I feel it's my fault. We should have been more patient with her."

"But my dear," Marji said, "we could not keep

her, not when she was stealing from us. We forgave her a dozen times, but she was never a true Renunciate in spirit. Going about with her tunic unlaced down to *here*—" she gestured, "and spending all her time gawking and giggling about with the boys instead of staying properly in the house and helping you with the children! We should have sent her to Neskaya or Thendara for proper training—we had no Guild-mistress here to teach her proper behavior. And then we went into her chest and found all your best holiday skirts retrimmed—and she had sworn she had not seen them—"

"Oh, I know; but still, I feel I failed here, I tried to treat her like my own child—"

"And so did I, and so did Lynifred," said Marji, "but done is done, and she seems happy. I only hope Janna does not follow in her footsteps."

"That's what worries me," said Lora. "But perhaps if she lives with her father for a year or two, she will appreciate the Guild House. Come, my dear, let's lock up for the night."

Lying sleepless at Marji's side, while her freemate slept, Lora thought of how they had established the first small Guild House this side of the river, with three women; herself—and her daughter Janna, then five, and the infant Loren, still at the breast—fleeing from her husband who had beaten her and abused her.

Worst of all, he had forbidden her to read, or to read to Janna . . . books, he said, only kept a woman from what was proper for her. When he had wanted to betroth Janna, at five, to the thirty-year-old lord of the nearby estate, she had rebelled and fled to the Neskaya Guild House to take the Oath.

Then she had met Marji, newly come to the Guild, pregnant at that time with Callie. When her husband kept on pestering the Neskaya Guild House, the Guild-mother had sent them both to establish a Guild House

here in this little village, with Lynifred, a veteran
Renunciate almost fifty years old. For more than a
year the village had treated them like outcasts, especially when they took in the runaway Cara at fourteen,
until Lynifred managed to save a dozen horses who
had been poisoned by witchgrass, and Lora went down
to the village and offered to teach women the special
skills of midwifery that she had learned in the Arilinn
Guild House. Now they had been, to some degree,
accepted; women in need of a midwife were as likely
to summon her as the dirty, slatternly old woman who
had been the village midwife since anyone could remember. Lynifred was now the local horse-doctor, all
the better liked because she was not not above removing a bone from a cat's throat, or splinting the leg of a
dog caught in a trap. "They are the Goddess' creatures, too," she said, "even if they are not riches like
horses or cattle."

The trouble had started, she thought, when Cara
discovered boys and in no Amazon spirit had decided
she wanted to experiment with them. This Janna had
heartily followed, too, against Lora's prohibition.

Cara had seemed interested only in catching a husband. Well, now she had one, and Lora honestly hoped
the girl was happy.

Marji hired herself out to work in the fields, which
was awkward, because Farmer Coll wanted to marry
her, and had accused her of trying to snare him with
spells; fortunately there was not too much superstition
in the village. Still it was an awkward situation, since
Coll was regarded as a good catch, and the local
women, many of whom would have liked to be Farmer
Coll's wife, felt angry because Marji scorned what
they thought so valuable, while Marji only wished Coll
would marry one of them, and be done with it.

Lora knew she must sleep; there were only three
more days before Loren must go to his father, and she

supposed Janna would choose to go, too. Deeply as Lora loved her daughter, she knew Janna was not happy; but she did not think Janna would be happy in her father's house either; and she shrank from the thought of losing both children.

She felt she had not slept at all when she heard sounds in the kitchen, and roused up to go and make up a fire; Lynifred had ridden in at dawn and with her was another woman, muffled in cloak and boots against the early chill.

"This is Ferrika, midwife at Armida," Lynifred said. The strange woman wore an Amazon earring but wore ordinary skirts, not the usual breeches and leather boots.

"I must work among ordinary people," Ferrika said. "There is no sense in antagonizing them before they know me."

Lora put on a kettle for tea, and cooked a big pot of oatmeal porridge, and with it fried a little of the bacon Marji had brought home. The women sat with their feet to the fire, drying their snow-stiffened cloaks, and Ferrika asked for the news.

"Only that a fosterling whom we had to ask to leave has married, and is running about already showing her pregnancy less than a tenday past the marriage," said Lora despondently. "It says little for our care of her."

"I am sure the villagers know her ways as well as we do," Lynifred said. "It is not a reflection on your quality as a mother, Lora."

"I am not so sure of that," Lora answered. "Janna is beginning to imitate her—nothing in her head but boys, and fussing with her clothes."

"Almost all teenage girls are like that," Ferrika said, "unless they have had an early and dreadful lesson in what conformity can bring on girls in this world. When Janna sees Cara a drudge to her husband she will be glad to know how she can escape that fate."

"I wasn't," Lynifred said, and Ferrika laughed.

"Nor I," said Lora. "Nevertheless I married when the time came, thinking it better to have my own house and kitchen than work in my mother's. And even so, if I had married a decent man—though I thought my husband good when we were married."

"And so he might have been," said Ferrika. "It is not his fault that he did as his father and grandfather had done before him. Be sure you raise your son better than that, to know what women need, and that women are human, too, and not slaves."

"But how can I raise my son to be anything at all?" Lora asked, finally bursting into tears, "when I must send him to be reared by Aric and turned into the very kind of man I most despise?"

"When does he go?" asked Ferrika.

"Day after tomorrow," said Lora.

"Why are you sending him? Why not keep him here?"

"It is required by the rules," Lora said.

"Whose rules? Tell me which provision of the Oath requires it?"

"I have been told since Loren was born that I must prepare myself to give him up to his father when he is five years old—"

"Yes," said Ferrika, "so they told you at Neskaya. In the larger Amazon houses it is a solid rule, yes—many boys of fifteen or more living under the same roof with many women, would indeed be disruptive. But tell me, are your two housemates pressuring you to send him away? Some Renunciates wish to be free of all male creatures, including little boys."

Lynifred turned from the fire and said, "No; I told Lora to defy the bastard and keep the boy herself. Marji feels the same."

"What I truly wish," said Marji, coming into the kitchen with Callie in her arms, "is that we could keep Loren, whom we all love, and send away Janna, who is turning this house upside down. I'm sorry, love; you know I love your daughter, but she's driving us all mad, and if she goes Cara's way, that's no credit to a House of Renunciates."

"She's right," said Lora, sobbing. "Why do we have to send a harmless baby away just because he's male, and keep that one because she had the luck to be born a girl?"

Ferrika said, "Under most conditions, boys—especially tough street-reared boys—cannot be housed with women without trouble; I could tell you some stories—there was a time in Thendara House when we kept boys till they were ten, and the experiment did not work. Even their mothers were glad to see them go. It was not safe even for the younger girls in the house; and when we let the boys stay past puberty it was disaster. So in general conference it was decided that they should be sent away before five, and *certainly* before puberty. But in this, every house may make its own rules." And she quoted the Renunciate Oath.

"*I alone shall determine rearing and fosterage of any child I shall bear.* If it goes against your conscience to send him to his father, then, Lora, it is your duty to find a foster father or guardian for him who will not—as you said—turn him into the very kind of man you most despise."

"I thought it was part of the Renunciate law that my son could not live with me after he was five."

Ferrika smiled. "No," she said, "you are confusing the law for all Renunciates, and the house rules of each group. In the larger houses it is established that no woman may be forced to live with men or boys; but here you may make such rules for your house as you all agree on. You might even make it known, so that some women who are considering leaving the larger houses because they cannot bear to part with young sons, could come to you here—"

"It's a thought," said Lynifred. "If young men were to be raised by Renunciates, some awareness of what women really are and what men can be might some day go into the world outside the Guild Houses." She drew on her boots. "I'll take Loren out with me and teach him horse-doctoring, now he's big enough to spend a day away from his mother."

Lora thought; Lynifred could raise a man better than most men could; certainly better than his father could. She'll raise him to be strong, honorable, hardworking, and to understand that a woman can be so as well.

"What will my husband say?" she asked.

Ferrika replied gently, "If you care what he says, Lora, you are in the wrong place."

"I don't really care what he says," Lora answered, "but I dread having to face him while he says it."

"I think we all do," Marji said, "but we'll back you up. I don't think any magistrate would rule that he is more fit to be a parent than you."

"Send Janna to him," Lynifred suggested, "and if a year of being a kitchen drudge, wash-woman, and baby-tender for her stepmother—and worse, treated as if she had no brains—does not send her fleeing back to us here, then perhaps she deserves to stay in that world."

"But I couldn't bear to see Janna go back to that—" Lora began.

"If it's what she wishes, you cannot keep her from it," said Marji. "Because we want this life, we cannot demand it must be for her."

Lora bent her head, knowing that Marji was right; Janna must be free to choose as she had chosen.

"So," said Lynifred, "we are all here; shall we call this a House meeting, and pass a rule that boys may live here, if the women in the house all consent, till puberty, and that girls reared here must live a year outside the house before they take the Oath? It makes good sense to me."

"And to me," said Marji. Lora wiped her eyes and said, "I am not yet able to determine what makes sense to me. I am only so grateful that I am not to lose my son."

"And your daughter," Marji said. "A year treated as girls are treated in, say, Neskaya village would no doubt, have brought Cara back to us. Janna will be back."

"I hope so," Lora murmured, but she was not so sure. Nevertheless if Janna wanted that kind of life she could not be denied it. And if other women came here with their sons, it could be a beginning for a nucleus of men raised not to despise women. That was worth doing whatever became of them.

"I agree," she said smiling, and began to cut leather for a set of boots for Loren. He would soon need a scabbard for his first sword, too.

To Challenge Fate

By Sandra Morrese

Here, by a new writer, is a story on a plot I get every year; but very seldom is it done well enough to print.

As I have said often elsewhere, there are only a few basic plots; and the one about a woman married off by her parents, when she would rather be married elsewhere (or not at all) has been happening since the beginning of time, up to—say—the beginning of the nineteenth century. Its very truth makes it hackneyed; a cliche after all, is something that's happened often enough to be proverbial. But by the way people keep writing about it, no one is bored with it yet; and if enough people keep writing about it, I assume they want to read it. (That's why I write. Don't you?) So here it is again. (MZB)

Allira found her grief almost too great to bear and controlling her tears too futile a task. It didn't matter. The hood of her cloak hid her face well enough and the escort of Armida guardsmen knew better than to intrude. The required lady-companion had also realized the girl's need for privacy and rode a respectful distance behind. Even so, Allira's pride prompted her to minimize the visible shudders running through her and keep her sorrow as silent and private as possible. The Tower lay half a day's ride behind her now and each step of her horse increased the agonizing emptiness she felt.

Why couldn't he let me stay? I was happy there!

In three years, Neskaya Tower had become her home. How could her own father so cruelly deprive her of it? Yet, how much of a father had he ever really been? *Sire* was a more appropriate term, not father, so why should it surprise her? Allira couldn't remember him speaking to her more than a handful of times in all her life. Not like he was with Larrisa, his favorite child. But she didn't begrudge her half sister the relationship she had envied. They'd grown up closer than most true sisters, even swearing the oath of *bredini* the day Allira left for Neskaya. And after all, Larrisa was legitimate, and Allira just *nedestro*. She could hardly expect Lord Alton to treat her as Larrisa's equal.

The wave of tears subsided again and she gazed at the unchanging view around her; tall resin trees so dense in parts she could see no more than a few paces past their edge. Strange how she'd noticed the same thing the last time she'd traveled this road. That trip, too, had seemed interminable. A frightened, lonely girl of thirteen, barely over the terrible threshold sickness that grips a telepath at the awakening of *laran*. But the Tower had been waiting at the end of that journey, the love and experience of the telepath circle.

Her arrival seemed both a day and a lifetime ago. She'd been sorely homesick for her mother, but the Tower's Keeper, Caillean Ridenow, took Allira under her wing. Caillean's gently guiding hands and mind had patiently taught Allira to control and master her psychic gift.

To Allira, the training had seemed to take forever. (Mastering first her own small matrix jewel, then the work of monitor and mechanic, finally the highly skilled and specialized work of a psi technician.) In actuality, her gift and talent for learning were so great, that by the end of her first year she had become one of Neskaya's finest matrix technicians.

Allira was happily useful. As Lord Alton's *nedestro* daughter, she'd been barely noticed in Armida. But in Neskaya, they knew her and loved her for herself. Even more important to Allira, they *respected* her, for her abilities and who she was inside. It became the emotion she cherished most.

Then, a tenday ago, a message had come through the telepathic relay screens for her. She was to return to Armida immediately. A marriage had been arranged for her to Coryn Ardais, eldest son of Lord Felix Ardais. The handfasting would be in three tendays, the wedding one tenday after that.

Allira was in shock. She tried to politely demur, explaining that she wished to stay in the Tower a few more years. The response she received was from her father himself: *An escort will arrive five days hence—BE READY!* It was like a physical blow crushing her life she'd built.

Other messages had come after that, from her mother. Attempts to soothe and encourage Allira. After all, how often was a *nedestro* daughter given to the heir of a Domain? She would be well provided for. Allira knew this already. Knew that any other girl, even legitimate ones, would have felt lucky. But all Allira wanted was to stay and work in the Tower. She'd hoped she was insignificant enough to be overlooked when her father began arranging marriages. After all, it wasn't as though she had any real lineage. She didn't even bear her father's name but her mother's, Syrtis.

Then her mother explained the reason she was suddenly so important. Years ago, the two lords had agreed that Coryn would marry the Alton daughter with the strongest *laran*. The youngest Alton daughter, Elorie, had just been tested, showing promising talent but no power so strong as Allira's, so they need wait no longer since *Dom* Felix was anxious for his son to have heirs with strong *laran*.

Allira hated this. Even though the old breeding programs of the Ages of Chaos were considered ancient history, many families continued to arrange marriages based on *laran* strength. She supposed everyone had assumed the children of Lord Alton's proper *di catenas* marriage would have a higher degree of *laran* than his daughter by one of his wife's waiting women. Now, because she, by chance of genes, had the strongest *laran*, she would be married off accordingly and expected to do her duty to kin and clan, passing her *laran* on to children for her husband's Domain, without complaint.

Like some brood mare being led to stud, she thought bitterly.

Her horse's lack of motion brought Allira back to the present and she looked up. They were in a small clearing beside the road and the leader of the six-man escort was saying they should make camp for the night. Allira glanced skyward and was a little surprised to see the blood-red sun far to the west and the first of the four moons visible in the east.

The woman companion, a fortyish and graying woman whose name was Margwenn, drew her horse alongside Allira's. The girl cringed inwardly for Margwenn, like the men of the escort, was head blind. Not the slightest scrap of *laran* among them. It made Allira uncomfortable, for she was used to the intense mental closeness of the Tower. Her father knew that, and Allira wondered if this wasn't some kind of punishment for having questioned his decision. At the very least it was an insult to any trained *leronis*. First, to be refused a companion of her own choosing from the Tower, then to be thrust into this group of head blinds.

"I'm sorry, Margwenn," she said, when she realized

the woman had been speaking to her, "what did you say?" Allira found listening with only her ears difficult.

"I said, Lady," Margwenn began, polite but clearly annoyed at having to repeat herself, "one of the men has camped here before and says a shallow stream lies two hundred paces or so up that path." She pointed into the trees. "We should go and refresh ourselves while the tents are set up."

Allira agreed, dismounted, then gathered soap from her saddle bag and followed the older woman. When they reached the water's edge they removed their cloaks, boots and heavy stockings, laying them on a large rock. Margwenn stayed by the water's edge, washing discreetly. But Allira undid her undertunic, tucked up her skirts and waded into the icy water. She also undid her long braid of bright, copper hair, wetting it a little and combing it with her fingers. Margwenn's expression showed obvious disapproval, but in the Tower, Allira had learned to disregard minor discomforts and unnecessary modesties, so she ignored the woman.

Neither noticed the tiny, blue, star-shaped flowers, hanging low and overripe with pollen, growing wild on the bank a little way downstream from where they bathed.

Though she should have been exhausted from traveling, Allira found sleep eluded her. Finally she rose and quietly left the tent she shared with Margwenn. The guard on night watch was facing the road, so she was able to slip unseen into the woods.

Perhaps a walk will clear my mind and ease the tension I feel.

It was late and all four moons were high in the night sky. Two were nearly full, shedding enough light for her to see clearly and not trip. She found the place where they'd bathed earlier and began walking downstream, figuring this the easiest way not to get lost in

the never ending forest. Surely there was no fear of
bandits this far into Alton lands.

The multicolored moons reflected rainbow patterns
on the water and she smiled as she wandered farther
along the stream. It was unusually warm for even early
fall and the night breezes seemed to follow her. The
sweet, intoxicating fragrance of flowers swirled all about
her, making her feel as though she could walk all night
and never tire.

Perhaps I shall walk to Armida, the amused thought
hit her, *and let the guard wonder where I am and
Father wonder where the guard is.*

As another pollen-filled breeze swept around her,
leading her farther and farther downstream, the moon-
lit surroundings took on a misty, dreamlike appearance. She felt her mind opening with a broader sense
of awareness than she'd ever experienced. The breezes
were like music, and she spun and danced around the
trees. And for the first time since she'd been ordered
back to Armida, Allira laughed. Laughed and sang
and danced.

She allowed her mind to wander, drifting free, touching every living thing about her. The flowers and trees,
sleeping birds and night prowling animals, touching
and embracing the essence of their life, touching . . .
another mind! After the day's seclusion within her
head blind escort, Allira was overwhelmed by the
sensation of the beautiful, wondrous rapport! As their
minds interlaced and mingled, she felt the last traces
of grief melt away in the loving rain of thought that
poured through her from this miraculous meeting. She
felt whole again, the void filled to overflowing. She
could not have said, later, exactly when their bodies
found each other. But it was only natural; with their
two minds, their very souls, so intertwined, that what
was mortal in them would also join.

*   *   *

Hours later Allira awoke still encircled by his arms. The pollen-laden breezes had died away, but their deep rapport remained. She gently touched the edge of his dreaming mind, caressing, careful not to wake him. She gazed at his pale, slender face, lightly touched his fine, long, white hair.

He was *chieri*—that most ancient of all Darkovan races. They who had been in the world ages before humanity and had long ago retreated to the deeper forests. Nowadays they were more myth and legend than reality, so rare was it that a human ever saw one. But songs and stories from the Valeron Plains to Nevarsin paid tribute to the fair folk. Revered as wise, they were the most highly developed telepaths in all the world. It was said it was the *chieri* who first gave the starstones to humans, teaching them the rudiments of matrix technology. Early human history told of coexistence with the *chieri,* and many Darkovan families still bore the traits of *chieri* blood—colorless gray eyes, six-fingered hands and incredibly long lifespans.

He awoke and smiled radiantly at her. She returned his smile, at the same time feeling the mutual sad acceptance that they would, in all likelihood, never see each other again. He could not live in her world and she could not follow him to his. But a part of him would always be with her in the memory of this night.

Suddenly her vision blurred and another took its place with the sometimes curse of *laran*—the unbidden seeing of possible futures. She saw herself in a strange room, lying on a bed surrounded by women, some in breeches, (which seemed quite odd to her, as she'd never seen a woman wear breeches before). They were encouraging and comforting her as her body was racked by the painful throes of birthing. The vision faded and she again gazed at the beautiful face of her *chieri* lover.

*Will being with child cause trouble for you with your
father? Or your betrothed?*

*Probably, but I will deal with it. I do not wish to
prevent her.* She withdrew her mind a little and sent
herself deep inside to monitor the cell divisions that
were becoming her daughter, awed at the speed of
development. Then she returned her mind to him.

*You should not be forced into a marriage you do not
desire. Our race learned long ago that each individual
has value and the right to choose his own destiny.
Perhaps your race, too, will eventually discover that.*

*Perhaps, but I must live in the present. No matter
what else happens though, the memory of you will for
all my life bring me joy. And when she is old enough
to understand, I will share this memory with her and
she will know her father.*

He touched her face gently with the tips of his
fingers, his farewell.

My mind will always be within your reach.

She stood watching the graceful being as he walked
into the dense trees, reluctantly turning away when he
disappeared from her sight.

Allira returned to the stream's edge and began following it back to the camp, only now realizing just
how far she'd wandered. Nothing looked familiar to
her. She cast her mind ahead and discovered it would
be at least an hour's walk. She looked up. Only the
huge, violet disc of Liriel still hung in the night sky
and to the east the faintest morning light was beginning to show. She'd never make it back to camp before Margwenn awoke to find her missing. Ah, well,
the inevitable was not something she needed to worry
about an hour before its occurrence. She would enjoy
her morning walk and let Lady Fate do as she wished.

As she walked, Allira reflected on the past few days
and how foolishly she'd been acting. She had allowed
her emotions to overwhelm her. She was not a Keeper,

subject to suppressing her emotions completely, but she *could* control herself better than she had. Indulging in self-pity was a pathetic thing, and for a *leronis,* inexcusable. *Nedestro* or not, she was a woman of Comyn blood, Tower-trained, and it was time she started acting like one.

As she approached the place where the women had washed the day before, she noticed for the first time the blue, star-shaped wildflowers and began to laugh.

Kireseth! No wonder! That indeed explains the strangeness of last night, my far wanderings, and why the chieri, too, could not refuse.

Kireseth was a flower as old as the world itself, its pollen a hallucinogen-aphrodisiac that could eliminate the strongest mental barriers of even a Keeper. Last night's breezes had carried the pollen in a Ghost Wind, named such because those caught in it are so freed of inhibition they appear possessed. If the winds had blown downstream only, as Allira suspected they had, the camp would have never noticed. Allira continued to chuckle softly as she neared the camp.

She sensed panic. The guards and Margwenn were searching frantically for her. Allira knew they were not so concerned about her safety as they were their own should they return to Lord Alton without their charge. When one caught sight of her and called to the others, their relief was almost physical.

"Lady Allira," Margwenn exclaimed, rushing over to examine her, "you gave us such a scare! Where were you?"

Margwenn's stern tone irritated Allira. How dare this woman publicly scold her like some errant child.

"I went to the stream to walk," Allira said in her coldest tone. "Since I wished to be alone, I felt no need to waken you."

The icy glare she turned on Margwenn had the desired effect.

As she turned toward the tents, she thought how stupid it all was. If any of them had had *laran*, they would have known she was safe. In fact, she probably wouldn't have gone in the first place.

But then, maybe last night would not have happened, she thought. And placing her hand to her belly, she was finally glad they were not telepathic.

By the end of the day Armida was in sight and the finality of the journey clawed at her heart. Allira had grown up in this castlelike house of the Alton Domain, but it did not feel like home. Home was two days' ride behind her now. Instead, as she gazed at the massive structure, she saw the scarlet rays of the lowering sun dripping like blood over the stones; a savage beast, reaching to rip the life from her dreams, trapping and devouring her. . . .

No!

Allira physically closed her eyes on the fear-induced vision, fiercely regaining control. Reopening her eyes she saw only a large estate bathed in the colors of a Darkovan sunset.

She sighed. What was she afraid of? Her father? Certainly he would not be pleased about her pregnancy. She knew nothing of Coryn Ardais. Would he still wish to marry a woman who carried another man's child, even a *chieri* child? And she could not be so dishonest as to try convincing Coryn it was his. No, she would tell them, for they would all know anyway should she be monitored or the babe be born looking like her true father.

So, the world goes as it wills. Merciful Avarra, give me the strength to endure, she prayed as the horses passed through the main gate of Armida.

Allira stood on the balcony of the apartments she shared with her mother and watched the large group of approaching riders. They wore the colors of Ardais and bore that Domain's banner. A familiar twinge gripped at her stomach, but she quickly mastered it—she would not give in to panic again. Dwelling on what might have been was not a luxury she could now afford. Her fate could not be dreamt or wished away, it must be dealt with.

Tonight, at a formal reception, she would meet her future husband and in three days more would be the handfasting ceremony. She had that much time to learn what kind of man Coryn Ardais was before revealing her pregnancy.

Feeling a familiar presence behind her, Allira turned, just as her mother reached the balcony.

Ysabet Syrtis was nearing her fiftieth year, though she hardly looked it. She had kept the figure and smooth complexion of a woman half her age and only the graying of her tightly braided auburn hair belied the illusion. Ysabet was a gentle, quiet mannered woman and seeing her again was the single joy returning here had brought Allira.

"Must you keep yourself so tightly barricaded, Allira, even from me? Surely you can relax in our own rooms."

Her mother was right, and it was exhausting to keep up the tight shields concealing the knowledge of her child. Allira relaxed some of the barriers, drawing her mother into a light rapport.

"The Ardais party is arriving," Ysabet said with a glance toward the balcony. "Have you decided what you'll do?"

"Not really. I must tell them, but I think I would like to find out more about Coryn before I do. Mostly it is Father's reaction that worries me."

Ysabet sighed. "Aye, he will not be pleased. He may not expect you virgin—but with child? I don't know Coryn. I have met him twice but briefly. Larrisa was fostered for two years at Adrais, perhaps she could tell you more."

Allira turned back to lean on the balcony railing as the riders passed out of sight within Armida's walls.

"I have not seen Larrisa since my return though I have tried to seek her out. It's strange, it feels as though she is avoiding me. I had expected to see her in Neskaya, why wasn't she sent?"

Ysabet shrugged.

"All I know is that she was trained in the basics here, by *Domna* Valaena. Perhaps they thought her *laran* did not warrant sending her to a Tower. Even sending you was difficult."

"Why?" How could it be difficult to send anyone *laran* gifted to a Tower? She'd always known it to be customary.

"Mikhail despises the Towers, Allira. He wanted them disbanded, even tried to convince Varzil himself to make it part of the compact. You see, his first wife died miscarrying their son because of bonewater dust poisoning. Then, a year later, he felt his younger brother burn to death at Hali. I think that's why he refused . . ." Ysabet cut herself off abruptly, but not before Allira could catch a scrap of what was left unsaid and know it concerned her.

"Why he refused what, Mother? What aren't you telling me?"

Ysabet turned away, feeling trapped, yet she could not lie to her daughter. A telepath simply could not get away with it. And perhaps it was time Allira knew. Certainly she had a right to. She turned back and looked at Allira squarely.

"Why he refused to allow you to be trained as a Keeper for Neskaya."

"What? Why wasn't I told this? Surely Caillean knew!"

"Yes, *Domna* Caillean knew, but she *couldn't* tell you. Please, listen to me, Allira." Ysabet could feel the suspicion growing in her daughter. "When Valaena

went before Lord Alton with the news that you should
be trained as a Keeper, he refused. So she told Caillean
of it and she came herself out of the Tower to argue
on your behalf. He still would not hear of it. He
blames the Towers, and all Keepers, for what happened to his wife and brother. As it was, it took all
Caillean's powers of persuasion, convincing him that
you would be a danger to yourself and all those around
you without Tower training, just to get you there these
past three years. And to win that much, she had to
vow that while you were there she would not reveal
her knowledge of your potential to you.

"And where was I while all this was decided?"

"Near to death in threshold sickness."

"I wouldn't have had to leave," she whispered, and
her bitterness cut like a jagged knife through their
rapport, making her mother flinch. Allira smothered
the emotion with difficulty.

"There is nothing you can do, Allira, but accept
things as they are. He is your Lord as well as your
father and you can't change that."

"If I were a Keeper, I would be responsible only to
my own conscience," she spat out. "I would *have* no
Lord over me!"

Allira turned away, slamming up barricades, painfully severing the rapport with her mother. She was
too angry, too hurt. With the Alton breed of *laran*
one could kill with an angry thought. A barricade was
safest until she calmed again, part of the control Caillean
had taught her. But would she ever be calm again? To
know all this torment might never have happened? To
know she could have been a *Keeper!*

The great hall of Armida lay elegantly decorated for
the reception of Ardais. Allira had been told it would
be even more lavishly done for the handfasting banquet; looking about now she found that hard to believe.

Gabriella, the Lady of Alton, had had her sewing women make Allira dresses. For tonight she wore a close-fitting gown of pale blue satin with a deeper blue velvet apron. The cuffs and deep neckline were elaborately embroidered and the hem trimmed with fur. Her hair was braided, wound and clasped at the nape of her neck with a fine copper clasp, a gift sent from her future mother-in-law. After the loose, comfortable robes of the Tower, Allira felt like one of the wall ornaments—or a doll, dressed up and put on display.

She sighed as her mother joined her at the top of the stair, similarly dressed in her own best ball gown. It had taken Allira several hours of strictly controlled meditation to ease her hostility after this morning. Finally, she'd accepted her inescapable situation. But she would never again be able to look at her father the same way. Always before, she'd felt inferior. Women were not regarded highly on Darkover, having very few and limited rights. The only women given equal status and rank alongside the Lords of the Domains were the Tower Keepers; and she could have been one. A little more training, that's all. She, herself, would have still been Allira Syrtis of Armida, still *nedestro* daughter of *Dom* Mikhail. Only her *laran* training would have changed, been more rigorous, more intense. She was *not* inferior to this man who'd sired her. Now she knew, within herself even if the law didn't, that she was his equal. Courtesy and custom might demand she act otherwise, but she would always know. And somehow, that newfound self-esteem gave her courage to face the life she had not chosen.

Closing her eyes, Allira quickly and carefully checked the mental barriers that guarded the information about her child. Then she looked over at her mother, who smiled reassuringly. Allira returned the smile and the two descended the stair hand in hand. At the bottom they waited for *Dom* Mikhail and *Domna* Gabriella to escort them.

Mikhail Alton seemed a dark, imposing man though it was much more his manner than his stature. He was actually a lightly built man with rather pale hair, but he was the Lord of Alton and it was evident in every move he made. A man in his late fifties, he conducted himself in a way that reflected the experience of his years and demanded respect.

Lady Gabriella was such a contrast to her husband it made one wonder how they came by one another. Gabriella was a small woman with a quiet, shy manner, easily twenty years his junior, with bright green eyes and vivid, red-gold hair.

They took Allira and her mother to where the Ardais family stood greeting the minor nobility of the Alton Domain who'd been invited to the banquet. They were first introduced, as courtesy demanded, to the Lord and Lady of Ardais, *Dom* Felix and *Domna* Deonara. Allira kept a probing portion of her mind open to learn all that she discreetly could about her future family. Lady Deonara received her with a smile and the gentle embrace of a kinswoman. Allira sensed kindness; yet she also sensed that while her outward friendliness was not ingenuine, it was more a matter of trained graciousness than true desire.

Lord Felix gave Allira an entirely different impression. His embrace was rougher and he held her a little more closely and longer than Allira would have thought proper. There were rumors that he was a lecherous old goat, lusting after anything in skirts, and his surface thoughts confirmed the rumors. She also sensed arrogant power, normal for a Domain Lord, and . . . something . . . she couldn't quite place. Then he kissed her lightly on each cheek, releasing her, and the feeling was gone, like water through her fingers, fading as quickly as a dream. She was still trying to grasp the last fragment, to understand, when she found herself in front of Coryn.

He certainly was handsome, her promised husband. Tall by Darkovan standards. Pale blue eyes looked out from a rugged, animated face and thick, curly red hair crowned his smooth brow. He was, at most, ten years older than she. Despite his beautiful features, Allira braced herself to read much the same in Coryn as she had in his father. She was surprised when she sensed only a detached, sadly resigned obedience to the duty put before him. It dawned on Allira that perhaps Coryn wanted this marriage no more than she did, so she pressed a little for more contact, hoping to learn why. Coryn, however, refused her mind's touch, forcing her to leave her questions unanswered.

Allira took her place at the table to the left of Lord Alton, along with his two legitimate daughters, Larrisa and young Elorie, as well as Ysabet and two more of Lady Gabriella's senior waiting women.

She wondered again at the elusiveness of Larrisa, who'd been her closest friend before she'd left for Neskaya. Being only a year younger than Allira, the two had grown up and been schooled together. Allira thought that perhaps tonight she could successfully renew their friendship. Looking over, she caught Larrisa's attention and smiled. Allira was shocked to see the glare of hatred Larrisa returned.

What could I have done to so offend her? Allira wondered.

At the head table, where the Lords sat with their wives and eldest sons, Allira saw Marius Alton. It had been his bearing which had called Allira's mother to Lord Alton's bed seventeen summers ago.

He is the heir to this Domain, she thought, *and he will be treated little better than me. Married off for the good of the Domain. At least he may be consulted about who is chosen. Women rarely have that privilege.*

After an elaborate feast of roast chervine and stewed rabbithorn, as well as every kind of exotic side dish and sweet bread imaginable, the tables were cleared and moved to the sides of the hall. Some of them were refilled with candied fruits, the mild shallan punch, and bowls of stronger wine as well. Allira couldn't believe anyone would have room for more, let alone the strength to dance, for she was stuffed and quite content to sit.

The dancing would remain segregated for a while yet, so Allira decided to seek our Larrisa to ask what was troubling her. She found Larrisa standing alone on the far side of the room, near the entrance to one of the long galleries. As Allira approached, Larrisa suddenly became busy with an imagined wrinkle in her gown. Allira reached tentatively out with her mind and touched Larrisa's vainly barricaded turmoil of emotions—anger, sadness, despair, anger again. Finally the girl raised her eyes, meeting Allira's with a savage gaze.

Why didn't you stay in the Tower? Why did you have to come back and ruin everything? Why!

Then her rage gave way again to the immeasurable sorrow that was its source and Larrisa turned away, running far into the gallery.

For a moment Allira could only stand there, stunned. She cast about to see if anyone had witnessed the exchange, but Larrisa had not broadcast; it had been for Allira's mind only. She followed after Larrisa and found her by the window at the end of the gallery, flung across a bench and sobbing uncontrollably. From her mind Allira picked up a memory:

Last midsummer's eve, Larrisa with Coryn in the gardens at Castle Ardais. Larrisa had been there two years, fostered to Lady Deonara. She and Coryn had grown closer than foster brother and sister; they had fallen in love. And that night, amid the blossoming

*flowers of the garden, they had consummated their love
and pledged themselves to one another. Coryn would
have petitioned Lord Alton for Larrisa's hand at Midwinter, when she was declared of legal age to marry.*

Allira stood motionless with the force of Larrisa's
pain reverberating within her. How could she have
been so wrapped up in her own problems that she
failed to see that more than her own life would be
affected by this unwanted marriage. How could she
have been so selfish?

Then her anger toward her father rekindled, burning as high and as strong as it had this morning. How
could he do this to his own daughter? His favorite
child? Surely he knew Larrisa was in love with Coryn.
Would it have been such a crime against his honor to
adjust his agreement with *Dom* Felix?

*Zandru damn him to the coldest hell! How dare he
so casually destroy three lives like this. Even a Lord
should not have that right!*

Larrisa looked up, sobered by the intensity of Allira's
barely contained fury.

"I'm sorry," she said quietly. "I shouldn't have
blamed you, I know this wasn't your choice. I'd just
hoped . . . hoped you'd be able to stay in the Tower
and refuse. You know, when *Domna* Valaena tested
me and said my *laran* would give me a talent for
healing but no more, I didn't think anything of it. I
really didn't want to go to a Tower, so I figured it
didn't really matter. Then I met Coryn," she smiled
wistfully, "and nothing else mattered. We were so
sure, we didn't know about . . ." Her voice faded as
she controlled another wave of tears. "When our fathers refused, we couldn't believe it. Mother tried to
change his mind, but he wouldn't listen."

Allira's anger softened in the face of Larrisa's heart-
break and she embraced the girl as she began to cry
again.

"Don't, *breda*," Allira soothed. "We will think of something. You are my sworn sister, I would not dare to tread on the hem of your garment. I swear to you, I will not take the man you love!"

The next morning Allira arranged a private audience with her father. Preparing for the worst, she asked Larrisa to set up a telepathic damper outside the door to Lord Alton's study after she went in. She told Larrisa it was to keep the meeting secret, but Larrisa suspected that was only part of it—one Alton's anger was bad enough, but an Alton against an Alton could be dangerous to every telepath in Armida.

Allira had brought one of her technician's robes back with her for its comfort. This morning she wore it as a statement to her father of who she was—and who she could have been.

Standing outside the study, Allira took a deep, calming breath, steeling her nerves, then knocked and entered when he acknowledged. She was relieved to see they were truly alone, with none of the stewards hanging about.

Mikhail looked up from his work, surprised, then annoyed when he met Allira's steady, direct gaze, instead of the respectfully lowered one women were taught. Then he read the hard resolve beneath the insolent gesture.

"What is it, Allira?" he asked with a surface calm.

"I came to discuss the marriage you've arranged between Coryn and myself."

"There is nothing to discuss."

"There is. Are you aware that Coryn does not wish to marry me? He is in love with Larrisa and she with him. They are the ones who should marry."

"What has love to do with it? Your *laran* is stronger. Our agreement . . ."

"Damn your agreement!" she interrupted. "You're treating us like mindless chervine being bred for endurance or tender meat. We're not animals, Father! You are ruining three lives with your accursed agreement. Doesn't that matter to you?"

Lord Alton was taken aback by her vehemence. He'd been unprepared for such an outburst from a woman, any woman, let alone this sixteen-year-old *nedestro* of his.

"Silence!" he ordered, anger being his only defense. He also used the compelling, *laran* projected *command voice*, and was shocked when it had no effect on her.

"No, Father," she answered quietly. "You have controlled my life long enough. I should have been a Keeper, but you denied me with your prejudice. I should have been able to remain working in the Tower as technician; they needed me there, and you denied that, too. But this I will deny you, I *will* not be the instrument that destroys my sister's happiness." She used the word *breda,* sworn sister, stronger than blood ties. "You want this marriage to breed strong *laran* into our lines, but I swear to you now, as Evanda and Avarra are witnesses, I will bear no children to the Ardais house. If I must destroy my own fertility to do it, I swear to you *I will*.

Mikhail rose from his seat menacingly. "You dare make threats to me?"

"What choice have I? You will not listen to reason, so I will be unreasonable."

He moved as if to strike her but stopped, met again by her steady gaze and unnerved by its force.

Allira took the opportunity to project to him Larrisa's pain and how much she loved Coryn. Then she reminded him of Larrisa's childhood. The bright, happy girl who'd been his joy, their special relationship that Allira had always envied. Had he forgotten how much he'd loved her? When she left for fosterage, he'd missed her terribly and plunged into the affairs of the

Domain in her absence, numbing himself. When she'd returned, he'd barely spoken to her.

"I am *nedestro* and unimportant, but Larrisa is your own and once you loved her. How can you hurt her so now?"

Mikhail sat down again, stunned and shaken by the revelations. He had loved Larrisa, still did. Marius was his heir and separate somehow, always taught independence, and Elorie was Gabriella's baby; but Larrisa, she had been his own. From the moment she could walk she'd followed him everywhere, unconditionally loving and admiring him. She'd never done anything to intentionally hurt him. Now he was hurting her, with a wound that might never heal. She would surely hate him. Yet, what choice did he have?

"I cannot dishonor my promise to *Dom* Felix, Allira. I wish, now, it could be otherwise but there is nothing I can do."

"If you could, would you allow their marriage?"

"I swear to you, if there were any way I could change all this I would, but it is already done. I'm sorry, truly I am."

Allira nodded. "So I thought," and left the study.

Allira was in her room packing two small bags as judiciously as possible. Her mother watched, worried but unable to express it. Allira knew. Knew also that it couldn't be helped.

"You know it is the only way, Mother. I cannot stay here. This will free Father from his agreement without dishonor to him. Have a servant find the note in the morning. It tells of my pregnancy and makes it appear I have run away in shame, not wishing to dishonor Coryn. It is not a lie. Marrying him while he loves another would be a grave dishonor. Tell Father, 're-member your promise.' He will allow Larrisa and Coryn to marry. I'm sure Coryn, too, will speak loudly of it being the only honorable alternative."

"But where will you go? A woman cannot travel alone, and in the dark of night?"

Allira laughed a little.

"I am a *leronis*, Mother, with the power of Keeper; I am better protected than if I carried a sword. But you are right, a woman alone is much too conspicuous. So I took some of Marius' old clothes to wear and will keep my hair under a cap. I am not tall; by casting a slight glamour I should be able to fool most into thinking I am just a boy on an errand for his master. If I stay to the less traveled roads I should be all right. I'm not really sure where yet. South I think. Perhaps to our kin in Valeron. Or maybe I will find a village somewhere thankful enough at having a *leronis* to heal them that they will not ask questions of my past or the strangeness of my child."

"Will I ever see you again, daughter? Or my grandchild?"

Allira could feel her mother's heart breaking with her own.

"Of course you will!" she said fervently, holding her mother tightly to her. "I will send you word whenever I can. Surely, in time, we can return."

They embraced a moment more, then Allira slipped out into the dim hallway. An hour later she was riding away from Armida.

The Devourer Within

By Margaret Carter

Every year I have the pleasure of seeing a few old friends; Margaret Carter made her debut with FREE AMAZONS OF DARKOVER, and has followed this up with a very different story for this anthology; a story of an almost unique story of the uses of laran; *one which presents it realistically as the not-unmixed blessing it can be. (MZB)*

Come at once if you would save your betrothed.

A priestess of Avarra, Kyria reflected, would not use such extravagant language lightly. And certainly not Kell's older sister Damrys, whom Kyria recalled as the most sensible and unimaginative of women. Yet the cryptic note delivered to Kyria less than a tenday past had sounded like a passage from a gory ballad sung by the fireside to frighten children: *I came home for a visit to find my brother in thrall. No one else can reach him, but perhaps you may be able to awaken his true self. This matter is too strange and complex for me to unfold in writing.* And then that urgent appeal—no more.

Kyria reined her chervine and paused to gaze up the mountainside at Kell's castle, looming fortresslike on its peak. She brushed a damp coil of coppery hair back from her forehead. Despite the snow on the ground, she was sweating from the exertion of the ride. The manservant riding with her as bodyguard said tentatively, "Shall we go on, *domna*? Sunset approaches."

She glanced aside at this solid, familiar bulk. "Very well, Garris." She spurred her mount to a slow walk along the rocky path to the keep. She had missed Kell Aldaran these past few months since he had left the Tower at his father's unexpected death to assume his position as lord. Had matters gone smoothly, Kyria would not have seen Kell again until the day, set for the following month, when she would have arrived here to become his bride. Though theirs was an arranged betrothal, fixed by their parents when they were children, Kyria felt no revulsion against it. Her father, a distant kinsman and minor vassal of the Aldaran lord, had been too kind to throw his daughter into the arms of a man she would meet a quarter-hour before the *catenas* were locked on her wrists. As soon as both Kell and Kyria were clearly past the danger of death in threshold sickness—his struggle with it had been by far the more severe—the boy had been sent to Kyria's father's hold for fosterage. By the time both had been ready for the long journey to Neskaya Tower, to serve their terms in the circle, they had been half in love. At the Tower, not being sworn to continence, Kell and Kyria had explored and deepened their affection. Then had come word of old Lord Aldaran's death, and the lovers had said a temporary farewell.

At the memory of Kell's delicate, six-fingered hands on her body, tingling warmth flooded Kyria's breast. This visit would be joyous if not for Lady Damrys' warning. *If he were in danger, surely I'd know.* But that was romantic silliness. Kyria's *laran* was not strong enough for long-distance rapport, however powerful Kell's might be. *I shall know when I see him, at least,* she comforted herself.

At the castle gate a boy trotted forward to take

charge of the chervines, and Garris followed him to oversee their stabling. The perspiration of Kyria's face and arms turned chill as she stepped into the coolness of the great hall. The tall, spare wife of the coridom, well known to Kyria from previous visits, came forward to take her cloak. "Thank the Lord of Light you're here, *vai domna*. *Dom* Kell will be much the better for it." She curtsied and dipped her head, almost, but not quite, kissing Kyria's hand.

"Surely it can't be that bad, Elena. Is he ill?" Kyria said, gratefully shedding her cloak into the older woman's hands and sinking into a chair next to the hearth.

Elena prodded the smoldering fire. "I cannot say," she muttered. "Under a curse, I might call it, being no *leronis*."

"Elena, you forget yourself," snapped a voice from the arched doorway.

Though short and slightly built, and clad in a simple green gown instead of sacerdotal robes, Lady Damrys radiated dignity. She gave Kyria a brisk embrace and a dry kiss on the cheek. "Thank the Goddess you've arrived safely, sister. Elena, fetch a cup of mulled wine."

"Yes, *vai domna*," said Elena, scurrying out of the room.

"What is all this, Damrys?" Kyria asked, resisting the impulse to hug herself against a more than physical chill. "Has Kell fallen sick?"

"You might call it that. Yours is a healing *laran*, and he won't let me near him for a proper examination. Perhaps for you—I remember how stubborn you can be when need arises—" Damrys broke off as the coridom's wife returned with the mulled wine.

Kyria folded her hands around the warm curve of the goblet, absorbing the backhanded compliment and waiting for Damrys to continue.

"But first you must persuade him to send Edric

away. Kell listens to none of us, and since he is lord now—"

"Edric Alton?" Kyria interrupted sharply.

"I see you trust our cousin no better than I do," said Damrys. "Yes, the same."

Edric Alton had been at the Tower with Kell and Kyria but had left before his time, for a reason not made public. "I know nothing definite to his discredit, but we heard that he quarreled with our Keeper."

"That's putting it too kindly," Damrys sniffed. "Edric defied the Keeper of Neskaya and was thrown out of the circle for his refusal to obey the most elementary safeguards in the use of *laran*."

"And he's here now?"

"As Kell's sworn *bredu* and trusted advisor. I never expected my brother to be so easily halter-led." Damrys shook her head. "Well, I won't try to explain what Edric has done to the boy. You'll understand when you see for yourself."

Kyria swallowed a few more gulps of the hot wine and set down the goblet on the hearth. "Now."

"Sure you're ready? Wouldn't you rather refresh yourself in your own room first?"

"I want to see Kell," said Kyria, fighting her rising annoyance at Damry's evasive manner. Despite her show of confidence in Kyria, Damrys obviously still thought of her brother and his bride as children to be protected.

Kyria followed Damrys across the cold stone floors and up the narrow, winding stair, built thus in an age of constant petty wars to deter intruders, to the bed-chambers. "He hasn't stirred outside the castle since I came home," Damrys remarked, "and he scarcely leaves his room."

When Damrys rapped on the door of Kell's chamber and opened it to a muffled reply from within, Kyria caught a dusty smell. Perhaps Kell allowed the

maids inside as infrequently as he ventured out. The
room was dim, drapes drawn so that Kyria could not
distinguish windows from the tapestry-hung walls. Heat
from a blaze in the fireplace made the air stifling. An
oil lamp on a writing desk gave the only other light.
Kell sat at his desk, wearing a russet house robe.

"Kyria! I didn't expect you—but by the gods, I'm
glad." He held out his hand.

Crossing the room to lay her fingers in his, Kyria
struggled to bring her shock under control and keep
him from sensing it. Kell had always been pale and
slender, more fit for study than for riding and hawking. Old Lord Aldaran, more liberal than many noble
fathers, had not made his son feel that temperament as
a defect. Kell had not been bred, after all, for crude
physical prowess, but for *laran*. At adolescence that
ability had revealed its raw force, and his family had
since waited eagerly to learn what form it would take—
both in Kell himself and in the children he would get
on Kyria.

*Laran—is that what troubles him? Some sort of exer-
cises he and Edric are doing? Sometimes I wish we'd
never heard the word! What would it be like to marry
for love alone and bring up children without watching
them every moment for signs of power—or doom?*

Now Kell's skin was not only pale but stretched
tightly over the delicate bones of his face. Had he
given up food as well as light? His hand, closing on
Kyria's, felt cold despite the fire. Her free hand clutched
her starstone through its protective silk pouch at her
breast. She focused on the lines of force rippling through
Kell's body. They looked faint, attenuated, wavering
beneath her eyes. He resembled the emptied outline
of a man.

He looks—hollow.

"I've missed you, Kell," she said, hoping her voice
did not reveal her concern. "Your letters haven't been

frequent." That sounded like whining; she hastened to amend the remark. "No doubt finding yourself so suddenly responsible for all this—"

He did not rise to kiss her, nor did he remember to release her hand or invite her to sit. "Yes . . . the accounts . . ."

He waved vaguely at the book open on the desk. From Kyria's angle the cramped letters did not appear to bear on stock-breeding or tenants' fees. "We must have a long talk soon, my love. Edric will be here in a few minutes, and he and I have much work to do. He's training me in the use of my starstone," he said with another half-finished gesture, confirming Kyria's guess. "You remember my cousin Edric?"

She nodded, puzzled at the warm tone in which Kell spoke of the man. In the Tower Kell had been no closer to Edric than she herself had.

"May we watch?" Damrys asked. Kyria jumped, having almost forgotten the other woman's presence.

"Yes, of course. Kyria, I know you'll be amazed by what we've achieved." His eyes glowed with an enthusiasm they had not shown at the sight of Kyria. "But now I have to meditate and prepare. Come back in a quarter of an hour."

Damrys led Kyria down the corridor to the room she had used on her former visits. Unlike Kell's chamber, the guest room had been ventilated, so that the fire only took the edge off the bracing air admitted by the open curtains. "Accounts, indeed," said Damrys as she tested the heat of the wash water in the bedside basin. "He leaves all that to the coridom and me. That was a book of Edric's he was reading, a compilation of results from questionable *laran* experiments."

"But what is it they're trying to do?" Kyria asked.

"Better let Edric explain his goals," said Damrys. "I wouldn't want to prejudice you." She paused at the door to add, worry replacing the ironic tone, "And I did tell my brother you were arriving today."

Left alone, Kyria washed quickly, then brushed and rebraided her hair. She was beginning to guess what Damrys had meant by claiming that Kell was "in thrall." The lady disapproved of Edric's influence over her brother. Kyria, too, remembering Edric as an arrogant, unapproachable young man, felt ready to share that disapproval, yet how could Edric be blamed for Kell's choices? Kell was of age and of sound mind. He might well resent Damrys' treating him like a headstrong boy.

Kyria caught herself staring into the fire, twisting her braid around her fingers like a child trying to recall a forgotten lesson. *This is a waste of energy—I'll know the facts in a few minutes.* She marched down the hall to Kell's chamber.

At his door she met Damrys. Together they stepped inside. Kell was still sitting at the desk, cleared of everything but a lit candle. In the shadows a few paces away stood Edric. He stepped forward to let the light fall on his lean face and the bleached, pale red-gold of his hair. He bowed to Kyria with a brief, tight smile. "Lady Kyria, it's a pleasure to see you again, *damisela.*"

She returned a silent nod of greeting. *He lies. He's thoroughly displeased to have me here. Not because he fears my power; he has nothing but contempt for that. Because I might be a distraction to Kell.*

She fixed her eyes on Kell's. "Won't you tell me what this demonstration is about?"

"Edric can explain so much better," said Kell. "All I can say is that he's opened up such depths for me. My love, I didn't know for certain what my *laran* was until Edric showed me." He cast Edric a glance almost worshipful, waiting for the older man to take over the discourse.

"My lady, what is the Overworld?" Edric asked Kyria.

"Are you conducting an examination?" she countered. "I was taught that it is a construct formed by the collective missions of all sentient minds that travel there."

"So we've all been taught. But suppose the Overworld has an independent reality, a character of its own? Suppose it contains regions not generated by human thoughts, never explored by any human traveler?"

"So?" Kyria shifted her gaze to Damrys, who kept her face expressionless. Only the priestess' eyes betrayed her impatience with a lecture she'd heard many times before.

"So," Edric mocked, "these regions may be inhabited."

"By what?" Kyria said. Her involuntary start of astonishment drew a gratified smile from Edric.

"An intriguing question, isn't it?" he said. "When I first found the gate to those territories, I didn't suspect there would be—inhabitants. As often as we've contacted them, or it, we still have no clear notion of its character."

"It? You claim you've seen—communicated with— some kind of inhuman intelligence?"

"It's no mere claim, it's true," Kell broke in. "Kyria, this is the most exciting—"

She interrupted, "What do you mean by 'gate'?" She silently prayed the answer wasn't what she suspected.

"That is what you're here to see, isn't it?" Edric smoothly replied. "Kell, are you ready?" The young man nodded and unwrapped the starstone suspended from a chain around his neck. Cupping the stone in his hands, Kell lifted it like a sacrificial offering into the circle of the candle's glow. Blue sparks flared from the stone's heart as it reflected the flame.

Shifting her eyes from the unsettling swirl, Kyria

stared at Kell's face. She clutched her own matrix, praying for strength, as Edric stood behind the chair and placed his fingertips on Kell's temples. At once Kell's breathing slowed and deepened. His eyes glazed over, and the energy currents outlined on his body became sluggish, muted. Kyria had never seen so deep a trance achieved so quickly. She drew a few long breaths herself, striving to disconnect her emotions and view her lover with a healer's eye.

His hands lay limp on the desk, his facial muscles equally slack. He resembled a snow-poppet melting in the sun. His lines of force began to blur, and a blue-violet mist seemed to rise from his motionless shape. At the same time Kyria felt a shudder in the air, as if the atmosphere had been snapped like a length of taut rope. The curtains and tapestries rippled, though she knew from the suffocating warmth that the windows were still shuttered. A log tumbled from the stack by the hearth and rolled to the center of the room. A book shelved over the mantel flew several feet and dropped. Damrys dodged with methodical ease, as if she'd seen this phenomenon many times and counted it no great threat compared to what lay ahead.

The fog exuded by the entranced Kell thickened and coagulated. It seemed to be trying to assume a shape, though one that constantly changed. Kyria thought she glimpsed hands, or perhaps claws, then the legs of an insect, then a many-lobed eye, then three eyes set in a triangle. She wrenched her gaze away from the vision to study Kell. His energy lines were faded almost to transparency. A fluid like slow lightning oozed out of him toward the creature—if living creature it were at all. Probing Kell's mind, Kyria felt emptiness.

Yes, he is hollow—and it eats him to a husk, more and more with every second.

She forced herself to grope for the thing's mind, if it

had one. She touched a maelstrom of violent hunger. Involuntarily pulling back, she fell into blackness.

She sensed it was only a few seconds later when her awareness returned. The mist was thinning and flowing back into Kell, leaving an aroma like mountain air before a thunderstorm. Kyria stared into Edric's icegray eyes. "How many times have you done this to him?"

The man shrugged. "This is nothing. Your presence is a disturbance—you hamper the materialization. Many times the vision has been clearer and remained longer. We don't know how to speak with it yet, but soon—"

"You fool!" Kyria raged in an undertone; she would have shrieked if not for fear of upsetting Kell. By now the atmosphere had returned to normal. To her dismay, Kell still stared at nothing, his jaw hanging open. "Bring him out of it," she ordered Edric.

"That isn't possible," he said. "Don't be concerned; the boy regains consciousness in his own time, and the process cannot be hurried."

Kyria leaned over to wave a hand before Kell's eyes. He did not blink. When she lifted one of his hands, it remained rigid in the air until she lowered it again. She turned to face Damrys, who watched with an expression of sorrow but not surprise. "Each time, it takes him longer to come to himself," she said. "On the last occasion he remained thus for most of the night."

Edric met Damrys' accusing stare with no flicker of self-doubt. "You are determined not to understand, *domna*. The importance of this discovery is well worth the risk. Hasn't Kell said to himself?"

"Kell is a misguided boy who'd leap into the coldest circle of Zandru's hells at a word from you. Come, Kyria, we can do nothing for him at this moment." With the stateliness of a woman one-third again her height, she swept to the door, adding, "I'll send up

Kell's body-servant. I know he can expect no care from you, Edric."

There Kyria thought her future sister misjudged Edric. The man probably took excellent care of his tools. Her head still had not stopped reeling by the time she and Damrys reached the older woman's chambers. A pot of tea waited in Damrys' sitting room, and she poured them each a cup before allowing Kyria to speak. "Now, sister, give me your thoughts on this— discovery."

Kyria cast her mind back to the display she'd seen, cutting through the chaos and suppressing her terror for Kell. She forced herself to process the images one by one. "Edric is lying to himself as well as the rest of us," she said finally. "He truly believes that—thing—is an intelligent visitor from the Overworld."

"And you think it isn't?" said Damrys in an unsurprised tone.

"Can't he see that it's a part of Kell?" Kyria burst out. "A piece of his own mind—split off—doubtless gaining more life every time it appears! And it's eating him alive!"

Damrys nodded. "I suspected something like that, but I don't have your sensitivity to perceive it. What do you advise?"

"Just what you did," said Kyria, taking a steadying swallow of her tea. "Get rid of Edric at once."

Damrys said with a humorless bark of a laugh, "So I've urged Kell over and over during this past month. Maybe he'll listen to you." She did not sound as hopeful as she had earlier in the day.

"I'll try," said Kyria. "The moment he's well enough to listen."

The following morning she invaded Kell's bedroom with that goal in mind. He lay in bed, guarded by his body-servant, who had barricaded the chamber against

Edric and would have barred the way to Kyria if he could. She shouldered her way past him, counting on his inability to use force against a noblewoman. "You may wait outside while I speak to my betrothed alone."

"That's hardly fitting, *vai domna,*" the man mumbled. A cold stare reminded him that Kyria was no longer the half-grown girl who used to visit the castle under a chaperone's supervision. He left.

Kyria sat on the edge of Kell's bed. "How do you feel?" She leaned over him, but drew back, flushing, when he made no move to kiss her.

"I don't know, much as usual." His voice sounded not only weak but flat, as though the subject held no interest for him.

"You mean, as usual after these—exercises?"

"Damrys has been at you, I see," he said. "She doesn't like Edric."

"Nor do I," said Kyria. "Can't you see he's killing you? Send him away."

The hardening of Kell's expression showed her that her vehemence had been a mistake. "Kyria, not you, too. I'll hear nothing against Edric. Do you realize what it was like for me, growing up, knowing I was good for very little aside from my *laran?*"

"Kell, that's nonsense. It's your illness talking."

"I am not ill. And you know as well as I do that I was bred for sorcery and nothing else. When years went by, and all the *leroni* could tell my father was that I had a powerful *laran,* but they didn't know what— Well, Edric had revealed my purpose."

"To be a link with creatures from other realms," she said dryly.

"Can't you understand how fascinating it is?"

"Perhaps I could, if that were actually what's happening," she said. "But can't you accept the possibility that Edric is mistaken? That the thing isn't from the Overworld at all?"

"What is it, then?" He sounded genuinely curious; perhaps she was reaching him.

Kyria took a deep breath. "A part of you. A projection of your own spirit, gone wild, feeding on you to build up its strength. A strength with no other purpose but destruction."

Kell's eyes grew distant again. "You're just like Damrys. Another small, closed mind—I wouldn't have thought it of you, Kyria. You may as well go."

She blinked back the angry tears stinging her eyes. No weak, womanly tactics would help. "Won't you at least give my theory a chance? Fairness demands that. Let me monitor your next experiment."

He gave her an indifferent nod. "You can't change the facts. Tonight, then."

So soon? After it drank so much of his life last time? She stifled her alarm. Persuading him to put off the confrontation might give Edric a chance of convincing Kell to forbid her presence altogether.

That evening Kyria gathered with Kell and Edric in Kell's chamber once more, Damrys standing by as witness. Viewing Kell with *laran* rather than ordinary vision, Kyria was appalled at how translucent he appeared. How could Edric ignore that creeping attenuation? Had it never occurred to him that he would soon lose his gate? Or that, if his attempts succeeded, he might loose a chaotic being fiercer than Sharra, the incarnation of Fire? Kyria wasted no energy trying to convince the man of his error. The sooner the experiment began, the sooner she could put a stop to the whole process. How, she was unsure, but she had resolved that this night would be the last time Kell would risk himself.

Before Edric arrived, she tried one more appeal to Kell's reason. "Do you remember what happens after Edric lulls you into a trance?"

"No," Kell admitted. "But I've been told all that happens."

"By Edric himself," Kyria pointed out.

"With my own sister as a witness," Kell shot back.

Damrys offered a reluctant nod. "Edric has not falsified the *facts*."

"The interpretation is his, though," said Kyria.

Again Kell gave her nothing more than a cool stare. "Do you know more about such things than a man who has studied them for years?"

Kyria gave up. A moment later, Edric entered and assumed his usual pose behind Kell, his hands on the younger man's head. Reining her fear and anger, Kyria sank into a pool of calm. This time she would not let her emotions stampede her into useless outbursts. Within seconds the trance enfolded Kell, and the life-force began seeping out of him. Instead of fixing her gaze on him, Kyria watched the entity as it formed. Again the room quaked. The candle flame dipped, and the glass globe of the unlit lamp crumbled into a pile of shards. A smell of lightning and hot metal slashed the air.

Kyria yielded to none of these distractions. She noticed that the thing immediately coagulated into a denser cloud than it had the previous night. Instead of blue-violet, it showed a turgid purplish red. Over the other scents crept a stench of burned flesh and dried blood. *Could my nearness be urging it to a more physical manifestation?* Kyria thrust the idea aside. For an instant she shifted her attention to Kell himself. He looked more than ever like a man sculpted out of snow.

It's draining him—I must act.

She took the one step most certain to disrupt the link between Kell and his emanation, though she had been warned of the hazards. She touched the naked stone sparkling in his hands.

Pain ripped through her. She felt the same agony convulsing Kell and echoing through Edric's nerves. A bone-jarring vibration threw her clear. Looking down, she saw her motionless body, one hand covering Kell's, which clutched the starstone. Kell's face was petrified in a rictus of pain. Behind him stood Edric, still holding contact. He froze as statuelike as Kell, except for the awareness glowing in his eyes. Damrys watched the tableau from her position against the wall, not daring to interfere lest she cause some worse injury.

Floating outside her body, Kyria watched the thing as it groped for a shape. It congealed into a vaguely human form, four-limbed and upright. In what should have been its head glimmered a pair of eyes. They shone with the blue of Kell's.

It wants to become him—it craves all of his life. Touching the creature's thoughts, she sensed a bottomless envy of all that walked the earth in corporeal substance. It could not be said to have a mind; it was all instinctive craving. If it swallowed up Kell as it yearned to, it might then acquire a mind.

An automatic fumbling at her breast led Kyria to the ghost—no, the soul—of her starstone. On this plane it scintillated as if a flame lived within it. She visualized it as a weapon, firing deadly rays at the voracious creature. At the first hit, the thing emitted a soundless screech that she "heard" inside her very brain. The cry seemed to sear the lining of her skull. She willed another ray to slice into the creature's vitals. It appeared to shrivel into itself.

It's weaker than I am. I'm a whole thing, and it's only a fragment.

Exulting in the thing's disintegration, she gathered her force for a final strike. From some corner of her mind rose the words Damrys had given her: "Yours is a healing *laran*."

So it has always been. And sometimes healing means killing the disease to save the patient.

This was no disease, though. It was part of Kell. Gazing into the shreds of its pseudo-body, she realized what part. It embodied all the violence buried within him and never released—the bite he could have gouged into his nurse's arm, the blow he might have driven into a playmate's face, the girl he might have ravished, the untrainable hound he might have beaten into a cripple, the insult he had choked down instead of spewing out. No wonder the thing fought for freedom. Yet it still had a right to exist in its own sphere. Repugnant as all those memories were, no person would be whole without them.

As Kyria wavered, the creature pulled its fragments together and loomed up before her. Concentrating on her starstone, she remolded the matrix from a weapon into a roll of endlessly unwinding filaments. She spun out a rope as fine and strong as spider-silk, whipping it around and around the thing's quasi-human shape. The captive writhed in the glittering cocoon, howling in pain that twisted her own vitals as well. When she had immobilized the things, she drew it toward Kell.

Life sprang up in his eyes. Though still paralyzed, he was awake. He knew what the creature was and what Kyria planned for it. His silent screams echoed the thing's. Unrelentingly Kyria shoved the two together. Against his will, Kell's mind opened up to absorb the ravening entity.

At the moment of union a burst of energy exploded from the pair. The flare of the forcible merging engulfed Kyria and Edric also. Kyria's head was still ringing as she snapped back into her body. She glimpsed Edric flung facedown on the floor. Damrys stumbled forward, falling to her knees beside the unconscious man.

Kyria found that she was no longer touching Kell.

Folding her hand over his, careful not to touch the
starstone again, she searched his face. He opened his
eyes.

"Kyria—you—you're not hurt? It's gone?"

"Not gone," she whispered. "Where it always was."

"Gods, you were right. It was—" His face crumpled. She leaned across the desk to him and held his
head to her breast. When he pulled free a minute
later, she noticed that his skin had already lost its
translucent whiteness. Though still pale, at least he
looked as if blood flowed through his flesh.

Kyria glanced at Edric. Damrys ran her hand down
his spinal column, not quite touching him. "He's alive,"
she announced, "which is more than he deserves."

"Thank the gods," Kell sighed. "You were right,
chiya, he didn't know what he was doing." His hand
tightened on Kyria's. "He was wrong about me. What
am I now?"

"Yourself." She raised his hand to her lips. "More
yourself than ever."

Sin Catenas

By Elisabeth Waters

Elisabeth Waters enjoys only one advantage in writing for these anthologies; since she lives with me, she can discuss the balance of the anthology with me, and write a short story or a long one—whichever I happen to need. Lisa has been writing Darkover fiction since the first of these anthologies—she wrote the title story of THE KEEPER'S PRICE—and personally I think that "The Alton Gift" is yet to be surpassed in any of these volumes. I'm not so sure that it is surpassed by any of my own work.

Like most of us, Lisa has written a novel; we're still waiting for a publisher. It's a good juvenile; and like most juveniles, I suspect it will outlast the writer—and me.

If Lisa has an advantage, she also has a disadvantage; when she's writing, she's right at hand, so I can stand right over her and tell her what kind of rewrite I want—and I do. (MZB)

Veradis Castamir chose her husband when she was nine years old. It was, of course, a serious decision. She was the only daughter of Lady Crystal Castamir and her husband, Dom Ruyven of Castamir, and thus heiress to all Lady Crystal's estates—or at least such portion of them as survived Dom Ruyven's profligacy.

Some men, Veradis knew, hunted forests into deserts, some gambled every coin and jewel they could lay their hands on, some drank until they were nothing but shaky shells. Dom Ruyven had a different hobby. He fathered bastards.

For as long as Veradis could remember, her father had had some girl or other living with them, each younger and dumber than the last. One would last about a year, then the current one would be married off to some small farmer or craftsman, with a dowry to support the bastard the girl was carrying, and Dom Ruyven would get a new girl and start over. Lady Crystal might not like it, but there wasn't much she could do. He *was* her husband—and she was too much a lady to do other than put a good face on the whole mess. Veradis wasn't so forebearing, which was why she was currently hiding in the woods.

Even in a life full of unfortunate incidents, today's had been particularly so. Veradis had disliked Asharra, her father's latest barragana, from the day she arrived, three years ago. What he saw in the woman Veradis couldn't imagine, but for some reason he had kept her, even when she bore him a daughter. Lady Crystal was fostering the brat, saying bravely how nice it was to have a baby in the house. Veradis thought it must be bad enough to get up at night to quiet your own screaming baby, but having to do it for someone else's, while she lay in bed with your husband, was intolerable. And today Asharra had come up to Veradis and announced, with a truly idiotic smirk, that Veradis was going to have another sister. Veradis had looked her straight in the eye, making no effort to hide her disgust, and said, "You are mistaken; I am an only child."

Unfortunately, her father had entered the room just then, overheard her, and beat her severely for "discourtesy to her elders." And her mother had cried over her and said that it was a woman's lot to accept whatever her husband chose to do.

Veradis, being in pain and thoroughly out of temper, had snarled back, "That makes it all the more important to choose a husband for something other than his good looks!" Her mother dissolved into floods of tears, and Veradis escaped to the woods to do her own crying in decent privacy.

Now she lay carefully on one side by the edge of a stream—she knew she wasn't going to want to sit down for several days at least—rinsing her face, and sobbing. "I just can't live like this!"

"In the woods?" a voice behind her said lightly. "I shouldn't think so; it gets too cold at night."

Startled, Veradis incautiously rolled over, yelped with pain, and struggled hastily to her knees. She faced a boy about her own age, dressed in clothes that, while plain, appeared to have been clean and neat before he spent most of the day in the woods.

"Are you injured?" he asked with obvious concern.

"Not really," Veradis sighed. "Just a beating, not the first, and I'm very much afraid not the last either."

"But why would anyone beat *you?*" he asked incredulously.

"My father didn't like the way I spoke to his barragana."

"Oh. You're Lady Crystal's daughter then."

"My father's activities must be notorious indeed," Veradis sighed. "I've never even seen you before, and you can identify me just from knowing that my father beat me because I was rude to his barragana."

"Well, I don't know your name," he admitted, "but my aunt did mention your mother as an example of—well, uh, ladylike endurance?"

"Idiotic stupidity?"

"I was trying to avoid saying that. My name's Cullen,

and I've come to live with my aunt, who is married to the tanner."

"My name is Veradis, and I'm happy to meet you. What happened to your parents?"

Cullen bit his lip. "My father is dead, and my mother's a Renunciate, so I can't live with her."

"Whyever not? And what's a Renunciate?"

"Renunciates are women who swear never to marry or be supported by men, so they live together in what they call Guild Houses, and boys aren't allowed to live there after they turn five."

"That's awful! Well, I can understand wanting to get away from men, but giving up your child . . ."

"Yeah." Cullen stared at the ground. "I wish my mother agreed with you. Children shouldn't have to live like this."

"No," Veradis agreed. "They shouldn't. Children are supposed to be a valuable gift from the Goddess, but the way some parents act, you'd think we were worth less than a rabbithorn!" To her surprise, she suddenly started crying again. "I hate them!" she sobbed. "I hate my parents and I don't want to be like them, ever, but I'm afraid I'm going to be because I don't know how else to be, and I don't want to hate them. They're all the parents I've got—but my father's an arrogant lecher and my mother's a nothing who lets him kick her—and me!—around. I mean, if she wants to look after his bastards, that's her choice, but what about me? If she cared about me at all, she'd at least send me away to be fostered somewhere, but when the *leronis* who tested me last spring suggested it, Mother said she couldn't possibly give me up! And I don't even have enough *laran* to go to a Tower. If Mother had to marry a man who'd abuse her, couldn't she at least have gotten one with *laran*?"

Cullen knelt beside her, held her against his chest, and patted her very gingerly on the shoulder. "Your father is a fool. He should be proud to have a daughter as beautiful as you are."

"And your mother should be proud to have a son as nice as you are," Veradis said, picking her head up and mopping her eyes with the edge of her shawl.

Cullen chuckled. "Well, at least we agree on the important things. Shall we get married when we grow up?"

Veradis looked at him in surprise, and watched as an older version overlay the boy's face in front of her. Suddenly she *knew* that this was what lay ahead for them, that they would marry and have children and grow old together. "Yes," she said solemnly, "when we grow up."

He looked at her and nodded slowly, and she wondered if he saw what she did. She shivered and realized it was getting dark. "I'd better go back before they miss me," she said.

"Right," he said. "We don't want a search party finding this place; we'll need it again."

She stood up and wrapped her shawl tightly around her. Just one question, Cullen," she said, smiling impishly. "You don't have any desire to be a father to your country, do you?"

Cullen laughed. "No, Veradis," he said, "the only children I want to father are yours. That will be plenty for me."

With her decision made, and with a place to escape to and someone to talk with, Veradis found life at home rather more bearable. It helped a lot to have a goal; she kept her mouth shut, and concentrated on learning all she could about housekeeping. She'd need to know it when she married Cullen. After her mother's death, of course, the Castamir estates would be hers, but there would probably be years when she and Cullen would have to live elsewhere, without any support from her parents. She had no illusions as to what her parents would think of her marriage, but they couldn't possibly think less of it than she thought of theirs!

She also learned how to take care of children; Dom Ruyven and Asharra provided her with plenty of practice. Over the next five years the number of their bastards grew from one to five. Lady Crystal seemed to age quickly and became less and less able to look after all the children. Fortunately, Veradis discovered that she liked babies and was good with small children, though she certainly would have preferred her own. Still, their unfortunate parentage wasn't the children's fault, and they were going to have enough trouble in their lives without Veradis' adding to it.

She and Cullen continued to meet secretly in the woods, and if they saw each other in town when Veradis went there on errands they pretended not to know each other. Cullen had been apprenticed to the tanner, and had worked hard and learned the trade well. By the time they were fourteen, Cullen was capable of earning a living and Veradis could run a house.

"So, when shall we marry?" Veradis asked one autumn day as they sat talking in the woods.

"As soon as we're both fifteen," Cullen said. "I asked my mother when she last came up to visit me what the law was on freemate marriages—I assume your parents aren't going to consent to our marrying *di catenas*?"

"I think that's a safe assumption," Veradis agreed. "That's why I've been careful not to let them know we even know each other. We don't want them looking for you when I disappear."

"Agreed," Cullen said. "I'll be visible earning a living, but you can be hidden pretty well. It's easier to find a tanner than it is to find someone who's not tied down to one trade."

"Do you think 'wife' isn't a trade?"

"Of course it is, but it's such a common one that it's harder to find one particular one." He made a face at her. "You know perfectly well what I mean. Don't be so difficult!"

"Sorry." Veradis grinned. "It's such a lovely change from meek and obedient daughter."

"Not too much longer now. I'll be fifteen next month, and you'll be fifteen in the spring."

Veradis nodded. "Our only problem is how soon my father will try to marry me off. Supporting his bastards is getting expensive, and as long as I'm heir to Castamir, I'm a rich prize for any of his friends willing to pay for the privilege."

Cullen nodded. "If he tries, you'll have to play for time. If we marry before you're fifteen, it won't be legal."

Veradis sighed. "If I'm lucky, he's forgotten how old I am. It's a good thing I'm small for my age. What's the form for freemate marriage? Do we need witnesses?"

"Not really. The simplest form is for us to share a meal, a bed, and a fire. Freemate marriage isn't valid until it's consummated, and the sooner we have a child, the better."

"Yes, that does tend to indicate that a marriage has been consummated."

"And once we have a child, the Comyn Council can't dissolve the marriage."

"Oh." Veradis thought that one over. "I shouldn't think they would; the Castamirs are just a minor branch of the Hasturs—but I certainly don't want to take the chance. It's a good thing we both want children anyway. So we'll elope on my fifteenth birthday, and have our first child as soon as we possibly can. Any ideas as to where we should go?"

"I've been thinking about that," Cullen said slowly.

"You probably won't like this idea, but I think I should leave as soon as I turn fifteen, set up somewhere south of here, and come back for you in the spring. That way, we won't both disappear together. I've been talking to my aunt and uncle about my desire to go out and 'make my own way in the world' so they won't associate my going with you."

"You're right on both counts," Veradis said. "I'll miss you horribly, but it's a good plan and you should go. Then when I leave, nobody will even know you were here. Just don't lose track of the days."

"Don't worry," Cullen smiled. "I haven't forgotten your birthday since we've known each other, and I certainly have extra reason to remember it this year."

"True enough," Veradis smiled bravely. "I'll meet you here at dawn on my birthday." She hugged him hard.

On the eve of her fifteenth birthday, however, Dom Ruyven called Veradis into his study and informed her that he had chosen a husband for her. Mindful of the undesirability of open defiance, Veradis temporized.

"But, *vai dom*, I can't possibly leave. My lady mother needs me here to run the household." This was at least partially true; Lady Crystal rarely left her bed at all now.

"Nonsense," he said briskly. "Asharra can run the place."

Veradis stared at him in astonishment. *Whatever is he using for brains? Aside from the gross impropriety of setting his mistress up as lady of the house, there are serious practical problems.* Aloud she said simply, "But Asharra hasn't any aptitude at all for household management."

"How much does she need?" he snapped back. "Isn't that what a housekeeper is for?"

"It isn't that simple, *vai dom*," Veradis said quietly, trying to maintain the appearance of filial obedience.

"Well, we'll just have to teach her then," he said. "You can stay here for a while after the wedding if necessary. Your husband is a cousin of Asharra's; he won't mind—it's all family, after all."

That did it. Wise or not, there was only so much Veradis was capable of tolerating. She lifted her head, looked him straight in the eye, and said firmly, "Asharra is *not* a member of this family!"

"Oh, yes, she is," he retorted, "and she'll be even more so once you're married to her cousin."

"I won't marry him."

"Nonsense, of course you will. Every girl dreams of marriage—and surely you want children."

"Yes, I do." Her lips thinned tightly together. "My children, not my husband's annual bastards!"

His lips tightened ominously, but she went on. "I've spent my whole life watching my mother house and feed your mistresses and care for your bastards—on her own estate! You chose well for your wife, but I'm not cut of the same cloth. I will *not* marry Asharra's cousin—or any other man you choose!"

He sprang from his chair with a snarl and slapped her hard across the face. "How dare you address me like that? That is not the way to address your father!"

"And your behavior is certainly no way to persuade me to marry anyone you approve of!" she pointed out, at the top of her lungs. "For my children, I want a father who doesn't think his job is done at the moment of conception!"

He grabbed her shoulder and shook her like a rag doll, shouting incoherently with rage. Veradis braced herself for a beating, hoping he wouldn't cause enough damage to stop her from traveling. *When, oh when,* she thought ruefully, *am I going to learn to control my temper and keep my mouth shut?*

Then she realized that the pounding noise she was hearing wasn't the blood in her head; someone was knocking at the study door. Dom Ruyven dropped her, fortunately into the chair she had been sitting in, flung open the door, and snarled at the steward. "You had better have a good reason for interrupting us!"

"I have," the man said curtly, looking disapprovingly at him. He crossed to Veradis and bowed to her. "I regret to inform you, *vai domna,* that your mother is dead."

Veradis didn't faint, not exactly, but everything went black momentarily and then came back in muted colors and she felt very cold. There were more people in the room now; the housekeeper was patting her hands and saying, "She didn't suffer, *chiya,* died quietly in her sleep she did."

"Yes," Veradis said faintly, "she was always quiet."

The steward came over with a glass of brandy and held it to her lips. Veradis took a gulp of it, choked a bit, and came back to full awareness of her surroundings.

Her father, looking suitably grief-stricken, came and tried to slip an arm around her shoulder. She shrugged it off. "My dear child," he said. "Don't worry about your marriage for now. Plenty of time for that when we're over the worst of our grief."

Veradis stood up and looked at him in contempt. "You must think I'm quite lack-witted. I've had ample evidence over the years of your feelings for me, and I believe I've made my feelings toward you quite plan this evening. You—and Asharra, if she cares to stay with you now that you're no longer lord of the estate— can live in Windmill Cottage. The tenant died in the late fall, so it may need a bit of repair, but I'm sure it can be made livable by the time the funeral is over."

She glanced at the steward, who said, "With pleasure, *vai domna.*"

"Good." She nodded at him, then turned back to

her father. "The cottage is a bit small for all the children, so, if you like, I'll keep the ones already living here. If you father any more of them, however, they're *your* problem. Now, if you'll excuse me, I have work to do."

She was busy working for the rest of the night. First her mother's body had to be washed, dressed in her best festival gown, and laid out in the household chapel. Then, after snatching a few minutes to change into mourning, Veradis took over the study and started writing to all of her relatives who needed to be notified of the death and bidden to the funeral. The sky was beginning to grow light when she finally laid down her pen, stood up, and stretched. She snatched up her cloak, told the steward she was going out for a walk, and went to meet Cullen.

He was there before her, pacing nervously. She called his name and ran into his arms.

"Veradis, what's wrong?" he asked, holding her shaking body. "You don't have your things—what's happened?" He held her away to look at her face and saw her clothing. "Who?"

"My mother." To her surprise, Veradis started crying. "Last night."

"Merciful Avarra." Cullen sat down on a nearby log, cradling her in his arms.

"I don't know why I'm crying," Veradis sobbed. "She wasn't a very good mother; all she ever cared about was my father, and he didn't care for her, and it's all so sad. . . ."

"Speaking of your father—"

"I told him that he and his barragana could live in Windmill Cottage."

Cullen chuckled. "Good for you. With all those children?"

"No, I'm keeping the children. *They* don't deserve

this." She twisted her head to look at his face. "Do you mind if they live with us?"

"No, of course not. Poor brats, what chance would they have with him? With his temper, shut up in a small cottage—he'd probably kill a couple of them." Both Cullen and Veradis shuddered, easily able to visualize that picture. "But—'with us'? Do you still want to marry me, now that you don't have to? I'm sure that your Hastur relatives would be happy to arrange a marriage for you, and surely not all Comyn men are like your father."

Veradis smiled and reached up to stroke his cheek. "Yes, Cullen, I still want to marry you. I've wanted to for six years, and I haven't changed my mind overnight. My mother made her choice, my father made his, and I've made mine, which is by far the best of the three."

Circles

By G. R. Sixbury

The computer age is indeed wonderful; Glenn Sixbury (of whom I had never heard before) is a fellow subscriber to a computer service called CompuServe, and this is what I found on my computer one morning, owing to the wonders of the computer age. (Of course I didn't know, until I asked him, that G. R. stood for Glenn Robert instead of, for instance, Gertrude Rose.)

Maybe a day will come when we will all be on computers and no longer dependent on the services of the U. S. Mail to submit fiction to editors. Just think: no stamps, no postal delays, just electronic impulses from one computer to another.

But by that time, there probably won't be any printed books—just a service where if you want a copy you just ask your own computer for a hard copy. But I dunno—maybe by that time none of us will be able to read. (Or write.)

I guess I am just old-fashioned; I have very mixed feelings about all the "blessings" of the computer age. (But then, I feel rather funny about the telephone, too; the idea that anyone anywhere can interrupt me, anytime.) I own a telephone, too; and, in spite of my many reservations about a word processor, have not yet (and I know nobody who has) thrown a word processor on the junkheap in favor of the old Remington.

For the real word processor, I keep reminding my-self, is still the brain; everything else, from a #2 pencil to a #2000 word processor—is just the tools. And they do keep changing. Even the typewriter would have been an innovation in the days of the quill pen.

The important thing is that once they're on paper no one can tell whether words came from the pencil or the word processor; that's how you can still begin to write with any handy pad of paper. Some few of my sillier colleagues say that no one should write without a word processor; they point out that a doctor or a lawyer has to invest a substantial amount of his chosen profession, and writing should be thus self-limited. But I think it would be a great pity if writing should be limited to anybody who can afford to buy six thousand bucks of hardware.

Latest light bulb joke: how many computer program-mers does it take a change a light bulb? Answer: None; that's a hardware problem.

And we all work with the software—the most valu-able software in the known universe, the human brain. (MZB)

I am Lord Aldaran now.

The thought pounded at Mikhael's brain. Put there by years of training, it had come automatically at his father's death; he could not drive it away, but he refused to welcome it home.

Mikhael's father had been a hard man, excellent with the sword, tough as an old banshee bird; but he had not possessed the gift they called *laran*. Today it killed him.

Mikhael's grandsire had inherited the gift of the *chieri,* the power of *laran*. Some said it was this extra ability that had helped him survive where others could not, that had helped him settle this part of the frozen, mountainous region of Darkover, justly named the Hellers.

It had been that first summer when his grandsire had painstakingly hauled the lumber to the top of this windswept, rocky crag, building the small hall where Mikhael now stood. Surrounded by a short, stout outwork, this first keep of Aldaran had been inaccessible, surviving attacks from Ya-men and bandits for over forty years.

Today the keep of Aldaran had fallen, and Mikhael wondered at what the people would think; the old ones that had first followed his grandsire, the ones that, as winters worsened and Ya-men grew more fierce, had turned for help to the man they chose to call Lord; the ones that had named this land Aldaran.

When the old man died, only weeks ago, Mikhael's father took his place, commanding Aldaran until a few hours ago, when Mikhael, less than fifteen, had inherited what was left.

Pacing to the open window, Mikhael looked out the window, thoughtfully bringing his fingers up to his face, his chin resting in one hand, an elbow resting in the other. From here, one could see the distant, ever snow-capped mountains standing proudly against the northern horizon.

Mikhael had always thought they were the most beautiful in early summer, their white tops rimmed in violet; but today they offered him no peace. Below, men stacked the dead in open wagons to await one last departure, *and one of them is my father*. Beside the wagons, a gaping hole wrecked the front wall, its blackened edges still smoldering in the stiff afternoon breeze. *It must be repaired before first winter's snow*. A bitter smile crossed Mikhael's thin lips. *The time to think of repairing the hall is not when you are locked within it*.

As Mikhael watched, a large, burly man, his sun-red hair and crimson cape fluttering behind him, marched across the small courtyard, halting here and there to give an order; proudly examining the damage he had

done. He was not an ugly man—in appearance; and
although Mikhael had always disliked him, Beltran
was kin. The ties were somewhat distant, going through
marriages and generations, but still obvious. Mikhael's
grandsire had not looked so very different from the
man who now walked below; fingering his own coppery hair, Mikhael failed to understand what could
have driven Beltran to his actions.

The attack was little more than a blur in Mikhael's
mind. It had come suddenly, in midafternoon. Beltran's
riders were spotted early, exposing themselves as they
labored up the narrow, treacherous road to the front
of the keep. Aldaran's men had been given ample
time to shut the great gate and to take up battle
positions on the wall; all was made ready, and then,
the world fell apart. Mikhael's memories were only
fragments; visions of men fleeing invisible demons;
echoes of shouted warnings about dragons on the wing;
shadows of loyal men, screaming from the pain of flames
that never were; tears on his father's face, dead but
unmarked.

When Mikhael fought back to his senses, Beltran's
men were inside the walls of the keep, scattered about
the courtyard. None laid a hand on him as they peace-
fully directed inside the hall, locking him out of the
way in his own bedchambers.

Turning from the window, he looked upon the only
family he had left.

The twins, Elholyn and Judith, sat by the door,
comforting each other in soft tones. Three summers
older than Mikhael, they both had lost husbands in the
battle; seeing them, their faces drawn and tired, put
knots in Mikhael's chest.

I should be dead.

His father and most of the men had been killed. The
others had been locked away or banished from the
keep; his family had been imprisoned.

I do not deserve to be Lord Aldaran.

Pacing nervously across the room, Mikhael wished for death. Then he saw Lori; his baby sister, her long blonde hair strewn about her shoulders, curled into a cowered ball of sleep on his bed. Mikhael's mother had died bringing her into the world; she was more his child now than his younger sister. A slight girl, she had seen her twelfth Midsummer Festival; soon, she would see her thirteenth; but she had been aged beyond her time. Living in the Hellers and growing up without a mother normally gave her the look of an adult, but sleeping, she looked only like the child she was.

Walking to the bed, Mikhael sat down beside her, petting her long hair, smiling without knowing it. Sensing his presence, she moved her head onto his knee, softly whimpering, the day's nightmare having followed her into sleep.

The sound was torment. Mikhael gathered a ball of down comforter in his hand, clenching it in his palm; setting his jaw, his breathing forced. He felt like a trapped animal, finally backed into a corner; it was time to fight.

Jumping off the bed, he pounded his way across the floor and flung open the door to the hall. Immediately he was stopped by two of Beltran's men, their swords drawn quickly to block his path. Mikhael tensed, raised a fist to strike, his eyes flashing like a verrin hawk, confronted for the first time in captivity; but before he had time to pounce, Elholyn and Judith appeared beside him, pulling him back inside, shutting the door.

Too angry to speak, Mikhael shook them off, dropping himself into a corner to think. *There is a way out of every cage,* he told himself, content for the moment to wait.

Two hours later, as the first night's stars began to twinkle outside the window, Mikhael rose, his eyes quiet, his head clear. In a calm voice, he outlined the plan to his sisters.

"No doubt Beltran will hold a victory feast tonight, probably in the main hall. Everyone will be there; drunk, loud, uncaring; sneaking out the back of the hall should be as easy as finding snow at midwinter; and once we get down the trail of stairs father cut from the cliff last summer, Beltran, even on horses and with his *laran,* could not track us through *these* mountains."

"What about the guards?" Judith asked.

"They are a problem; but if Elholyn will help me. . . ."

"I have not tried that trick since I was a child," she said, reading his thoughts. Nervously she stroked the stone which hung about her neck. "I can't do it; especially not to both at once."

"I will help," Mikhael said, tapping a finger to his chest. "If you can get one, I will get the other."

Mikhael's voice was confident, but inside he was deeply worried. He and Elholyn had often played games with their starstones as young children, taking advantage of the mind gifts they had been given. Never had they depended on the power of their inherited skills for their survival; but Mikhael's grandsire had done it, and today he had seen with his own eyes what *laran* amplified by a starstone could do. It could be done, but could *they* do it?

Elholyn began first, looking deep into the large, beautiful blue stone; all emotion draining away as she concentrated on sending her thoughts into the crystal. Old Lord Aldaran had brought many such jewels from the forests when he had first traveled here; but Elholyn, as the oldest, had received the largest of his collection.

Following his sister's example, Mikhael took his own jewel into his fingers, staring intently at the blue fires that danced within. As he concentrated, sending his thoughts deep into the stone, he felt the world around him grow quiet, gradually fading away until all Mikhael knew was the life inside the stone. Even as his senses dulled, they became more intense: Sight, sound, scents disappeared into the background while the *feel* of things intensified; and suddenly Mikhael was part of the very fabric of the world, stretching out beyond his body, beyond the room, into the hallway.

Mikhael could actually see the guards now, relaxing, slumped heaps upon the floor, mugs of mead in hand. Beltran had permitted them to drink, perhaps as compensation for missing the festivities. It was a good sign; it meant he did not believe a young boy and three women capable of escape.

Beside him, Mikhael could *feel* his sister, sensing the outline of her shape as she approached the first guard and went to work. Concentrating his own attention on the other man, he focused on projecting his thoughts into the stranger's mind. Mikhael created pleasant sensations, relaxing waves of energy, flowing from him to the area around the guard, surrounding him in the protective fabric of sleep. Mikhael continued until the man's head began to nod and his eyelids started to slowly flutter. A moment later, his chin sank to his chest, and his breathing grew heavy. Turning, Mikhael saw the other guard was sound asleep.

Back in his body and conscious, Mikhael breathed a sigh of relief and rose with great effort to his feet. The effects of using his *laran* had drained his energy. He and Elholyn needed food and rest, but there would be no such luxury for any of them this night. By morning, they would need to be many leagues away if they were to evade Beltran's inevitable search. Gathering blankets for cloaks against the freezing night air, they slipped quietly from the room.

Mikhael paused, carefully taking a sword from one of the slumbering guards before leaving him to his dreams. Moving quickly to a rear staircase, they crept silently down two flights of stairs, slinking around to the back of the hall. Mikhael reached to open the outside door; but stopped short. Judith started a question, but he waved it sharply into silence.

This route had been chosen, because it was the farthest from the main hall and Beltran's men, and it had worked well; they had not seen or heard anyone. It had been quiet—too quiet; as if no one else was in the house at all. It didn't feel right; and Mikhael found himself suddenly wanting to turn and run the other way.

"What are we waiting for?" Judith whispered. "What's wrong?"

Mikhael started to speak, but stopped himself. There was nothing to say. How could he explain *he* was afraid while asking *them* to be brave? Shrugging his shoulders, Mikhael opened the door and peered out into the darkness.

Glowing softly green, Idriel hugged the horizon; Mormallor stood above it, casting silvery shadows across the small courtyard to the back wall. The other two moons were not in the sky tonight, the larger being the most happily missed. Darkover's three smaller moons paled against the brilliance of Liriel.

Checking the walls for guards, Mikhael turned to his sisters, putting a finger to his lips. Carefully, the four forms crept out into the courtyard. Quickening their pace as they neared the rear gate, they reached it unseen; Mikhael grabbed the brass handle and pulled the thick door open.

A loud burst of laughter cut the crisp night air and lantern light brightly flared around them, revealing a crowded courtyard. Two men blocked the gate, and as Mikhael turned, Beltran stepped from the shadows. Instinctively, he moved to shield his sisters, brandishing his sword, but more men stepped from the shadows, surrounding the small party. Indecisive, Mikhael fought anger with reason; slowly he lowered the sword, reluctantly allowing the blade to fall.

Beltran strode arrogantly across the courtyard. "Where are you headed on such a chilly night? You might catch your death of cold!" He laughed loudly, his teeth shining, and then quickly allowed the smile to drop from his lips. Motioning sharply with his hand, Mikhael's sisters were taken away. "Put them in the cellar and guard them well. I will attend to them shortly."

"As for you," he said, turning to face Mikhael, "you *will* accompany me to dinner. There are—matters to discuss." Beltran turned his back to Mikhael, his head held high, the insolence in his fluid movements draining Mikhael's courage; he was in total charge of the situation.

Mikhael meekly followed Beltran inside to the formal dining hall and to the feast which lay in waiting. His men, all denied their celebration while they waited impatiently in the bitter cold, were now released to rejoice as they wished. As raucous laughter irritated Mikhael's ears, he noticed that Beltran had only a handful of men for what he accomplished. The man had made his own victory; aided only with his *laran*.

After checking to assure the men did not destroy *his* new hall, Beltran relaxed into place at the head of the table and turned his attention to Mikhael.

"So, kinsman—"

Mikhael scoffed, interrupting, and the older man's brow wrinkled up in anger. "You will learn respect, *boy,* and you will learn it *now*. I am your kinsman. I will be treated as such." Beltran allowed the scowl to slip from his mouth, showing his teeth. "Come here. Give your long lost uncle a proper greeting."

"Greeting? When you deserve death? You are nothing more than a lowland—" The last words choked in Mikhael's throat, leaving him gurgling and gasping for air. Before him, Beltran sat calmly in his chair, shining starstone in hand, the edges of his mouth turned up in what may have been a smile.

"Come." His teeth glimmered from across the table. "Give your uncle a kiss."

Mikhael fought hard against the sudden pull that dragged him toward Beltran. Searching deep inside himself, he called upon the will power he knew he had, and it worked; he pulled away. Lifting his head, Mikhael wanted to see the bitterness of defeat in Beltran's face, but the man was grinning smugly. *Like a cat playing with a mouse!* Mikhael's knees turned to water. *He* is *too strong.* The thought passed away quickly, but it had been enough. Mikhael surrendered, giving Beltran complete control.

Pulling him around the table, Beltran forced him to bend low, his lips close to the older man's cheek. "Not too much, now," Beltran said, his eyes dancing. "I wouldn't want people to think my new nephew was a lover of men."

Mikhael closed his eyes, shamed to the bones. It felt like he had been stripped, and Beltran was laughing at what he saw. No longer able to fight, Mikhael leaned over, felt his lips on Beltran's rough cheek. His entire body ached; he had just given a kinsmen's kiss of welcome to the man who killed his father; and he could feel Beltran holding him there, relishing the moment.

When Beltran finally freed him, Mikhael was unprepared, and he stumbled, almost toppling over backward. Climbing slowly back into his chair, he cast a tired glance across the table; Beltran still smiled broadly, his face bright with victory. "You see, you cannot resist me."

Wearily turning back to his plate, Beltran shoved a greasy piece of roasted meat into his mouth and took a long swig of wine from the nearest bottle. As the juice from the meat rolled down his chin, he drew the back of his hand across his lips.

"*Laran* is draining, my friend," he said, his mouth full. "You must be starving. Eat. Drink. Keep up your strength."

Mikhael resisted, but when Beltran raised a hand to his neck, he began to eat. He thought the food would taste bad, sticking in his throat, but once he started, his hunger took over, and he ate greedily, trying to ignore Beltran as he spoke again.

"Kinsman, I bear you no ill will. In fact, I feel that some day we may become friends, of a sort."

"Never," Mikhael mumbled through a mouth full of food.

"No matter. Either way, you will stay here the rest of your life; *however long that may be.*" Mikhael raised his eyes at the comment, but said nothing. Beltran continued, "Don't you realize I don't cause harm just for harm's sake? Haven't you wondered why I chose to risk my life to take this meager hall on this overgrown pile of rocks? Of course you have," he said, taking joy at the sound of his own voice.

"Your grandsire was a smart man; he chose the most defensible spot in the Hellers to build this hall." Mikhael thought he detected true admiration in the words. "But I can make this place truly defensible. With high stone walls and *laran* to protect them, no one could ever take this hall again." Beltran paused a moment before he added, "That is where you come in."

Mikhael had finished eating, and now sat glaring at Beltran from across the corner of the table. "You do not understand, my young kinsman," Beltran continued. "You have not seen the things I have seen. In the lowlands, there are men who have discovered ways to use this power of ours to do things you would not believe; *laranzu* people call them; the ones who taught me how to do the things I can, the things which enabled me to take this stronghold so easily. There is incredible power in *laran*, and all you need, my young kinsman, is the gift to take advantage of it.

"Even now the *laranzu* in the lowlands are seeking methods to breed new and better *laran* into the children. Do you realize the power one man will hold when the *ultimate laran* is developed?" Beltran breathed deeply, pleased at the thought.

"You and your sisters have both Aldaran and Ridenow blood. Don't you see? I am not interested in you for yourselves, but for your lineage." Grinning, he added, "I want the children you will father and your sisters will bear."

A look of horror started across Mikhael's face, which Beltran purposely ignored. "With a great castle, set upon the site where this hall now stands; guarded by *laranzu'in,* loyal to me by direct lineage; I will control this land. I know it!"

Beltran's eyes grew distant. "I have the gift of sight, my friend. I knew how you would attempt to escape before you did; that is also how I know what this land will become. "Someday," he said, turning his eyes back to Mikhael, spreading his hands into a fan above the table, "people will be scattered across this land from the plains in the south to the great mountains of the north; and all will pay homage to the man who sits in castle Aldaran. I want to be that man—or at least be the father of that man. Now, *I will be.*"

As Beltran finished, one of his men appeared, leading Lori by the arm. After she was brought to the table, Beltran took her by the wrist, pulling her to him, taking her in with his hungry eyes before sliding one of his greasy hands up beneath her skirt.

Lori tugged at his hold and called out to Mikhael. Her older brother was already on his feet, but as his hands reached for Beltran's throat, two men grabbed him from behind. Struggling helplessly, he could only watch as Beltran's hands groped across his baby sister's body. "Yes," Beltran said, smiling broadly, "this one is still young and firm; she will be a pleasure to bed." Lori tried to pull away, terror in her face; but Beltran just drew her more tightly to him, enjoying her struggles and the pain and desperation in Mikhael's face.

At last, Beltran released her to one of his men with orders for her to be taken to his room, *and prepared.* "I will kill you for that," Mikhael growled, still pulling against the men who held him.

Beltran just grinned. "I think not," he said, rising from the table.

Beltran led the way as his men dragged Mikhael out of the hall and down a steep, narrow staircase to the cellar. Pulling open an old oaken trap door to the storeroom, Mikhael was dumped inside; landing hard, he lost his breath. Rolling over, gulping air, he spotted Elholyn and Judith pressed against the wall next to the stores of food and the cobweb-covered extra wine barrels.

Above them, Beltran chuckled softly. "This time," he said, his eyes cast down, "there will be no escape. Before, I was interested in how powerful your *laran* really was; now that I know, I can no longer be bothered with such inconveniences. I will personally see to it you do not leave this place until *I* wish it."

With that, he swung the huge hatch closed, shutting off the light. As Mikhael hauled himself to his feet, a blue glow filtered into the room from around the crack at the door. Above, Beltran's resounding laughter faded away into the distance.

After he was gone, Judith pulled Mikhael to his feet. She was frantic. "Where is she? They came and took her away. Did you see her? What has he done with her?"

Mikhael let a heavy sigh fall into the room, and turned away. "It's a long story," he started, "something about a breeding program; one he apparently plans to start with Lori. She is already in his bedchamber."

"But she's so young. Surely he wouldn't—"

"Yes, he would," Mikhael said, cutting her off. "He says even I am to be bred, although I know not how." Absently rubbing a forearm across his lips, Mikhael changed his mind. "Perhaps I do know; but it does not matter. Beltran will not live to see the crimson of the sunrise."

Feeling his way up the old wooden ladder, Mikhael pushed against the top with all his strength. It didn't budge. "We might as well try to move a mountain," Mikhael called back as he climbed down. "He must have spelled it, and I am too tired to do much."

The mental contest he had fought with Beltran had drained him more than he thought. At once Mikhael's face brightened. *It must have drained Beltran, too.* "Elholyn, see if you can counter Beltran's magic."

As she pulled her starstone from under her clothes, a blue light slowly spread across the room. Letting her mind go deep into the stone, she searched upward, looking for the mental block Beltran had placed against their escape. As her mind-body drifted toward the ceiling, she felt a blow to where the top of her head should have been; looking up, she found a huge blue-tinted plate, sealing the door, locking them in. In this state, she could usually pass through any of the real world's solid objects; but the plate above was solid in this world, too. She dropped back into her body, exhausted. "It won't work. The spell is too strong for me to handle."

"Your turn, Judith."

"But I've never been as good at those things as you or Elholyn." Judith felt more than saw Mikhael's strong eyes on her through the darkness. After a moment, she relented. "I'll do my best."

Judith took longer than Elholyn, but the result was the same. The situation was hopeless; and Mikhael blamed himself. If he had listened to his feelings, if he had trusted in his *laran*, they could have walked out the front gate of the hall and sauntered down the main road, leaving Beltran and his men to freeze in the night air.

Muttering softly to himself, he dropped in a bundle onto the floor, giving up. It was just too much. Beltran really was stronger—there was nothing they could do.

The mind battle he had lost at dinner continued to haunt him; the complete defeat; the knowledge that Beltran could control him, could possess his mind.

And Lori.

Lori's face swam before him; it was the image of his baby sister when Beltran mishandled her; the look of pain in her eyes; the helplessness he had felt; *and Beltran had her now!*

Mikhael snapped.

Jumping to his feet, he scrambled up the ladder; straining against the weight of the door; beating it with his fists; no longer caring what it took, he was going to get out.

His mind racing, he called down, "Elholyn, Judith, help me. Maybe we can push it open." The two sisters struggled up beside their brother, and all three of the bodies stretched upward until a loud crash of splintering wood bounced around the room; the ladder had given way, piling them onto the floor.

All three lay twisted into a heap, breathing hard, saying nothing. *How can Beltran do this?* Mikhael asked himself in the dark. *He is only* one *man.*

Suddenly Mikhael understood.

Untwisting himself, he stood up. "I have it."

"What?"

"If we all try together, it should work."

"We just did that," Judith complained, rubbing her arm where she had fallen.

"No, I meant we could try to break his spell together—using our starstones."

"How?"

Mikhael shrugged his shoulders. "I don't know, but there must be a way; we have no other choice."

All three moved to the center of the room; briefly touching to position themselves before settling down cross-legged, forming a circle on the floor.

Mikhael began first, focusing his thoughts into the crystal which hung about his neck. As Elholyn joined in, it caused a disturbance, an eddy, a conflict of wills, forced together, trying to come apart. Judith's weaker influence slowly entered the swirling mesh, and it quickly became impossible to keep the three blended together. Taking control, Mikhael forced them to intermix; but as he did, the delicate process collapsed, causing a backlash and knocking all of them flat on their backs.

Immediately Mikhael said, "Again."

"But this will never work. Every time I try to join in, you fight me."

"It's not us," Elholyn disagreed. "It's the stones. They seem to be—they don't—fit," she said, struggling for words. "Maybe it is the difference in size; one overpowers the others."

"She's right. It won't work, Mikhael."

"I didn't say that," Elholyn corrected her. "I just meant it wouldn't work using all three stones. If we were to use only one—like mine. . . ."

"It is worth a try," Mikhael said. "Elholyn, put your stone where we all can reach it."

She obeyed, pulling the chain and dangling jewel over her head; placing it between Judith and Mikhael, keeping her own fingers lightly touching it on one

edge. Judith added her touch to the jewel first, and
the air in the room immediately changed, charging itself, as if it were alive. *This might work,* Mikhael
thought. Reaching out, he touched the edge of the
stone and Elholyn let out a small yelp, jerking it from
his grasp. The energy in the room immediately died.

"What's wrong? What did I do? Did I hurt you?"

"Yes. No. I'm not sure." She stuttered; her voice
shaky. "It didn't exactly hurt; it felt more like your
fingers were digging into my heart. I'm—I think I'm
all right now. Let's try it one more time, but without
you actually touching the stone."

Mikhael agreed, and once again he sensed the stable
energy from Elholyn's thoughts around him; then Judith's shakily joining in; the power moved through
him as it spread across the room. Cautiously, he
stretched out his fingers, close to but not touching the
stone, sensing even at a distance, he disturbed the
energy flow. As he concentrated on blending in with
his sisters, he suddenly felt Elholyn's thoughts reach
out, helping them all to mesh together.

Suddenly small electric sparkles danced before their
eyes, and Mikhael sensed more than energy from his
sisters; he sensed their presence, their thoughts;
Elholyn's fierce concentration, her fight to control the
sudden flow of power they had created; Judith's smaller
effort, a reflection of Elholyn, providing support. He
could *see* the joint forces as they flowed, moving slowly
in a circle; spreading out in satiny webs; enclosing all
three of them; passing through them.

Mikhael felt dizzy, as if he were spinning upside
down from a great height, and then Elholyn was there,
steadying him, joining them, directing his actions. As
they settled down, he *heard* Elholyn's voice *or is it her
thoughts?* drifting in the air around him.

*I think we have it, Mikhael. I feel so much power; I
never dreamed this was possible.*

The door. Blast the door.

All three of them moved as one, their thoughts gripping the mental door Beltran had built to lock them in, crushing it into bits of energy, watching as the burning chips flew away, like sparks from a black-smith's hammer.

We've done it.

Mikhael wasn't sure if it was Elholyn's thoughts, or Judith's, or his own.

Now for Lori . . .

Lori.

Suddenly, Mikhael was with her, trapped inside her body as she was trapped in Beltran's chamber; and Beltran was there; his body covering hers. Mikhael experienced the pain; the terror; the revulsion; Beltran's weight crushing into his, or hers; he could no longer tell. He opened his mouth to scream and found himself again in the cellar, his older sisters around him.

It's Lori. I must get to her. Help me.

I will send you. . . .

Mikhael was never sure what happened next; the dizziness grew worse, the waves of power pounded at him, and the webs of energy seemed to collapse, wrap-ping him in a cocoon of light. Then he was in Beltran's chamber, sitting on the floor as he had been in the cellar, still not sure if he was really there, or if it was only in his mind.

Beltran had rolled to the edge of the bed, and for a moment gaped open-mouthed at what he saw. In the next instant, Mikhael felt as if his head were being ripped from his body. Through the pain, he was dimly aware of Beltran, standing above him, shining crystal in hand, content on crushing his skull like an eggshell.

Too late, Mikhael fought back, furiously trying to barricade his mind against Beltran's attack; but the effort to escape the cellar had been too much. Reach-ing out with his thoughts, he tried desperately to find help from Elholyn and Judith, but he could no longer sense their presence. He was left alone, confused and helpless.

Beltran increased the pressure, fiercely concentrating on the glowing matrix in his hand. Mikhael rolled senselessly on the floor, his head in his hands, knowing he would die; but just as Mikhael thought his eyes would pop from their sockets, Beltran released him and staggered where he stood.

"You will pay for this," he said, stumbling over to stand directly over Mikhael. Breathing heavily, he grabbed Mikhael by the hair, jerking his head back, forcing him to look directly into his fiery eyes. "I told you; *I* am the stronger." But the air of confidence was gone; Beltran was obviously shaken. Grabbing Mikhael at the collar, the stronger man was forced to struggle, finally pulling the younger to his feet.

Beltran's breath was hot in Mikhael's face, and as he tried to raise his chin, his eyes were drawn into the fires of Beltran's starstone, causing his head to swim once more. The lights danced within the stone, mocking him.

Beltran growled. "That was a most impressive trick. Most impressive; I will find out how you did it—and then you will die." Turning to look toward the bed, he added, "Say good-bye to your older brother, my new wife. You will not see him again."

Mikhael heard the words, but they did not register. He saw only Beltran's stone, glowing softly on the other man's chest.

"Did I hurt you?"

"It felt more like fingers were digging into my heart."

Suddenly Mikhael reached out, wrapping his fingers tightly around the brilliant blue crystal, squeezing as hard as he could; in one motion, he jerked the jewel from Beltran's neck.

Beltran immediately released his grip and staggered

back a step, clutching wildly at his chest. His eyes rolled back into his head and his face went white; wilting, he crumpled into a heap, lying still upon the hardwood floor.

Mikhael breathed a sigh of relief, looking down at the crystal burning in his hand. As he watched, the dancing fires within it dimmed, twinkled, and finally went out, leaving only a blackened, lifeless rock. As he tossed the useless stone away, his sister, her night-gown torn and bloody, leapt from the bed, pouncing on top of Beltran, sobbing, screaming she would kill him, pounding his warm corpse with her small fists.

Reaching out, Mikhael wrapped her arms up in his, pulling her away, cradling her to his chest. "He's dead, Baby," he whispered, "he's already dead."

Soft snowflakes swirled gently around them, accumulating just enough to make the stones slick and their boots crunch as they walked along the wall.

Stopping suddenly, Mikhael admired again the castle he had built.

"It took over ten years, Domenic, but now that it is done," Mikhael paused, breathing deep the crisp air, "I have a sense of security I have not felt since my father was alive." Stooping to fluff his young nephew's hair, he added, "I do not think this castle will ever again fall into the hands of our enemies."

Domenic did not lift his gaze, but peered out upon the valleys and peaks about the castle, his head tilted slightly, his eyes distant. Slowly, in a voice too deep for his years, he said, "It will fall many times; from fire without and lightning within."

Mikhael stiffened at the serious voice, and an eerie ripple crawled up and down his skin. When Domenic looked up, Mikhael saw only the eyes of the boy's dead father.

The moment passed quickly; Mikhael saw only

Domenic once more; a simple boy of nine, his youngest sister's child, his sole heir to Aldaran. Turning, they headed inside, yielding to the worsening storm. Outside, snow pelted the new stones, quickly filling in the tracks they had left behind.

Festival Night

By Dorothy J. Heydt

Dorothy Heydt made her first bow in the second Darkover anthology, SWORD OF CHAOS, with the excellent "Through Fire and Frost." After that she wrote several very well-received stories with an ancient Greek— or maybe an alternate-world Greek background—about the sorceress Cynthia, for the SWORD AND SOR-CERESS anthologies. We're glad she still has time for other writing projects in the middle of work on a novel; now she has written this very fine story of the Keeper Marguerida and the Terran Donald for this latest anthology.

Dorothy Heydt is local—she lives in Berkeley (which is a good place for a writer) and has a big house full of computers, cats, and children, all of which could be called the necessities of life for a Berkeley writer. (MZB)

The south wind was warm only in comparison to the icy breath of the Hellers, but Marguerida drew it into eager lungs and threw back her veil to feel it against her face. "Smell that," she said. "There's goldenthorn on the wind, and roses. It's spring, Donald, do you realize that? Spring, and a conjunction." She turned her head to see the moons riding the sky, three close together and the laggard fourth hurrying to join them. *"Cozid'Evanda dia vivais: sovrei dovan al deyn'*

anvada!" Raising her arms to greet them, she took a
step, and tripped, and sat down suddenly. "Damn,"
she said: the first word of Terran she had learned.

"Are you all right?" Donald appeared all in haste
from beneath the wing of the small bedraggled plane.

"I'm all right." She pulled herself upright and tucked
the grimy hem of her formal Keeper's robe around her
feet. "Only tired."

"Me, too," he said. "Rest yourself; we may have a
walk ahead of us . . . oh, yes, that's torn it." He
stepped away from the wing, out into the moonlight.

It would have taken a second look to recognize him
for a Terran. The mingled light of the moons spilled
like silver over his black hair. He had the rugged
bones of any mountain man. But he had seen twenty
worlds, and the light in his blue eyes was strange.

"I was right," he said. "It's the aileron cable that's
snapped; the metal crystallized with fatigue. Even if
you could get the plane in the air again, I couldn't
steer it. We'll have to walk. There's some kind of
habitation over that way; I can see lamplight. A mile
or two, no more. Can you manage it?"

"Can you?" A tenday stranded in the mountains,
fighting off blood-poisoning and what came as close to
pneumonia as made no difference, had done more to
weaken Donald than a few hours' matrix work could
do to Marguerida. *Crystallized with fatigue*, she thought.
That's us.

"And who are you?"

Marguerida looked up, and peered into the darkness. The man was sitting in a cart laden with boxes,
drawn by a dispirited-looking stag pony. "And why
aren't you in the Hall?"

"We just got here," Marguerida said, getting to her
feet. She shook out the stiff red skirts of the robe, and
put her veil over her face again. "I am Marguerida
Elhalyn, sometime Keeper of Alba Tower, and this is

my servant Donal." ("Sorry, Donald," she murmured
in a voice that would not carry two feet. "I'll explain
later.")

"Well, get in the cart," the man said after a pause,
and I'll take you to the Hall. *Dom* Jeral will want to
see you."

"We thank *Dom* Jeral for his offer of hospitality,"
Marguerida said sweetly. "Just a moment while I col-
lect a few things." She stepped back into the plane,
and Donald followed her.

"Donald, I apologize for giving you less than your
proper rank," she said as she swiftly coiled up the long
strips of the matrix drive that had brought the plane
here. "I think it's best no one knows you're a Terran,
not till we get to Thendara; there has been some bad
feeling."

"*Domna*, I haven't any rank and I admire your
restraint in describing planet-wide rioting as 'bad feeling.' I shall be pleased to be anything you choose to
call me. In fact, it might be better if I didn't come with
you at all."

"Whyever not?" She glanced at him. She was not
the telepath her foremothers had been, but the man's
emotions were as tangible as pease-porridge. Doubt,
fatigue, a double measure of embarrassment, and the
lucid fragment, *If they see us together, they will think*—
She averted her mind from the rest.

"Are you concerned for my reputation? I forget
you've only been on Darkover a year. No one accuses
a Keeper of misconduct; at least, not without wagon-
loads of evidence. There's a very old saying: 'Who
shoots at the king had better kill him.' I shall say
you're my paxman, sworn to protect me, if you're
worried about your own good name. Is there anything
here you want to take with you?"

"There's the medikit, what's left of it. I used up the
bandages and the antibiotics, but there might be some-

thing of use." He tucked the flat box of Terran metal into his loose-fitting jacket, and they left the plane together. Donald lifted Marguerida to a seat beside the driver, and climbed in behind with the boxes.

Up close, the source of the lamplight was neither farmstead nor village, but a large building in a bastard style: walls of the local stone, corrugated Terran plastic for its roof. It had been a warehouse of some kind, a storage depot for the trade that had gradually increased in the recent years of Empire membership. Trade that had dwindled to a trickle again in this plague year. Emptied of goods, the place was full of people; their voices could be heard in the still cold air outside.

A stocky man stood at the half-open door like a guard, his thumbs hooked in his belt. He wore a conical helm, a battered antique that shaded his eyes. A sword hung at his side. "Get inside, you two," he growled as Donald and Marguerida approached. But as Marguerida stepped into the shaft of lamplight before the door, the man started, and muttered, "Zandru! *Another* one!" Then he smiled, showing broken teeth. "Welcome, *vai domna*," he said. "You lend us grace. Please go inside; supper's almost ready."

The man's voice put up the fine hairs along Donald's spine. But Marguerida only inclined her veiled head, and passed by the grinning guard as if he were a tree. Donald followed without a word.

Inside, most of the building was one huge room, with heavy timber beams supporting a loft that ran around the near wall and sides. The far wall had a single door, leading perhaps to what had originally been the warehouse's business office. A rough dais had been constructed against the far wall, with a table on it that could seat perhaps a dozen. Something hung from the roof overhead; Donald had to blink a few times before he recognized it as a block and tackle, drawn up to the ceiling and out of the way. The fall rope that raised and lowered it stretched down to the loft over his head; tied to a beam or something, no doubt.

The center of the floor was clear, but all the space under the lofts was filled with people. Thin-faced, tired-looking people with the stain of fear on their faces: refugees from fire, from plague, from the ecological disasters that were striding across Darkover like the Fifth Horseman—and from the vicious winter that was only now coming to an end. Their breath showed faintly in the cold air, but it was warmer inside the building than outside. Each family had staked out a bit of space and spread blankets across it. Emaciated women sat holding children with shadows in their eyes. Their men stood against the outside wall, looking about the room as if it were the woods outside. A child began to cry, and its mother hushed it quickly, looking from side to side.

A rough kitchen had been set up to one side of the door, with firepits and a plaster bake-oven. Women were bending over big country-style caldrons set over Terran energy packs whose radiating surfaces glowed dull red. The woman nearest Marguerida started when she saw the tattered Keeper's robe, and wiped her hands on her apron as she hurried up to her.

"*Vai domna*, how did you come here? Oh, but I shouldn't say that; you lend us grace, I'm sure. Have you only just come in, you and the other? Oh, you'll be starving of the hunger. Here, start in on these, and supper will be ready soon. *Dom* Jeral provides for us most generously," she added in a louder voice, her eye on the door.

"Oh, and *domna*, are you a healer? There's a poor woman in labor up there in the loft, and the midwife says she can't sort her. Could you go up to see her?"

"I'll see what I can do." Marguerida took the basket

the woman gave her and led the way up the ladder into the loft.

"I haven't even met this *Dom* Jeral, and already I don't like him," Donal said.

"Me neither," said Marguerida, "but I wouldn't mention it just here."

The loft floor just above the kitchen area had been cleared for an infirmary: it was the warmest place in the building—unless the mysterious *Dom* Jeral had a Terran space heater in his little room behind the dais. The rest of the loft was full of crates, hay bales, old pieces of abandoned Terran machinery. Donald noticed with some amusement that the fall rope from the block and tackle had been secured around an anvil whose design hadn't changed in three millennia.

There were four people in the infirmary area. Two of them were plainly suffering from some kind of stomach upset, and they lay curled up in the blankets, groaning softly, with beakers of water and sour-smelling basins laid beside them. The third lay flat on a pile of straw matting, her fists clenched above her head, and the fourth was the midwife who knelt beside her. Marguerida put back her veil and went to speak to her.

The midwife was a hillwoman, with an accent so far removed from the Thendara dialect that Donald couldn't understand a word. He took his share out of the basket—dried fruit and slices of bread spread with nut paste—and settled himself with his back against a post.

After a week's semi-starvation he could cheerfully have devoured the carter's stag pony horns, hooves, and all, but he made himself eat the fruit and bread slowly lest they all come back up again. Besides, the leathery fruit took its fair share of chewing. He laid a golden raisin next to a deep red cherry on a slice of Terran pineapple, and admired the effort: like unpolished jewels. After the second bite of nut paste, he began to smile.

The laboring woman's teeth were clenched, and her face was gray with exhaustion. Marguerida held her matrix between the fingertips of her right hand, and passed her left hand slowly over the woman's body. The midwife crouched beside her, hands clasped reflectively under her chin.

"The baby is lying crosswise," Marguerida said in a low voice. "Perhaps you already knew that?"

"Suspected it," the midwife said. "Is the baby alive?"

"Yes," Marguerida said. "The heartbeat's strong, and all the signs are good."

"Avarra have mercy on us all," the midwife said. "Now I've got to choose which of them to save. I should've been a plumber, like my mother.

"If I'd only had my hands on her earlier! But she came in last night and went into labor this morning, like the rest of them, poor souls. Or perhaps you already knew that?" She gave Marguerida a sidewise glance, not without humor. Her short hair was spattered with gray and she'd run a linen thread through her earlobe in place of the earring she'd had to sell, but her spirit was undaunted. "A pregnant woman who's been in danger or on the run, if she's within a month of her time, will go into labor within a day and a night of reaching shelter. If I'd gotten to her sooner I could have turned the baby, but now her womb's clenched tight around it. Unless—" she glanced at Marguerida again. "Unless you could stop the contractions for a few minutes."

"Maybe," Marguerida said. "Donald, come here, please. You've got that box of medications; what's in it?"

He pulled the box out of his jacket and opened it. "No antibiotics left, as I said. This, umm—" he read the label on a vial— "this will speed blood clotting in a wound. I used half of it when I crashed, but the other half would be still good. Sunburn lotion. Hay fever medicine. Practically everything that would be useful on Darkover has been used up already. Scissors. An instant ice pack for bruises and sprains."

"We can use that afterward," Marguerida said, "if we get that far. Nothing that makes contracted muscles relax?"

"Nothing like that. Wait a minute, this—" he pulled the last vial from its place— "my god, it's a Mickey Finn. For bone-setting, I suppose. There must be ten or fifteen doses here."

"Mikhail who?"

"Michael Finn was a legendary Terran innkeeper who put sleeping potions in the drinks of unruly customers. He would have used chloral hydrate, I guess, and this is Edrin, but the principle is the same. But I wouldn't use it on your patient; it'd knock her out for hours, and I don't suppose it'd be good for the baby."

"No. Thank you, Donald." He returned to his post, and she to the midwife.

"You said you could turn the baby, *mestra*? I didn't know that could be done."

"Ah, well now." The midwife grinned. "There's them that says it's possible, and there's them that says it's impossible." She stretched her fingers and wiggled them, as if to warm them up. "And as for me, I've done it."

Marguerida smiled back. "Let's try." Her hand stretched out over the woman's abdomen again, and her attention slipped between her fingers, down toward the nerve centers that ruled the smooth muscle fibers. *Knots, be loosed; rivers, flow; doors, stand open.*

The woman drew a deep breath and let it out again. "Ah," the midwife said, and laid her fingertips against the swollen abdomen. She pushed at the hard lump that marked the child's head, firmly but without haste.

The lump shifted a trifle. A push on the other side, where the folded legs lay flat against the rump. Another push to the head, and another perceptible shift, east-by-south to east-southeast. The patient grunted, and the midwife said without looking up "Shout all you want to, but don't go tense!" She pushed again.

Donald, having finished his bread and fruit, had almost fallen asleep when the gong sounded: a bar of salvaged Terran iron struck against another that hung from a rope. The inner door had opened, and two men came out. Like the guard who had let them into the place, they wore bits of armor: helms on their heads, an old mailshirt on one and a Terran riotproof jacket on the other. (There was a great deal of Terran material around this room, one way and another. He was beginning to suspect where it might have come from.) Spears in hand, they stood to either side of the door like an honor guard.

The man who stepped out between them was also dressed in a mixture of Terran and Darkovan, but exaggerated almost beyond belief. He reminded Donald of a fellow who'd come to a costume party once as an "Explosion in a Time Machine." He'd belted a brocaded tunic over a pair of Terran military trousers; a white fur cloak lay over his shoulders; a golden belt held an antique longsword to his side. A crown of gold and garnets that must once have belonged to a real king was perched on a Terran police helmet with its faceplate removed. His face was pasty white, paler even than most Darkovans' after the long winter, and smooth and unlined as a baby's. His eyes were small, a pale ice-blue, and expressionless, but his mouth smiled.

The room rustled as the people got to their feet and bowed. Four more men in motley armor followed their chieftain out the door and up the rough stairs to the table on the dais.

Marguerida joined Donald at the loft's edge, just far

enough from the edge for safety's sake—and out of the light of the torches below. She was eating the last of her bread and licking the nut paste off her fingers.

"Do you know what that stuff is?" Donald said. "Terran peanut butter."

"Yes, most of the foodstuffs here are Terran. Dried and potted and—what was the word?—freezedried emergency staples, and I gather there are rooms full of the stuff in Thendara. I should like to know where it was when my people were starving in the Hellers."

"Where it is now," Donald said. "They've been feeding the refugees that get as far as Thendara, but there isn't enough air transport to carry it out into the countryside, and your ground transport is limited to pack animals on narrow mountain trails. I'm sorry."

The crowned man went to the center of the dais and turned to face the room, his arms spread wide. "My people," he said. "I welcome you to our Festival Night. Spring is here, and in this spring we shall go forth and conquer. The Domains will rise to aid us as we go forth, sweeping all opposition before us, till we have burnt out the nest of the usurper, Hastur of Hastur!"

"He's insane," Donald said.

"I know," Marguerida said. "He thinks he's living in the Ages of Chaos."

"Hastur is gathering *leroni* in Comyn Castle, to channel their witchery against me. But he's doomed to fail. We'll see what *laran* can do against blasters!

"Tonight, however, it's a time for celebration. Eat and drink—I believe our cooks have come up with something exceptional—and dance and be merry. Remember—" the pasty face creased into a roguish grin that made him look like a diseased cauliflower— "what's done under the four moons will never be held against anyone. Let the feast begin!"

The people dutifully cheered. *Dom* Jeral seated himself at the high table, and his men took seats around him. The two guards by the inner door closed and locked it, and took up positions at either side of the table. The people began lining up with their wooden plates and bowls, to have them filled at the kettles. A nervous-looking serving man brought to the high table what looked like a brace of rabbithorn, roasted and gilded with egg yolk and surrounded by herbs. The rat-faced man on *Dom* Jeral's right rose to carve them.

"I don't want to be seen if I can help it," Marguerida said. "Donald, could you go down and get our share? There are dishes over there by the water pot."

"Sure." He rose and bowed. "Z'par servu." He collected three sets of dishes and made his way down the ladder. No one noticed him but the doorward, but that one looked at him suspiciously, as if trying to put two and two together and coming up with at least three and a half.

There was a stew rich in meat and onions, fragrant with Terran chocolate and cinnamon, and loaves of bread green with vegetables, and little pies filled with fruit that had been soaked till it was soft. Donald brought it up to the loft and served Marguerida and the midwife before he sat down to his own portion. For long minutes there was no sound in the loft but the grunting of the woman in labor, and the soft encouragement of the midwife.

The stew was dark and rich, and the pungent gravy soaked happily into the soft heavy bread. The pies were crisp outside, soft and juicy inside, full of dried fruit that had died and gone to a heaven of honey and spices. "Where did this all come from?" Donald asked when there was nothing left but the warmth of the bowl.

"More of your Terran emergency supplies," Marguerida said. "Mostly it's big boxes of ready-made stew, just add water. They eat it practically every day. But for tonight's dinner they had the children picking over the bits, separating the meat from the vegetables, for two days to be able to make this. People will go to extra effort to celebrate a festival, even in thin times like these.

"Donald, I'm frightened to think of what this madman may do. He is not, of course, a Comyn lord, or even petty hill-nobility. Nobody knows where he came from, but about fifty days ago he turned up with that band of cutthroats and a wagonload of Terran food. It's assumed he stole it. Whatever, it made him very welcome to the people, and he took over this building and started bringing people into it. He does feed them; he takes care of them. He sent two of his men, trained to tell a plausible lie, all the way into Thendara to fetch that midwife. He believes they really are his people, and he their lord.

"But he also believes he's the rightful King of the Domains, and he intends to lead an army against Lord Regis Hastur as soon as the weather is a little warmer. I don't know whether the men will march, and be slaughtered by the Guard, or refuse to march and be slaughtered by Jeral's men."

"It's worse than you think," Donald said. "Didn't you hear what he said about blasters? I don't know where he's getting his Terran food supplies, but if he's half as clever a thief as he seems, he may have entry into a spaceport armory as well."

"Then Aldones help us," Marguerida said. "And he won't let any of them leave the building, Donald. Not even to go to the necessary—there are privies there in the far corner, but they're not enough for so many people. Already, as you see—" she gestured toward the two enteritis patients behind them— "sickness is beginning to spread. We have to do something."

"We? You and I?"

"Do you see anyone else? We'll simply have to think of something."

"On my planet," Donald said, "there's an old piece of folklore, a drawing that's been redrawn hundreds of times. The picture is always the same: a dungeon where two poor wretches are chained, hand and foot, to the wall. One says to the other, 'Now, here's my plan. . .' "

Marguerida smiled. "We'll come up with something. We have to."

Midway through the meal the guard changed, so to speak; three men got up from the table to relieve the doorward and the honor guard. The doorward knelt before Jeral and said something to him, and the chieftain's head snapped up. His tiny eyes peered into the loft without finding anything. He rose.

"I've just been informed that we have a noble guest this evening," he said. "A powerful *leronis* from out of the hills, come to fight at my side with the power of *laran*. A gift from the Gods for our righteous cause, an answer to Hastur with his pack of traitors in the Castle! Let her come forth at once."

"Don't move," Donald said. "You rank him, that's the line to take. I'll go."

He hurried down the ladder and went to the middle of the open floor. He bowed deeply before the suspicious-looking Jeral. "*Vai dom*, I serve the noble lady, Marguerida Elhalyn, Keeper of Alba Tower," he said. "What is your will?"

"Let her come before me, curse it!" the chief spat. "I've no time to waste with underlings; I want the *leronis* where I can use her!"

"I will say so," Donald said, and bowed again, and returned to the loft.

He found Marguerida veiled again, her hands tucked into her sleeves, her head high. "You stay here," she said. "Let me deal with this."

Donald said nothing. His eyes searched around the loft, as if something might suddenly appear from under hay bale or scrap heap and suggest a better plan. His battered medikit lay open where she had been sitting. He looked a second time. "Marguerida," he said, "where's the Mickey Finn?"

Marguerida looked up, her eyes masked by the veil. "Mikhail?" she said innocently. "He had to leave. He said to give you his regards."

Shaking his head, Donald sat again at the edge of the loft. He had to assume she knew what she was about; God knew there was enough in that vial to lay out a dozen men. If she could give it to all of them simultaneously— He crossed his fingers.

Marguerida crossed the floor and approached the high table, greeted the chief with the graceful nod of one slightly higher in rank. "*Dom* Jeral, I greet you, and I thank you for your hospitality. May the Gods look on your endeavors, and grant them the reward they have earned." (*Ouch*, Donald thought, but the jibe seemed to pass over the chief's head.)

"Welcome, lady," Jeral said. "Come and sit at my side. We'll drink together—" he indicated the Terran bottle the serving man had set on the table—"and make our plan of battle. Can you make me *clingfire*?

"No, milord," said Marguerida. "Nor can any other; the secret is lost." *Thank the Gods*, her tone suggested, but not her words. She took the seat the rat-faced henchman held for her, her hands still tucked modestly into her sleeves, and bent forward to examine the bottle on the table. Donald could not read the label from where he sat, but the shape suggested whiskey.

"I fear I cannot drink with you, *vai dom*," she said, "lest I set my powers in disarray. But I will pour out for you and your men."

She picked up the bottle, only the tips of her fingers visible, and went up and down the table, filling each man's cup. She even called up the servers to carry cups to the doorward and the table guards. "To victory!" she cried, holding the bottle high, and set it down. "Victory!" the men shouted, and drained their cups.

Marguerida stood waiting. One breath drawn, two . . . and Jeral and his men slumped into their seats and let their heads rest on the table. The standing guards fell to the floor in a rattle of armor. The people, watching, caught their breath and began to murmur with the beginnings of hope. And one inarticulate shout of rage echoed through the building, as one more armored man leaped onto the dais, spear in hand.

He had been in the privy, maybe, or annoying some woman among the refugees. Now he strode up to Marguerida, and his spearpoint was at her throat.

"You did this, witch!" he cried. "What did you do? You can undo it, or you can die."

Marguerida held up a hand. "Be warned," she began.

"I know," the man said, with an ugly smile full of rotten teeth. "If I touch you, I die. So I won't lay a hand on you, only this." He raised the spearpoint a finger's breadth.

For a long instant Donald could not move. At last he stretched out an arm and touched the cold iron of the anvil beside him, the anvil tied to the fall rope of the block and tackle. From where he sat, the man's ugly face was cut in two by the line of the rope.

But Marguerida was beside him, half-covered by his shoulder; if he loosed the thing, it would strike her as well. Maybe she would move. Would he let her move? Donald got silently to his feet and looked around for a pole.

The guard's face was contorted, and oily sweat ran over his skin. Marguerida stood tall and silent, unmoving. Then suddenly the palms of her hands turned up, and she slumped to the floor like a dead woman. The guard stood stupidly, clutching his spear, and in that moment Donald pried up the anvil and let it fall.

The rope stretched and creaked under the sudden weight, but it held, and the anvil swung across the room in a graceful curve that cut the space in half. The people drew breath with a sound like wind in grass. One foolish voice cried out, and the guard raised his head, just as the anvil swung over the table and caught him in the face. It carried him bodily to the wall, and stopped when it reached the beam that supported the roof. There was an audible crack. The anvil swung back and forth, back and forth, slowly losing momentum, while the people began to shout and sing, and Marguerida picked herself up and got off the dais before the blood could soak into her hem.

Behind him, almost drowned by the noise below, Donald heard a thin sound like the meowing of a cat. He turned to see the midwife laying the newborn child in the arms of its mother. The woman was breathing hard, and could hardly raise her arms to hold the baby, but her face shone. "Congratulations," Donald said. "Do you know, if this were only winter instead of spring, it'd make a great Christmas story."

"A what?"

"Never mind." He showed the midwife how to strike the cold pack into action, and hurried down the ladder so that she could apply it where it was needed in privacy. By the time he reached the floor his knees were weak with reaction, and he had to clutch at the loft pillar to keep on his feet. Dizziness swept over him, and receded. When he could see again, Marguerida was standing before him.

"I told you we'd think of something, did I not?" she said. "Let's go get some air."

She took his arm and led him outside. The air was bitter cold, but many of the people had already run out of the building, to sing and dance in a ring. Overhead, the four moons lay as close as buttons in the palm of your hand.

"As soon as we get to Thendara," Marguerida said, "we've got to have you tested for *laran*."

"Whatever for?"

"You foresaw where the anvil would hit, just as I did, and knew when to fall out of its way. Precognition is one of the old Gifts."

"Precognition, nothing," Donald said. "From where I stood, I could see him bisected by the support rope. A pendulum will always pass beneath its point of suspension and swing in a straight line. That's simple physics."

"Physics? What's that?"

"I'll explain later. Do you suppose we could sit down?"

"Of course." They pulled up two empty containers marked MEAT AND VEGETABLE STEW/ADD WATER/MAKES FIFTY GALLONS and sat on them. One of the refugees, a wiry man with knotted muscle along his thin arms, came up to them with an armload of hardware.

"We took care of them, *vai domna*," he said. "These are their weapons." He laid them at her feet: spears, swords, daggers. Marguerida looked them over. She selected a serviceable-looking dagger and a shortsword the length of Donald's forearm.

"Do you suppose you could kneel a moment, Donald?"

He shrugged. "Why not? Easier than sitting up." He slipped to his knees before her.

She put back her veil again. "Now, pretend for a minute that this one's yours, and this is mine." She handed him the dagger, and took it back. She laid the two weapons hilt to blade.

"Donald Stewart, be from this day paxman and shield-arm to me; may this blade strike me if I be not just lady and shield to you. The Gods witness it, and the holy things at Hali.''

She put the sword into his hands, and stopped, suddenly realizing what she must do. *What do I know about Terrans? What will he think?* But the rite demanded it. She leaned forward and gave him the brother's kiss on his cold cheek.

After a moment he returned it, and bowed his head. The dance whirled about them while they sat there, silent as moonlight under the dancing moons.

A Laughing Matter

By Rachel Walker

One of the complaints I make most often about these anthologies is that I too seldom get anything with a breath of humor.

Granted that Darkover is a pretty serious place and the ordinary slapstick story doesn't often work (and I get all too many of them), when I get something I can use that is in any way humorous, I am just a sucker for it. I have been told too often that I don't have a sufficient sense of humor, because I do not appreciate sitcoms, pratfalls or practical jokes; but my funny bone, though hard to reach, is there; as can be seen from this story. (MZB)

Caitlin MacAran did not want to see anybody. As Neskaya's new Keeper, her duties were weighty enough in these strange new times without the constant problems of the Tower workers. Yet she could feel the bristling impatience on the other side of the door curtain—too strongly to ignore it. "Come in," she called resignedly.

Belloma, one of Neskaya's handful of technicians, came storming in like a Hellers' gale. "I can't bear it anymore, *vai leronis*," she said tightly.

Caitlin sighed. "What has Cassalina done this time?"

"She stitched the sheets of my bed to the mattress!"

Belloma managed to control her surrounding psychic cracklings, but her eyes still flashed with anger. *"Vai leronis,* I know she's young, but she's been here for two years and has yet to learn discipline! If you can't find some way of controlling her—her— "

"Sense of humor?" suggested Caitlin mildly.

Belloma sniffed at the phrase. "Shall I say, her exuberant youth, *vai leronis?* Whatever you choose to call it, if you cannot persuade her to curb it, I will be forced to speak to Regis Hastur himself, if necessary!"

"You'll do no such thing, Belloma," said Caitlin sharply, a seldom-heard hint of steel in her voice. "I am still Keeper here, and I am aware of Cassalina's penchant for—shall I say, tricks, inappropriate for a Tower. I will deal with Cassalina in my own fashion. Regis Hastur is far too busy to deal with something like this. Do I make myself clear?"

Belloma looked rebellious, but bowed her head meekly. *"A ves odres, vai leronis,"* she murmured.

Caitlin frowned a bit, then waved a negligent hand. "You are dismissed," she said brusquely, turning her eyes back to the papers scattered on her desk. *Confusing as our Ages of Chaos were, I'll wager no Keeper then had to deal with paperwork!* she thought ruefully. The young Keeper understood the Telepaths Council's need for knowledge, and agreed that the Towers had to build up their numbers again. She even was in favor of the Council's gathering information from each Tower to see where was the greatest need for help. She agreed with everything in theory. It was when she was confronted with the blank reports that she began to entertain thoughts of running away.

A deep chuckle was heard from the other side of the curtain. Caitlin looked up, annoyed at this new interruption. "Either come in or go laugh some other place," she said crossly.

Alessandro, her under-Keeper, entered with a wry

grin still on his face. "Pardon my laughter, *vai leronis*, but your image of running away from the Tower was so vivid that I could not help myself." He sat down in his usual sprawling manner. "So, what are we going to do about Cassalina?"

Caitlin rested her head in her hands. "If I could, I'd send her back to her family—"

"Hardly a viable option," Alessandro pointed out.

The Keeper nodded. Cassalina's family was no more tolerant of her *laran* than Belloma was of her pranks. "Sending her to another Tower would only shift the burden to another Keeper's shoulders," she continued. "But we are so short of people here!'

"Even Belloma must admit the girl has a talent for being a monitor," Alessandro agreed. "Her empathy is quite extraordinary, yet she manages to keep herself free enough to help when in the circle." He leaned forward, propping up his head with his right hand. "But all of our talking is worth a handful of sand in the Dry Towns if you cannot help Cassalina learn discipline. What are you going to do?"

Caitlin pursed her lips thoughtfully, then a clear light spread over her face. "Do you think you can find Cassalina? Quickly?"

"Of course."

"Then go and tell her I wish to speak with her at once."

Alessandro stood up immediately, but turned back before he pulled aside the curtain. "I don't suppose you'll share this idea with me?"

"Patience," admonished Caitlin. "You will hear it in time."

Cassalina peeped around the edge of the curtain, her expression telling Caitlin the young monitor was fearing punishment for her foolishness. "Oh, come in and sit down," ordered the Keeper exasperatedly, waving the girl to a chair. "Avarra's mercy, child, I'm not going to eat you!"

Cassalina laughed gaily, then set her face in a more sober fashion. "Your pardon, lady." She sat down, her hands folded and her eyes down; she was in the very picture of propriety.

Alessandro slipped in quietly, standing a little behind and to the right of Cassalina. "Here she is, just as I promised," he announced needlessly.

"Thank you, Alessandro," Caitlin replied gravely. She turned her gaze back on Cassalina. "Did you really sew Belloma's sheets to her bed?" she asked curiously.

Cassalina flushed. "Yes, *vai leronis*."

"Why?"

"Because she's such a prune-face! I couldn't resist!"

Caitlin sighed in confusion. "Cassalina, I cannot understand how you could go through the discipline necessary for becoming a monitor, yet you persist in these pranks of yours."

The girl squirmed. "I—I'm not sure," she confessed. "When my family told me to come here to Neskaya, I thought how wonderful it would be to be a part of the Tower Reconstruction, and I worked hard. But I just couldn't stop playing my jokes." Cassalina lifted her chin in pride. "I never played any of my pranks when we were in the circle, *vai leronis*."

"That is true, but you have often played a prank on someone who has just returned from strenuous work. I hoped that you would learn control, and sometimes, when several moons would pass without one of your pranks, I believed you had." Caitlin leaned forward, her eyes serious. "But today I think I am forced to say that you can no longer stay here at Neskaya."

Cassalina gasped in shock. "No! Please—let me have just one more chance—"

Caitlin raised a hand; Cassalina fell silent. "You can

no longer stay here at Neskaya," Caitlin repeated, "but there is a way for you to prove yourself worthy to come back, if you choose to accept it."

The monitor had a desperate look on her face. "I do! I do!" she cried eagerly.

Again Caitlin raised a stern hand. "Will you accept something without knowing its true value?" she asked in gentle reproval. "Hear me now: There is a small village nearby, Gaelan. Their healer-woman is growing old, but as yet she has no replacement. I propose to send you to Gaelan, for you to serve as its healer, and if by the end of a year you have proven yourself to have learned control and discipline, you may come back to Neskaya. Do you accept?"

Cassalina hesitated only for a second. "Yes," she said firmly.

Caitlin breathed a small sigh of relief. "Then go and pack; you leave tomorrow."

"I swear I will not fail you," Cassalina vowed fervently, nearly knocking over the chair in her haste. "Thank you, *vai leronis*, I will not despoil the reputation of Neskaya or bring shame upon you. I swear I will prove myself worthy of your trust!"

"Do you think this will work?" asked Alessandro as soon as the girl had gone.

Caitlin turned in her chair and stared out the window. "I certainly hope so. I cannot afford to waste such talent as hers, but neither can I have dissension in the Tower. Perhaps this taste of responsibility is what Cassalina needs." She looked back at Alessandro. "I only wish I was more sure of my decision."

Cassalina reined in her horse, cocking her head curiously. Eavesdropping was bad manners, but no one had visited her in the three moons she had been in Gaelan. She was lonely for conversation.

"—he'll be abed a few tendays more, but the healer

said his feet won't be any worse after the skin grows back."

"Could've tried taking him to the Neskaya girl," said another male voice.

"Her?" scoffed the first. "She may be Tower-trained, but she's too flighty. Did you hear her giggle when she came here? Only reason Neskaya sent her here must've been she's too weak for proper Tower work."

"Or too scatterbrained," agreed his friend. "Morag may be old, but her skills are still sharp."

Cassalina did not stay to hear more. Angrily she snapped the reins and rode back to her small house. Flighty! Scatterbrained! Her? Ignorant, ungrateful peasants—

"No," she said aloud. "They are right. I am scatterbrained." She sat beside her window, hugging her knees to her chest. "Very well," she said to the silent room. "If they don't respect me now, I'll make them respect me!"

For the next tenday, nobody would have guessed that the sober, quiet girl who went about her business politely had been the giggling Cassalina of the past three moons. Gradually, people came to see her; first with smaller injuries, then slowly with more serious ones. The villagers stopped referring to her as "the scatterbrained girl from Neskaya." Now she was "our young *leronis* from Neskaya." Morag visited her from time to time, sharing a seventy-year accumulation of healing knowledge. Cassalina had the respect of the village.

"And that's what I wanted, isn't it?" she asked of her reflection. "I have been a model of Domains propriety." She set down the hairbrush. "I have helped the people I was sent to heal. I only need to continue this way until the end of the year, then I can go back to Neskaya." Cassalina sighed at the thought of never laughing again, for she knew that if she returned to the Tower, she dared not repeat the behavior that had sent her to Gaelan.

A knock sounded at her door. Cassalina rose, preparing herself once again to play her role. "Please come in," she said quietly. "May I be of some service?"

"My thanks, lady," the farmer said awkwardly. "I am Derik; I farm the north side of the hill?"

"Yes," Cassalina said encouragingly. "Have you or a member of your family had an accident?"

Derik looked flustered. "Not to say, lady; it's my daughter." From behind him came a small girl, no more than ten or eleven years of age. "You see, m'lady, she hasn't talked since she was a wee one."

"I cannot cure dumbness—" began Cassalina in apology.

"She's no mute, m'lady, she used to talk—babe talk o'course, but now she won't speak at all." He swallowed. "Morag couldna help her—said it was no illness she knew, an' I was hopin' you could do something, since you're Tower-trained.'"

Cassalina knelt before the little girl, putting a hand on her forehead. "What is her name?"

"Graciela—we call her Shaya, m'lady." The plain man's face struggled between keeping his stoic outlook and giving rein to the helplessness and sorrow that raged inside him because he could not help his daughter. "Please, m'lady, if you can do anything—"

"I am not sure," said Cassalina slowly. "Would it be an inconvenience if you left her in my care for a few days?"

His face showed a faint glimmering of hope and gratitude. "No m'lady, if you're certain she wouldna be in your way—which she won't," he added hastily. "She never gives trouble—she just sits all day, staring at her fingers an' twiddlin' 'em, or stands at a window, like she's lookin' outside, but y'can tell from her eyes that she isn't—"

"She will be no trouble," Cassalina assured him. "If I cannot discover what ails her, you might consider sending her to the Tower."

Derik looked abashed. "I don't know, m'lady, bothering them for a little thing like this—"

"It would be no bother, Derik," she corrected him. "The Towers are here to serve the people of Darkover. I will do my best for your daughter."

"Thank you, m'lady." He ducked out quickly, then reached across the threshold to fiercely embrace his daughter. Graciela did not even respond to her father's gesture; she stood still, slightly swaying from her father's attention. He wiped at his eyes hurriedly, then went off down the street.

"Shaya," said Cassalina gently, "my name is Cassalina. You're going to stay with me for a few days, to see if I can discover what's wrong with you."

The little girl gave no sign she heard. The monitor sighed. "Shaya, I'm sure you can hear me. I don't understand why you can't—or won't—talk, but I think I will keep talking, even if you don't answer."

Shaya still did not seem to care. For the rest of the tenday, Cassalina kept talking, trying to draw the little girl out. But Shaya only sat and watched her wiggling fingers, or stood staring mindlessly at the window. Not even an attempt at telepathic contact produced any results. Cassalina could only determine that Shaya had had no injury that prevented her from speaking. She kept up a constant flow of talk every day in hopes Graciela would respond, but the girl remained wrapped in her own private cloud.

The end of the tenday was drawing near, and as Cassalina sat darning her stockings, she despaired of ever reaching Shaya. Then, as the monitor glanced at the stocking in her hand, a memory came back from her childhood—watching a puppet show in her home village.

She immediately slid her hand into the knitted tube, folding in the toe for a mouth. "Graciela!" she said brightly, forcing her voice into a higher register. "Do you know what the Terran said when he saw a horse?"

Shaya stared at her.

"He said, 'Where's the steering wheel?' "

Graciela stared at her, then gave a small laugh. "Cassie silly," she said.

With a low cry Cassalina hugged Shaya. "You did it, *chiya*," she sobbed. "You did it! And it wasn't even that funny!" She felt two small hands touch her lightly on her back. She held Shaya away from her, looking her straight in the eye. "Now, let's find out what has kept you from talking all these years!"

"Laran?" asked Derik in disbelief. "M'lady, her hair is not—"

"You don't need red hair," Cassalina told him. "And I'm not suggesting she's Festival-born, either. But somehow she has the Ridenow Gift—had it at such an early age that she was frightened. I imagine she assumed everyone could read her feelings as clearly as she read theirs."

"But m'lady, I never treated her bad, nor did her mother—"

"But you have been angry, am I right? I know you were not angry with her, but she only felt the anger, and to protect herself she stayed in her own private world." Cassalina looked affectionately at the young girl gathering flowers. "My home is insulated by telepathic dampers, and the only emotion I had was concern for her. She never felt anger from me, and when I played that silly trick with her, I believe she knew she could trust me, and that is what has opened her up, Derik, not some technique of the Towers." She looked at the farmer seriously. "But I cannot teach her to use the Gift, and it must not be wasted. I think you should send her to Neskaya for training."

He hesitated. "I don't know, m'lady—the Tower—"

"—will accept her," Cassalina finished gently. "Eagerly will they accept her. In time, she will learn to control her Gift, and then she will be a very happy little girl."

"Can't you teach her?" Derik asked pleadingly.

Cassalina shook her head. "No, I do not have the skill or training for that. She must go to Neskaya, else I am afraid she will retreat once again."

Derik bowed his head, then he, too, looked at his daughter. "If you say so, m'lady." He turned to Cassalina again. "Will you take her there—make sure she'll be safe?"

Cassalina smiled reassuringly. "Of course, I would be honored." She knew what else she would tell Caitlin; that she had decided to stay here in Gaelan for more than her one year—stay to help the people she had grown to love. Some day, perhaps, she would return, but not for a while.

She walked over to Shaya. "You must pack your things, Shaya. We're going to Neskaya."

"Cassie come, too?" the girl asked her.

Cassalina laughed. "Yes," she answered. "Cassie come, too."

Mourning

By Audrey Fulton

There have been, in general, few stories about Darkovan children—though, come to think of it, with the precedent of STORMQUEEN, I don't know why there haven't been more. The only one I can think of offhand was in last year's anthology, Elisabeth Waters' "Playfellow." Here, in quite another vein, is a story about children— but not a children's story. There's a difference.

And Audrey, like so many of us, is also working on a novel. (MZB)

Ranwyn Hastur was dead. Wellana Hastur stared in shocked disbelief at the crumpled body of her young daughter. Only a few short hours ago Ranwyn had been a healthy, happy nine year old. Now she was dead.

"When will it end?" The question echoed within Wellana's mind. Her husband, King Regis III, gently touched his wife's shoulder. His eyes reflected not only Wellana's grief but his own as well. Ranwyn had been so full of life and joy. Now there was only a hollow emptiness.

At least, Regis and Wellana consoled each other, they still had their son: twelve-year-old Regis-Ranyl. He had suffered the backlash of the assault which had so brutally claimed his sister's life, but he would survive.

"Something must be done to stop this," Wellana said aloud. "We must put an end to *laran* warfare."

Regis sighed. While he personally abhorred the practice and felt the Towers could be put to better use than developing more destructive weapons, he knew, too, it was a matter of survival. Nor was he immune to the horror; his own *laran* heightened his awareness, but he had forced himself to accept it. Now, because of that same *laran* warfare, his only daughter was dead. "Do you seek revenge?" he asked grimly.

"So that more innocents can die?" Wellana said bitterly, her emotions raw. "Do we truly know what they feel? What she felt? I heard her scream, Regis. Within my mind I heard her terror and felt her pain. I felt her death. What does it matter if it came from one of our enemies, or from one of our own *leroni*? Ranwyn is just as dead. *Laran* killed her, but it cannot bring her back."

The King felt his wife's anguish. The two were in close rapport with each other, and with the spirit of their dead child. No weapon devised by man could be as cruel as the awareness that a child who should have lived was now dead.

"Revenge?" Wellana's voice was deathly quiet. "In a way you could call it revenge. I want an end to this misuse of *laran*, Regis. Surely the Gods did not give us these gifts in order for us to see how brutally we could destroy each other, not to mention what it's doing to our world. We have both seen what the *clingfire* does, and that is nothing in comparison with other weapons being devised and used. Where will it end, Regis? Are we all to die as Ranwyn died? You cannot let her death be in vain. You cannot."

Regis understood his wife's feelings. Within his own mind it was too easy to see those who had died in battle, and those who had suffered the terrible aftermath. *Clingfire*, deadly chemicals, unseen terrors striking the minds of their victims; the land laid to waste and the survivors wishing they had been among the dead.

Regis felt Wellana's pleading with him to stop the slaughter. Again he sighed. It was an argument he had had with himself many times since he was younger than his son. "What you are suggesting cannot be, Wellana. In our fathers' time and in their fathers' time there were wars, wars in which the use of *laran* made the difference between success and surrender. They liked it no better than we, but it has always been the only way to ensure peace."

"Peace?" Wellana spat. "When a nine-year-old child dies in a war not of her making, you call that peace? Regis, there has to be another way."

"What would you have me do?" Regis asked sadly. "Go to our enemies and ask each of them to fight me personally? I could be killed, Wellana. You wish to risk that?"

Wellana shuddered. Losing her daughter left a terrible, empty space in her life, but losing her husband. . . . The man she had married more than fifteen years before, the man she loved and cherished even if she did not always agree with him. To think now of losing him. . . . She pushed the thoughts deep within her mind. "I cannot answer that," she barely murmured. Together they both thought, "Perhaps there is no answer. . . ."

"I'm worried about Regis-Ranyl," Wellana confided to her husband nearly a tenday later. "The *leronis* Mharyelle says he has recovered from the attack on Ranwyn, but he is far too quiet and keeps to himself more than he should."

The elder Regis agreed. He did not like the change

in his son, but any attempt at communication resulted
in the boy becoming more sullen and withdrawn. "I
know he still mourns for Ranwyn, we all do." He met
his wife's gaze. "Surely he cannot be afraid of us as
well. . . ." He knew she shared the unspoken thought.

In addition, Regis and Wellana both knew their
son's own *laran* had begun to awaken. Too well did
Regis-Ranyl know that *laran* could kill. Was he afraid
of what his own untried powers could do? His parents
could only wonder.

"I'll talk to him," Regis comforted his wife. "The
fighting has subsided and I know he is anxious to go
riding again. Here Ranwyn's death still haunts him.
Perhaps we could go up to the old hunting lodge for a
few days. That might give him time to put his grief
behind him and let me know what's bothering him."

Wellana nodded, her eyes reflecting her love for her
husband. He had always been so gentle and understanding with both children, had always known just
how to comfort them and had always taken the time to
share even the smallest things in their lives. And the
hunting lodge was a good place. Wellana had pleasant
memories of the few times she and Regis had been
there, and knew it to be a place of peace and content-
ment.

The next morning Wellana said farewell to her husband and son. Already the boy's eyes were less fearful
as he hugged his mother, then followed his father to
the stables. Wellana watched the two mount their
horses, and continued to watch until they disappeared
into the woods. She could follow them with her mind,
she knew, but they needed this time alone. Father and
son. Her own duties and those of the household would
keep her occupied until they returned.

Sitting with her sewing, Wellana was sadly reminded
of Ranwyn. The child had possessed Wellana's talent
for the *rryl* and would often sit and play the instru-

ment quietly while Wellana and the other women sewed. Forgetting the embroidery in her lap, Wellana lost herself in the memory of her daughter. "Oh, Ranwyn," she sighed.

A terrified scream suddenly erupted in Wellana's mind. Briefly she wondered if she was again experiencing her daughter's death, at the same time feeling terror and intense pain. "Regis!" she cried, afraid for both of her loved ones. The sewing dropped to the floor as Wellana rose and ran toward the stables.

"Saddle my horse!" she commanded the groom.

He hastened to do the Queen's bidding, and helped her to mount. Briefly Wellana wished for breeches instead of her heavy skirts for riding, then turned her attention to her husband and son. "Regis, where are you?" she called mentally. Only an empty silence answered. "Regis!" she screamed within her mind. Unaware of the few guards who followed, she raced along the path her husband and son had taken. Again and again she called mentally to her loved ones, each time hearing only a hollow silence.

The path led into forested hills. In the distance a waterfall rumbled. How often had a much younger Wellana and Regis gone riding through these woods, following this same path. Here the two had found a deep and lasting peace, reminding them that a few of the Old Ones yet lived deep within the woods. Haunted by her memories and by an unseen terror she pushed on.

Gradually the path began to climb. The horse had to pick her way among the rocks, and fretted at Wellana's uneasiness. Conscious now of the guards behind her, Wellana let them be. If her husband and son were in trouble, and she was quite sure they were, she might need those guards. The path seemed endless, winding its way up through dense woods toward a meadow Wellana remembered well. She and Regis had spent many brief summer days there. "Regis, where are you?" she mentally called again. She was answered only by the stillness of the forest, and by her own increasing fear that her husband and son were dead. "NO!" she screamed within her mind, urging the horse onward.

Finally, Wellana recognized the rocky outcropping which bordered the meadow. Extending her consciousness she felt no danger, only a deep sense of loss. Cautiously, almost fearfully, she forced herself to go on. Following, the guards kept a close yet respectful distance behind their Queen.

Both the King and his son lay motionless in the field. With one swift movement Wellana dismounted and hastened to the still forms. She did not need her starstone to tell her that her husband was dead. The scream, she now knew, had come not only from her son but had been her husband's own excruciating pain and sudden death. Her son was alive, but how long he would remain so Wellana did not know. "Merciful Avarra," Wellana prayed, wishing desperately for knowledge of the healing arts.

Wellana had no time for grief. Although her first thought was for her son's welfare, there were also instructions to the guards concerning the return of the King's body to the castle.

It was a slow procession which made its way down the steep path; a ride made more difficult by the horses' fear of death, and the raw emotions of their riders.

Wellana was never sure how she endured the next few hours. Upon returning to the castle she was both relieved and apprehensive. With the terrible ride behind them, her son could get the rest he needed, and Wellana was grateful for Mharyelle's knowledge of healing. The King's own servants would see to the preparation of the body for the funeral, while Wellana comforted the rest of the household and accepted their condolences as well. Fear of uncertainty and of dark times ahead was foremost in every mind. As Queen, Wellana had to reassure the others, while inwardly she asked herself many of the same questions. Vision and hope alike rested with the unconscious prince.

Mharyelle's face was pale and grave when Wellana finally joined her. "How he survived is beyond me," the *leronis* said. "He had to have felt what was happening to his father, and must have acted as a shield. It's a miracle his mind was not completely shattered."

Within her own mind Wellana felt the *leronis'* fears mingled with those of young Regis-Ranyl. What the boy had seen and how he had suffered. . . . Wellana had only to look at Mharyelle to know the ordeal was one he would relive in nightmares for years to come.

"You have done what you can, Mharyelle, and I fear we shall all need your strength in the days ahead," Wellana said gently. "See if you can get some sleep. I'll stay here with him."

Mharyelle met the Queen's gaze. The *leronis* thought, and knew Wellana heard the thought, that the Queen would do well to heed her own advice. The women shared a grim smile of understanding before Mharyelle left the room.

Alone with her son, Wellana forced herself to remain calm. Gazing into her starstone, she focused all of her awareness on the boy. With a shudder she recoiled from the intense terror and complete hopelessness she felt within his mind. All she could do for him now was send thoughts of reassurance and comfort, and visions of peace.

The first dim rays of sunlight were filtering into the room when Regis wakened with a terrified scream. For a long time he cried like a wild thing, his body racked with grief.

"I tried to be brave," he sobbed at last. "I tried to save him, but. . . ." Again the terror claimed him and

Wellana felt him quail at her gentle touch upon his mind. "NO!" he screamed. Fighting the vivid images of his father's painful death, Regis cried, "Don't make me remember! Please, mama, don't make me remember. . . ."

Pained by her son's pleading and by the images in her own mind, Wellana shielded from him her thought that eventually she would have to know what had happened. Again her primary concern was for her son, and she sought only to comfort him. She nearly cried aloud in anguish when he suddenly closed his mind to her, shattering the close mental contact between them.

"I hate *laran*!" Regis declared angrily. "And I don't see how you can use it after what it did to father and to Ranwyn." Before Wellana could reply, the boy continued, "Is that what I'm to become when I learn to use my own *laran*? A monster who deliberately tortures and murders its victims?"

Wellana shook her head. Sadly she recalled the last conversation she and her husband had had on the subject. "In our fathers' time and in their fathers' time there were wars," Regis had said. And throughout the long history of those wars *laran*-created weapons had been used. Little wonder Regis-Ranyl was afraid to develop his own powers. Wellana met her son's gaze. His eyes were filled with fear, and with questions.

"Originally I believe the Towers were designed as places of learning," Wellana gently explained. "Places where those with telepathic powers could go and be with others of their kind and learn to use those powers. I don't believe the Gods gave us these powers so we could kill each other. Certainly your father never believed it. He felt that *laran* should be used to help rather than to destroy."

Regis' fear had subsided and he gazed thoughtfully at his mother. He had never known either of his parents to misuse their own *laran*, yet he knew too well the destructive forces.

"It cannot be right," he said at last. "The Towers cannot be allowed to turn us into monsters, devouring each others' minds. Isn't there something we can do to stop it?"

Wellana felt the determination behind her son's words. He was young for the responsibility being forced upon him, but she had no doubt that he would accept it. "When Ranwyn died, your father and I talked about this very thing, Regis. He had an idea that no one could kill another without putting himself in danger of being killed. You can see the risk involved."

Regis remained thoughtful. "But at least father would still be alive, and Ranwyn, too. Do you think it would work, mother?"

"It wouldn't hurt to try, but it won't be easy. Too many generations have been using *laran* to create more deadly weapons. Our enemies won't easily accept the change."

"But we can try?"

"We can always try, Regis."

His eyes were shining with eagerness, his mind filled with visions of a Darkover free of the terror of *laran*-created destruction. "You'll help me?"

Wellana nodded. "I'll be here for you. Your visions are as much your father's and mine as they are yours. Regis, if anyone can accomplish this thing, you will be the one."

Aware of his mother's periodic flashes of precognition, Regis asked seriously, "Promise?"

Wellana smiled. "I promise."

The Death of Brendon Ensolare

By Deborah Wheeler

Someone once said that there were only half a dozen plots in all, to be endlessly reshuffled. I don't know whether or not this is true, though in my own writing class I am likely to say there are basically three: man against nature, man against man (which, of course, includes man against woman) and man against himself.

One of the oldest plots around is the one whose most famous incarnation is "Lieutenant Kije"—an old Russian story which deals with the creation of an imaginary individual on a bureaucratic roster somewhere—who must then, somehow, be gotten rid of again. Like the sorcerer's apprentice, the creator usually finds that such creatures are easier to create than to be rid of.

The best known one in science fiction is probably the Hugo winner "Alamagoosa" by Eric Frank Russell. And now that I've given away the gimmick, on with the story.

Whenever feminists say that motherhood is incompatible with writing, I cite not only my own case, but that of Deborah Wheeler, who (in addition to being a chiropractor) has two young daughters.

She is also a writer, having sold to every one of these anthologies, as well as a martial-arts expert, and is therefore as well qualified to tell this story of the cadets as anyone could be. (MZB)

"Hey, Raimon! Welcome back, you old *cralmac*!"

"Same to you, Edric." Raimon Valdizar grinned, showing white teeth in a darkly handsome face, and clapped his friend on the shoulder. At sixteen, he was one of the younger third-year cadets who stood a little apart from the mature Guardsmen, waiting for the formal ceremony that would begin the Comyn Council season. "Anyone seen Bredan yet?"

"Didn't he stay with your family over the break?" asked Felix Macrae, a slender youth with reddish tints in his strawberry-blond hair.

"Yes, and damned near convinced my parents to handfast my oldest sister to him," Raimon laughed. "But she didn't care for his freckles." Lanna actually liked Bredan well enough, but was too spirited to do anything which would please her older brother without putting up a token resistance. She knew that nothing would suit Raimon so much as the *bredu* of his heart becoming his brother in truth.

"Who's cadet-master this term?" someone wanted to know.

"Not Di Asturien again—I heard one of the officers say he's temporary Commander," Edric said.

"They ought to let the old man retire. He must be almost ninety. Even the Comyn can't expect—"

"Bredan, quick! You're just in time. We're about to start!" Raimon grabbed his arm and pulled him into line. Bredan Escobar was wiry and good-looking, a golden shadow to Raimon's darkness.

The old man walked into the hall with stately grace and the entire assembly—officers, mature Guardsmen, and cadets—came to attention. The first-year cadets, brazen and unsure, stood in a little knot where the light from the great fan-shaped windows highlighted their multicolored civilian clothing.

Raimon heard their muttered comments and glared at them. *They think he's a doddering old fool. They*

*don't know how lucky they are to have him now that
Lord Alton's gone off-planet with his son—we could
have Dyan Ardais, or worse! Di Asturien may not be
as young as some, but at least he's honorable.*

Domenic Di Asturien finished his opening remarks
and began the formal process of the roll. He held
himself as proudly as any officer in the full strength of
youth as each Guardsman came forward and repeated
the ancient ritual of loyalty. It took a long time to go
through the list and toward the end the pauses grew
longer, the old soldier's voice less sure.

The next order of business was for the cadets to
stand forth in order of seniority.

"Valentine-Felix, cadet Macrae . . ."

"Here, sir!" Felix answered, with more enthusiasm
than necessary.

The old man looked up, his eyes reddened with
strain of so much reading in the difficult polychromatic
light. For a moment he seemed uncertain. Or was he,
Raimon wondered, remembering some other cadet who
had stood before him in this very hall, long since
grown from boyhood with sons of his own?

The roll went on until Di Asturien stumbled again,
over a name that was not quite legible. "Bre- Brendon,
cadet Ensolare."

Bredan cleared his throat. "I think—" he began,
clearly meaning to say, "I think there's been a mistake." But he could not bring himself to shatter the
illusion of the old man's competence.

"Here," he finished lamely.

At the same moment, Edric MacAnndra burst out,
"That's Bredan, cadet Escobar, sir."

"Bredan, cadet Escobar?"

"Here, sir," said Bredan, confused.

The old man glanced down at the parchment in his
hands. "Then where's cadet Ensolare? His name has
been omitted from his list. See to the correction, cadet-

master." Gabriel Lanart-Hastur, standing at Di Asturien's elbow, nodded gravely.

After the ceremony, the third-year cadets returned to the barracks to unpack the belongings they had taken home over the break and prepare for dormitory inspection.

"Hey, Bredan, one of you's not enough for us, eh? You had to be signed up for the Guards twice!" laughed Edric.

"You!" Bredan rounded on the taller boy. "You should have kept your fool mouth shut and everything would have straightened out! Now we're stuck with an imaginary thirteenth cadet—what are we going to do when Bredan, cadet Ensolare, fails to show up for his assigned arms practice?"

"I—I was only trying to help!"

Raimon said equably, "There's no harm done, 'Dan. Di Asturien may have ordered the name of Ensolare to be added to the lists, but the other officers know he doesn't exist. They'll fix things up quietly and we'll never hear of him again."

The next morning the assignments for arms practice were posted. Raimon elbowed his way forward to peer at the list.

"Oh, my aching backside, I've got Padraik for sword, and right before dinner," he groaned. "I'll never get out in time for a decent meal. You banshees will have eaten it all by the time he's finished with me—assuming there's anything left of me to want dinner." Then he noticed the expression on Bredan's face. "What's the matter, who've you got?"

"Rai. Look!" Bredan pointed halfway down the schedule, where Brendon, cadet Ensolare, was scheduled for a lesson with a new instructor, Timas Wellsmith. "You said they'd catch the mistake. We'd seen the last of him—your very words."

Raimon grinned engagingly and shrugged.

"I feel responsible for this whole mixup," Bredan said. "I should go in and straighten it out."

"Tell Di Asturien he's made a mistake? To his face?"

"He's right, you know," said Mikhail Castamir, a serious boy from the Kilghard Hills. "We can't let the Commander be humiliated that way, even if you told him in private. And he would be, if he learned he'd made a mistake like that."

"I can't just let it go on—" Bredan protested.

"Look," Raimon took him by the shoulders, his voice soothing and persuasive. "It was a simple mistake, not anyone's fault, let alone yours. Let's get out of here, before all there is left of breakfast is cold nut-porridge and no honey. Besides," he added, as they trooped down to the refectory, "I have an idea of how some good might come of the situation after all."

Later that afternoon, Raimon, clad in old clothing and carrying a battered sword, presented himself for arms practice. Timas Wellsmith, he had learned, was a former Guardsman who had tried breeding *chervines*, but turned out to be allergic to their dander and was forced to return to the only occupation he knew.

"Cadet Ensolare?"

"Well, not exactly," Raimon said, flashing his most engaging grin. "He had an emergency of an—um, personal nature, and rather than inconvenience you by being late, he asked me to trade session times with him."

Timas looked dubious. Perhaps, Raimon thought, in his day such things weren't done—you showed up for your assigned workout even though you were blind, lame, and loaded with *kireseth*. As a point of fact, switching times was occasionally although unofficially allowed, but any change in instructors was definitely not, and Raimon knew it. He tried to look earnest as he said, "I know I won't disappoint you, sir. I've been looking forward to the opportunity of training with you ever since we heard you'd rejoined the Guards."

Finally Timas nodded, his features softening a little. "All right, then, lad, let's see what today's cadet standards are like."

Raimon passed a thorough if unimaginative workout with Timas and then happily presented himself to his own, stricter instructor. Padraik, who had known him from past years, may have had his doubts, but the dust and scrapes Raimon so proudly displayed proved that he had indeed already had his lesson.

At dinner that night, Raimon took his usual place between Bredan and Felix, looking very much like the proverbial cat set to guard the dairy.

"I thought you had the last shift with Padraik," Bredan said. "And I can't imagine he let you off early for the sake of your empty stomach. How did you manage this one—you didn't cut training, did you?" That would be a serious breach, even for a cadet with Raimon's reputation.

"Oh," Raimon replied airily as he dabbed his stew with a hunk of bread. "I swapped times with our old friend, Brendon Ensolare."

His sworn brother gazed at him wide-eyed, and for a moment Raimon was afraid that he'd outraged even Bredan's sense of propriety. But Bredan was doing his best to suppress a whoop of delight. "You didn't!"

"I did, Aldones' own truth. I have a feeling this is just the very beginning—for all of us—"

Bredan protested, laughing, "The last time you got one of these ideas, we ended up with a solid month of latrine duty."

"I remember that," growled Mikhail from the other

side of the table. "I still don't understand how you managed to talk me into it, let alone Felix."

Raimon refused to be baited. "But it was worth it, wasn't it, to see the first year cadets' faces the next morning? Even you enjoyed sneaking into the Terran Zone to buy the voice recorder."

"Whoo!" chortled Bredan, relishing the memory of his *bredu's* most notable prank. "You set the thing to go off just past midnight. *"Beware, this dormitory is haunted! Beware the ghost who stalks these halls!"* Complete with rattling chains and a great rendition of a banshee. They looked like they'd actually *seen* a ghost!"

Felix, sitting on Raimon's other side, said shyly, "How do you think of such things, Rai?"

"I stay awake all night plotting them. Now, I've been thinking—"

"I have a feeling we're going to be very, very sorry we ever listened to you," Bredan said.

"The problem we had last time," Raimon continued, undaunted, "was that one of us had to buy the voice recorder, and that meant registering it by name."

"Technically, we shouldn't have brought it out of the Zone at all," Mikhail said. "Ever since the Sharra uprising at Caer Donn, the *Terranan* have been fanatic about upholding the Compact."

Raimon said, with unwonted seriousness, "If I thought that a simple voice recorder could be used as a weapon, I'd sent it to Zandru's coldest hell before I touched the filthy thing."

Bredan reached out to touch his shoulder, and Raimon relaxed under the pulse of steady love and support that flowed from the brief contact.

The conversation then changed to the latest scandal involving The Golden Cage, Thendara's most notorious brothel. At least in the Darkovan sector, Raimon said. He had heard there was a place in the Terran Zone that could give it some competition.

"The Greek Dancer."

"What does it mean, Greek?" Felix asked.

Mikhail said, "Some ancient *Terranan* custom. Who cares, with dancers like that?"

"How come you know so much about it? The man is full of surprises!" Raimon dug an elbow into Mikhail's ribs, prompting a round of sputtering. "Since we've got a personal guide, I think we ought to check this *Terranan* wonder out."

The blood-red sun was just dipping behind the rooftops of the Darkovan sector as the four cadets approached the gate to the Terran Zone. A black-suited guard stepped forward and addressed them in barbarically accented *cahuenga.*

"You can't bring those weapons into the Zone. Either take your swords back home, or check them here. And by the way, you boys are minors under Terran law, and subject to curfew. Be back by an hour after sunset, or you'll get reported."

After checking their weapons, the four friends wandered through the gaggle of eating places and small shops gearing up for an evening's business. In comparison with the natural lighting of the old city, the neofluorescents cast eerie, almost supernatural shadows. They paused to inspect some goods prominently displayed on open tables.

"Cheap trade stuff," Raimon sniffed.

Felix bought a stick of spun-synthesugar candy. "This isn't bad."

"Eat enough of that stuff and you'll end up as fat as Alban the Miller—and with as few teeth!" Bredan laughed.

"I think what we want is over this way," Raimon flung an arm around Bredan's shoulders and, ignoring the disapproving stares of the Terra merchants, started down an even more garishly lit avenue.

The Greek Dancer was not difficult to find, even in a mass of buildings of various degrees of taste. A woman leaned from the balcony window, calling lewd suggestions to passers. The Terrans in the street looked up and shouted equally obscene replies, but the Darkovan boys kept their eyes averted. Felix blushed furiously as the blonde, her breasts barely covered by gauze and glitter, offered to relieve him of his virginity.

"C'mon, Felix, it's not as if you'd never been to a brothel before," Raimon said, keeping his voice low so the woman could not hear. The precaution was unnecessary, as she had already turned her attention to more promising prey. "I dragged you there myself for your fifteenth birthday."

"These *Terranan* have no sense of decency," Mikhail said somberly.

"By Aldones, no!" Raimon agreed enthusiastically. "That's what makes them so much fun!"

They elbowed their way into the dimly lit central room and stood for a moment gaping at the decor, especially the glittering fabric wallpanels. For Darkovans raised in airy, open buildings of translucent stone, the undulating, closed-in room was momentarily disconcerting, repellent. Then Raimon's eyes dark-adapted and he spied an empty table near a dais which could only be a stage.

A server approached them as soon as they lowered themselves into the sculpted plastic seats. Raimon turned his head to see a length of naked thigh topped by a brief tunic of metallic fabric. Dark eyes glittered behind a feathered mask and the reddened lips curved in an inviting smile.

"What's the matter, cat got your tongue, sweetie?" One hip brushed against his cheek in unmistakable suggestion.

Raimon just stared, for the melodious, honey-sweet voice, like the bulging crotch placed so strategically near his face, was unmistakably male. Raimon was neither a virgin nor a prude, nor was he uncomfortable with the physical expression of love with his *bredu*. But for a man of such dubious morality to approach him in a public place left him momentarily speechless.

Making a noticeable effort to keep his face serious, Bredan told the server, "My friend's tongue seems to be paralyzed. I think spiced wine all around would help."

"We don't have anything that tame, but I can get him a lady's cocktail if you boys aren't up to anything stronger."

Raimon recovered his voice. *A lady's cocktail, indeed!* He searched his memory for the one Terran drink he knew to be suitable for grown men. "Forget that," he snapped. "We'll start with a Callahan Special. All around."

The server glided back toward the bar through the thickening crowd, his hips swaying to an astonishing degree. Bredan said, "Maybe the crazy *Terranan* have an operation like the illegal *emmasca*, only in reverse— instead of becoming neuter, you become both."

The drinks went down like frozen fire, with a peculiar aftertaste at the back of the throat. Raimon sipped his as the first act began. A thin woman, who seemed to him to be practically naked to begin with, did an elaborate strip-tease with two feather fans. He noticed that Felix was blushing furiously, his eyes downcast. Finally the dance ended and Mikhail leaned forward to say, "This is only the teaser. It gets better—"

"Mikie, honey-lips! Where you been so long?" Squealing in delight, an unambiguously female server threw her arms around Mikhail's neck and swung her legs on to his lap. The other boys watched, astonished, as she kissed him on the lips. "You boys lookin' for a good time? I'm Kitten, and I'm real friendly!"

"Mikhail, you old—" began Raimon.

"Listen, baby, you seen the show before, you don't need to waste time on it again. Last time you were here I promised you a special treat, much better than the show tonight. What d'ya say?"

After some enthusiastic coaxing from Kitten and not much resistance on the boys' part, they followed her past a layer of rippling wall coverings and down a narrow hallway to a tiny but sumptuously furnished private room. Raimon sat beside Bredan on the low couch which was obviously designed for more than sitting.

"Now you boys just wait a moment and I'll be right back. I been saving this little surprise for Mikie's next visit."

"What's this 'little surprise'?" Raimon asked after she left.

"I don't know. She said she knew something that would 'loosen me up,' whatever that means."

Kitten returned in a few moments with a small black box. "Stygian bloodroot, the real stuff. You never tried anything like it, I guarantee that. No free samples, but you'll never regret it." She named a price that would have left the boys gasping if they had not been so determined to impress her with their worldliness.

Inside the box lay a pile of thin gray threads. Kitten separated one out. "You put it under your tongue," she said. "Don't chew, or we'll be scraping you off the ceiling. Hold it there and in a few minutes—wowie-zowie!"

Gingerly, Raimon picked up a piece. He'd never heard of Stygia, let alone its bloodroot, and he had no idea of what to expect. Whatever it did, he reasoned as he placed it beneath his tongue, it was sure to make a great story back at the barracks.

Several things happened at once. Raimon's ears felt as if they'd been shoved in a pot of boiling water, he felt a strong urge to giggle, and there was a brassy honking from the hallway.

Kitten scrambled to her feet. "Oh, shit, we're being raided!"

"Raided?" Raimon blinked at her, and then giggled. There was a strange echo in the room that magnified his own laughter.

"Yes, you idiot! It's the narcs!" She slammed the lid of the box shut. "Do you have any idea how illegal this stuff is? I don't know what they'll do to you, but they'll send *me* someplace very boring for a long, long time."

She yanked open the door and disappeared.

"Some friends," muttered Bredan, his speech strangely distorted, almost bubbly. "Leavin' us to take th' blame."

Raimon tried to think, but his vision was beginning to dance with tiny pink butterflies. "We'd better get out of here."

The hallway outside seethed with bodies in various degrees of undress, each apparently trying to go in a different direction. Raimon, first out the door, paused. Someone grabbed his arm, firm but not unfriendly. He recognized the male server who had flirted with him.

"Come on, this is no place for kids!" The server pulled him down the hallway to the main room. Raimon reflexively grabbed Bredan's hand, an island of security in a world gone bizarre. The server shoved them toward the back of the dais. "We've got a secret exit— What's the matter with you?"

Mikhail, breathing heavily, stammered, "K-Kitten—"

"That bitch! Did she try to pawn spidercrack off on you as bloodroot?"

Raimon nodded as a sudden wave of nausea knotted his stomach.

"You poor innocents. Half the fun and twice the pain, but it won't kill you. Through here—"

Felix and Mikhail dove behind the matte-black curtain, Bredan hesitating only a moment to make sure Raimon was following.

"Freeze where you are! Terran Vice Squad!"

Suddenly the server shouldered his way past him and Raimon fell retching to his knees. A moment later he was hauled to his feet by two heavily muscled Terran officers.

For the next hour, as the server had foretold, his stomach and balance centers were in utter revolt, but he managed not to disgrace himself by vomiting. He sat, wrists bound by lightweight force-cuffs, waiting to be formally charged. By the time he had to face any questions, the worst had worn off, although waves of nausea still seized him at irregular intervals. It took all of Raimon's guile to keep his jailers from detecting his illness and treating him medically under the emergency care provisions of the Treaty.

"Name?" snapped the grim-looking officer at the desk.

Raimon straightened his shoulders. He was the last of the small group of Darkovan customers to be processed, and his gastrointestinal symptoms were beginning to give way to deep muscle tremors. The last thing he wanted was to appear frightened before this bureaucratic rabbithorn of a *Terranan*.

"Brendon, cadet Ensolare . . . sir."

"Cadet, you are charged with violation of Terran anti-crime law. Consorting with known prostitutes, on the premises where illegal hallucinogens—" Raimon did not even twitch—"were seized, present in an establishment serving alcohol to minors—and I don't doubt that you yourself consumed some. Those are fairly serious charges, enough to get you sent to Juvenile Rehab if you were in our jurisdiction. But the

Darkovan authorities insist we turn you over to them. We will file formal charges against you tomorrow. Until those charges are dismissed by your own superiors, or they inform us you have completed whatever penalty they give you, you are not welcome to return to the Terran Zone. Is that clear?"

"Perfectly, sir."

Somehow Raimon managed to make it, escorted, to the border of the Terran Zone and then, unescorted and undiscovered, to the barracks. Bredan was still awake and waiting for him. Raimon knew, without having to kindle a light, that his *bredu* felt no better than he did, but with the added burden of worry for his friend.

"What in Zandru's seventh hell happened to you?" Bredan hissed through the darkness. "You were right behind us, but when we came out in the alley, you weren't there. And neither, by the way, was that thrice-bedamned *bre'suin*—"

"He did us all a favor when we got into that mess on our own. But there's no harm done. I was the only one caught and—listen to this, 'Dan—tomorrow the Terran authorities will be registering formal charges—against Brendon Ensolare!"

Raimon felt Bredan's astonished glee like a wave of warmth and he wondered for the hundredth time if one or the other of them might have a trace of *laran*—not enough to show up overtly, but enough to account for the amazing sympathy between them.

Bredan whispered, "What do you suppose Di Asturien will do to him?"

Raimon took off his clothes, stuffed them in the narrow wooden chest at the foot of his bed, and slipped beneath the covers. "Let's just pray it's something he doesn't have to show up in person for."

The next morning, the cadetmaster's aide stuck his head into the third-year barracks just as they were finishing dressing for breakfast. "Cadet Ensolare!" He saw the puzzled faces and sniffed. "No one's seen him, eh? Well, you can tell the miscreant that he's assigned double latrine duty for the next month, Commander's orders." And then he withdrew."

"You can't say Di Asturien's entirely lacking in a sense of humor," Raimon commented. "He clearly means that those who voluntarily choose the—er, pits, ought to have their wishes granted."

The four friends managed to pick up the extra shifts of latrine duty, so the absence of cadet Ensolare went unnoticed by the inspecting officers. As the weeks passed, the last residue of the "Stygian bloodroot" faded into a humorous memory, and Raimon's old confidence began to reassert itself.

"It's nearly the end of the Comyn Council season . . ." Felix began shyly. He stood together with Raimon and Bredan outside the practice fields, waiting for Mikhail to finish his lesson. Having been raised in Kilghard fashion to fight with two knives, Mikhail found the stylized cadet swordwork frustrating. When surprised, he would automatically reach for his second blade which, unaccountably, was always somewhere about his person. The armsmaster was making a concerted effort to teach him decent lowland technique.

"Too bad, no more honor guard duty," Raimon said lightly, watching Mikhail go through one more timing drill. "Still, it would have been nice to see them in all their splendor at least once—another story to tell the grandkids, right, Bredan?"

Felix took a deep breath and blurted out, "I've been issued an invitation to their closing ball, tomorrow night, and I can bring one guest, and I was wondering if you'd like to attend with me, Raimon . . . that is, if Bredan doesn't mind."

Raimon and Bredan stared at him. It was one of the

longest, and certainly the most astonishing speech they'd even heard him make. Bredan said, "How did you manage an invitation? I didn't think cadets were included in those affairs."

Felix blushed, but less than usual. "You've probably guessed from my hair that there's Comyn blood in my family. My grandmother was a *nedestro* Elhalyn, although usually nobody remembers. I went—I saw Lady Callina about Tower training after I finish this year, and she said I ought to be included."

"A Tower?" Bredan and Raimon exclaimed in unison. "How'd that happen? C'mon, Felix, give!"

The boy looked down at his dusty boots. "I had threshold sickness much worse than my older brother, but everybody said it was because I was so sickly as a child. When I was fourteen, my mother wanted me tested by a *leronis*, but my father said it was more important to make a man of me, so he sent off to the Guards. It wasn't all bad—I mean, I met you two, and Mikhail. But I feel these things—as if I'm a featherdown blown by other people's emotions. I think it would be better to find out how to manage it, even if it turns out to be worthless."

"Aldones!" Raimon breathed. No wonder Felix was always blushing!

"So," said Felix after a long pause, "what do you think?"

"Bredan?"

Bredan grinned and punched Raimon gently on the shoulder. "Go ahead, have a good time. I've got city patrol tomorrow night, anyway."

Raimon sang softly under his breath as he and Felix made their way back, three parts drunk and very pleased with themselves. The ball with its Comyn lords and ladies, officers, and even a crimson-robed Keeper, seemed like a dream. Raimon had worked up enough nerve to dance with several of the young noblewomen, too overwhelmed to notice the details of their gowns that Lanna would certainly question him about. Old Danvan Hastur himself had been there, along with his young heir. Commander Di Asturien had been gravely polite to both boys, and they had seen Dyan Ardais in the famous sword-dance. All in all, a night to tell one's grandchildren.

Felix managed to open the barracks door and they went in. Mikhail, Edric, and a few of the others were clustered around a shielded light. Mikhail looked up, his breath coming in a sob.

"Raimon, thank Aldones you've come."

Something in his voice stung Raimon like ice water, sweeping away the last traces of the wine punch. "What's wrong?"

"It's Bredan," said Edric shakily as Mikhail hid his face in his hands. "I wish I didn't have to be the one to tell you—"

In one movement Raimon shot across the floor, grabbing Edric's shoulders with such force that he lifted the taller boy from the ground. "Damn you! What's happened to Bredan?"

"He's hurt—badly. Maybe dying—we don't know yet," said Mikhail.

"There was a fight down by The Golden Cage," Edric cried. "A bunch of damned fools drunk on some stuff they'd gotten illegally in the Terran Zone. Bredan was alone—he tried to separate two of them. One knifed him—under the ribs, I think. They've sent for a healer from the Tower, to try to save him. Rai, I'm so sorry."

Raimon opened his hands, barely feeling Edric slump and then catch himself. Images seared his vision, images of darkness and bloodshed. Bredan knifed down in the street, bleeding, calling out to him, Bredan lying in a pool of his own blood.

Bredan dying . . .

"Why—how could he be alone? City patrol is always by pairs."

Mikhail put one hand on his shoulder and said in a low voice. "His assigned second was . . . Brendon Ensolare."

Raimon reeled in shock. There was no Brendon Ensolare to fight at Bredan's side, the difference between life and death, and no Raimon Valdizar to make up the absence, because he was enjoying himself at the Comyn ball. Bredan had never gotten over feeling personally responsible for Ensolare because of the confusion over his own name, so he hadn't asked for help.

If 'Dan dies . . . if he dies it will be my fault. I didn't let him clean up the mistake and I wasn't there when he needed me.

"He's in the infirmary," Mikhail said gently.

Raimon tore through the door at a run. The infirmarian recognized him and let him in without any questions. He showed him to a small, well-lit room. A young woman wearing a loose white robe, her copper hair spilling over her shoulders, knelt at the side of the bed on which lay a waxen-pale figure, blurred in Raimon's sight.

"Can I go to him?" he whispered.

The infirmarian shook his head, but the woman, without opening her eyes, said, "Yes. You can add your will to live . . . to his."

Raimon sat on the low stool as the head of the bed, looking down at Bredan's face, so white and still, as if his life fires were already extinguished. Only the slow, almost hesitant rise and fall of his bandaged chest told Raimon that he had not come too late.

The *leronis* shifted her position, her thin, six-fingered hands outstretched over Bredan's body. "Take his hands," she said. "Let him know you love him."

Bredan's fingers were cold, almost stiff. Raimon willed them to warm with life, with his own life.

Bredan, my brother, my heart, don't leave me. I don't know what I'll do if I lose you because I was so damned cocky—

Tears were running down his face freely now, spilling over onto their joined hands, but if the *leronis* noticed, she gave no sign.

I thought this whole Ensolare prank was a game, the biggest joke of my career. But I never meant to hurt anyone, never meant it to come to this. If there's a price to pay for my stupidity, let it be me that pays— Oh, Avarra. Dark Lady, let it be me and not Bredan!

"Raimon." The voice was low, female, shattering the passion of his agony and guilt. "Raimon, go back and sleep. You can do no more here tonight, and your *bredu* will need all your strength in the morning."

"He will live?"

The *leronis* smiled.

A somber Raimon Valdizar stood before Commander Di Asturien in his private offices, his face still drawn from the weeks of ordeal behind him.

"As you know, sir, cadet Escobar has still not recovered sufficiently to continue with his duties. The infirmarian suggested that he return home for the rest of the term. I would like permission to accompany him and remain with him until he has regained his health."

"I understand at one time you wished to continue in the Guard as an officer. If you leave now, you'll have to repeat the entire year."

"I—I know that, sir. I'm willing to pay the price."

"Very well, then, as long as you understand the consequences."

"That I do, sir." *Possibly for the first time in my life.* "And sir?"

"Yes . . ."

"Cadet Ensolare asked to come along, too."

"Cadet Ensolare . . . ah, yes. That rather brash young man who got himself embroiled with the Terran Vice Squad. I've been meaning to speak to you about him, cadet Valdizar. You're his friend, maybe you can talk some sense into him. Do you think there's any hope for straightening him out?"

Raimon said with a perfectly straight face, "I think he's learned his lesson, sir."

"Learning a lesson and putting it into action are two completely different matters. Nevertheless, permission is granted to both of you to accompany cadet Escobar. *Adelandeyo*, go in peace."

Despite the slow pace, Bredan was nearly exhausted by the time his family's small estate came into view. "I need to rest before we take that last downward stretch," he said, grasping his saddle with white-knuckled hands.

"We should have arranged for a travel litter," Raimon said, and sent their hired servant ahead to announce their arrival.

Bredan shook his head, smiling with a trace of his old spirit. "That would have frightened my mother out of her wits for sure. As it is, she'll fuss over me worse than if I were Aldones himself. Believe me, it's better that I arrive sitting up."

They halted their horses in the little paved court-yard between the house and the smaller workshops and stables. Bredan's mother, a tiny woman with iron-gray hair, rushed to his side as Raimon helped him to dismount.

"You've come at last—I've been so worried—look at you, you're as pale as a sheet—Raimon, you take his other arm—we've got to get him lying down, maybe with some hot wine—that's good for rebuilding the blood—what a pity Pietro isn't here to help, but he's gone with your father up toward Gray Hill, looking for

stray stock and the other men are at Armida, helping
with the hay harvest—I can't imagine what your father
will think when he comes home and finds you here
already and him not back to welcome you—there!
mind the step," she said in a single breath.

Bredan looked up at Raimon. *You see what I meant.*

I've got to do something about Brendon Ensolare,
Raimon thought as he watched Bredan's mother
bustle about the solarium, tucking him in with blankets
and exhorting him to drink the heated wine. *Each
moment I see Bredan like this I'm reminded how it
happened. I can't forgive myself until the whole game is
finished.*

Later in the day, when red shadows were lengthening
across the courtyard and Bredan had sunk into a restful
sleep, Raimon jerked awake from his own dozing at a
clatter on the threshold. He found his way to the front
door, where a haggard Pietro stood, gesturing wildly to
Lady Escobar.

"I ran the poor beast half-dead gettin' here, but the
Lord canna hold out for long, not agin those de'ils."

"What's going on? Can I help?" As he drew closer,
Raimon saw deep welling scratches through the rents
in the man's heavy shirt.

Lady Escobar said, "Catman attack. Since Corresanti,
they've come farther south, but usually toward Alton
lands, so we thought we were safe. My husband's trapped
in one of the Gray Hill caves. There's only women and
one old man to send, since Pietro's wounded." Gone
was the fussiness, replaced by a quiet fatality.

"I'll go. Bredan showed me where it was on my last
visit."

She looked at him, her gaze measuring. "You don't
owe us this."

"Your son and I are *bredin*," he said, using the
inflection that meant "sworn brother."

Minutes later Raimon was pounding up the trail, his sword slung across his back. It was almost dark when he pulled his lathered horse to a halt, scanning the fractured granite of Gray Hill. The caves lay along the east side along the switchbacks which crossed its creviced face. He saw the glimmer of torchlight aloft, and spurred his panting mount forward.

Two catmen, armed with curved Dry Town blades, held the sloping, pebble-strewn apron at the cave's entrance. They whirled, alert and ready even before Raimon leapt from the saddle, sword in hand. The horse, snorting in outrage, bolted back down the trail.

One catman uttered unintelligible curses and hurled itself through the air toward Raimon. He parried its blade, but it tossed the sword away and sank its extended claws into his shoulder.

Raimon staggered under the sudden impact of the catman's weight, twisting aside so that the deadly hind claws swept through empty air instead of his own belly. He fell to one knee as the creature spun away with inhuman agility to renew its attack. Suddenly the catman's battle cry turned to a scream of panic as it clawed frantically at the loose, sliding rock.

The apron of pebble and weather-crazed stone tumbled free in a miniature avalanche. The catman went with it, flailing and yowling, but unable to regain its footing on the treacherous slide. It sank from view as its voice fell silent, and no further sign of life came from below.

The rock beneath Raimon's knee began to give way with a sickening wrench. He scrambled to his feet on what was left of the narrow trail, coughing on the acrid dust. The remaining catman crouched before him, blade raised and glimmering in the failing light. It sank into a fighting stance, blocking the entrance with clear malice. Just inside the cave lay a pile of dark, unmoving bodies, evidence of Escobar's defense.

"Lord Escobar! Are you all right?"

"Aye, for the moment, but m'leg's broken."

"There's only one of the things left—"

With a murderous growl, the catman shot forward, aiming not for Raimon but for the remnants of the trail at his feet. A quick slash outward sent Raimon jumping backward, and the catman dug its sword tip into the loose stone and pushed outward. A flurry of rock tumbled down the hillside.

Sliding his feet to feel his way, Raimon inched forward. If only he could get close enough to reach the cursed thing before it pried loose so much of the trail that he either suffered the same fate as the first catman or else was cut off completely from the cave. The catman, seeing his intention, jumped forward in open assault.

Instantly Raimon met the attack, his muscles flowing into the patterns Timas Wellsmith had drilled into him. Without thinking, he parried, disengaged, and thrust clean through the catman's guard. A scream and sudden wavering of the curved blade told Raimon his own sword had found its mark. He was fighting by instinct and feel rather than sight now, could barely see his opponent in the near darkness. Part of him wanted to break off this impossible battle and go running back down the trail to safety. Any moment now he might go tumbling down the hillside to break his neck on the rock fall, or miss a lightning thrust of the catman's blade and die in a pool of his own blood.

But Bredan had very nearly died that way . . . .

Raimon brought himself up with a start, realizing that the catman had suddenly disappeared. He stepped forward, expecting a renewed attack at any moment. The torchlight from the cave guided him, for a moment illuminating the entire arch of the entrance. Then he spied the catman in silhouette, clinging to the upper wall. It was using its sword as a lever, the point thrust deep into the crevice.

Even as Raimon's blade sped upward toward its unguarded belly, the catman twisted and lost its footing in a shower of granite slivers. Raimon flinched, raising his free hand to protect his eyes. The catman's hind legs churned madly against the stone face, fighting desperately for purchase while its weight fell against the sword.

Raimon slashed upward again. This time his blade met living flesh. He felt it glance off bone and jerk forward, almost out of his grip.

A sudden *crack*! brought another shower of fresh rock as the catman loosened its grip upon the sword and jumped free. A huge piece of stone from the overhang came hurling outward. It caught the catman even as it leapt for the entrance, and disappeared downslope.

Raimon watched in horror as the entire outside face of rock began to break up. Without thinking, he dropped his sword, whirled, and dove into the cave. Lord Escobar had hauled himself upright, standing on one leg, his face set and grim in the last of the dying torchlight. He hobbled forward as Raimon shouted, "Let's go!" and hooked his arm under the old man's shoulder.

In the few seconds it took them to reach the entrance, more stone had fallen, almost closing the passageway. Lord Escobar hesitated in the fall of dust and rock. "No use, lad."

"It's our only chance!" Raimon cried. He couldn't give up, not with Bredan's father depending upon him, not even if he died in the attempt. He shoved the old man bodily through the rapidly disappearing opening.

Loose rock pelted them and Raimon ducked, trying to shield the old man. A chunk of granite struck

Escobar on the side of the head with a sickening *whap*! and suddenly he went limp in Raimon's arms.

Raimon did not feel the shower of stones battering his own body, or the shrieking pain in his arms as he hauled Escobar's inert body to the last strip of clear trail. He had only a moment to sling the old man across his shoulders before that, too, began to slide under his feet. Half-running, half-scrambling, he somehow kept going down the nightmare trail until he reached level ground.

Gently Raimon laid the old man down on a patch of grass. His breathing was shallow and regular, but he did not rouse when Raimon, using strips cut from his own undertunic, lashed two pieces of fallen wood to his leg to brace the fracture. Then came a more difficult decision, for even though further movement might worsen Escobar's head injury, Raimon could not leave him, not with the night chill already seeping into his bones and possibly more catmen prowling the darkness.

Dredging his memory for the details of Gabriel Lanart-Hastur's tales of mountain rescues, Raimon used what was left of his shirt to tie Escobar so that he could carry him more easily. How he made it through the night, staggering up one hill and stumbling down again, he never knew. He stopped counting the rest stops he was forced to take when he simply could not make his legs move any further.

Some hours past dawn, Raimon's ordeal came to an end. Pietro met them along the trail with whoops of joy and an extra saddled horse. The return of Raimon's riderless mount had caused near panic, and he had been sent to see if anything could be done before sending to Armida for help.

Bredan and his mother rushed forward to meet them before they set foot in the courtyard. Clearly, neither had slept all night. As the injured lord was put to bed, his fracture set and his other wounds tended, Raimon sat silently by the fire, holding Bredan's hands with one hand and a cup of hot wine with the other. He had eaten and bathed, and the scratches on his shoulders were bandaged, but he was far from sleep.

"Raimon, I cannot thank you enough. You—you have saved his life, you know." Lady Escobar stood in the doorway, her face careworn but radiant. "You have proven yourself a true hero—"

"He's going to be all right?" Raimon asked, ignoring the gratitude in her eyes.

"Evanda willing, he will outlive us all. His skull is not broken, only stunned. He is awake now and wants to thank you himself."

"It was a brave rescue ye did, lad," said Bredan's father. His dark eyes sparkled beneath his bandaged forehead, although he seemed a little confused about what happened to him.

"No, it wasn't," Raimon replied in a low voice. "I mean, it wasn't me."

He took a deep breath and said again, "It wasn't me that saved you. It was Brendon Ensolare, a fellow cadet, a friend to Bredan and me. He was delayed on the trail, but he followed me to Gray Hill. He fought at my side against the catmen and carried you out when I couldn't get past the cave entrance. But he was caught by the landslide, buried in the rock. He died saving us both."

For a fleeting moment Bredan looked confused, and then he said, "That would be just like Ensolare, to show up when he's least expected. But unlike you, Raimon, to give away the credit when you might be acclaimed as a hero. You always loved being the center of attention."

"I—I can't accept what I don't deserve," Raimon stammered. "The important thing is that your father is alive and recovering."

"I am pleased that my son and his *bredu* had such a

friend. We must send word to his family," said Lord Escobar.

"I don't think he has a family outside of the Guards, Father," Bredan said.

"Sad, but he will not be forgotten," the old man commented, and drifted into sleep.

Raimon Valdizar stood in the great hall of Comyn Castle, waiting for the formal ceremonies to open the next year's season. He was old for a third-year cadet now, and he could tell by their expressions that the younger boys considered him stodgy. He didn't care, for at his side stood Bredan Escobar, alive and well.

Domenic Di Asturien stepped forward to begin the ceremony, just as he had on that fateful day a year ago. But this time there would be no Brendon Ensolare on the roll.

Raimon had visited Di Asturien in private upon his return to Thendara to inform the Commander of the heroic death of cadet Ensolare.

"He died bravely, a credit to the Guards. Lord Escobar sent this letter of commendation."

The old soldier took the note. "We'll miss the lad, but perhaps it's all for the best."

And then, suddenly, "Do you like nuts, cadet Valdizar?"

"Sir!"

"Nuts—ambernuts, hazels, pitchoos."

"Y-yes, sir."

"The principle thing about nuts, Valdizar, is that each requires a different technique. Pitchoos, now, they're covered with such a delicate skin that even a fingernail can mar the fruit inside. Barknuts are sweet enough, and easy to crack with a common nutcracker. But ambernuts are a different matter. To get at the meat, you have to throw them in a fire. Nothing less will break through that hard shell, but when you're done, you have the best eating of all. Do you understand me?"

"I think so, sir." *Aldones, he must have known all along.* . . .

"Then run along. I'll see you and your friend at call-over. And cadet Valdizar . . . Don't either of you forget your names this time. I don't think the Guard could survive another season like the last one."

Sort of Chaos

By Millea Kenin

Whenever I get a manuscript from Millea Kenin, I am always on the alert for the roving pun. I don't know how Millea does it; she is a local writer/desktop publisher and, like many of us, has a couple of teenage children. In fact, though I didn't set out to confound those people who think writing doesn't go with being a mother and housewife (and I certainly don't recommend it), this anthology certainly contains ample proof that it happens. (It's about all you can do if you're bitten by the writing bug, and the kids are there. Maybe we should think about these things first.) Millea publishes market listings and many other things, including the small magazine Owlflight.*

She also knows that I like to end my anthologies with something short and funny; and at least once before, it has been with one of Millea's bad puns that I have done so. (While it may be possible to chain a dragon for roasting your meat, it is not well done—arggggh!) So forward—but you have been warned. (MZB)

Please don't bar me from all the Towers forever. After all, Lisandra wasn't really hurt—she turned the backlash back on me—and I was able to protect myself well enough. I'll be perfectly all right in another day or two. So don't give me that *reish* about it being for my own protection.

The thing is, it won't happen again, if Lisandra and I are never in the same room again. We communicated for years through the relays without any problems, as every telepath in the towers of Darkover can confirm. All of you here at Dalereuth can also confirm that I've been a perfectly reliable matrix technician here for ten years, that I've never gone out of control before, that I've been easy enough to get along with. According to the relays, the people at Neskaya were looking forward to having me work with them. So just let me go there, as originally planned, and nothing will go wrong.

Nothing ever has gone wrong between me and anyone but Lisandra. And nothing serious would have happened, even now, if she hadn't come out with that awful *cristoforo* quotation just as I was packing up to leave. . . .

Lisandra and I don't hate one another, never have, though it's been hard for people to believe that. I've nothing against her, even now, and I'm sure her feelings about me haven't changed. What we both have always hated is what happens when we're together. Neither of us ever did it on purpose and neither of us ever could control it.

We're twins, the youngest in our family, which has Comyn connections—particularly to Ardais—not too far back. Given our red hair, everyone pretty much expected us to develop *laran*, but it had been happening for a long time before anyone realized what it was. When we were together, things spilled on us without either of us touching them; stones rolled into our paths to trip us; cups fell out of our hands to smash on the floor. Since as little children we were together almost all the time, it took a long time for us to realize that we were never clumsy at all when we were apart, and still longer to realize that what happened when we were together wasn't clumsiness at all, but something worse.

I remember the day I did realize. I was sitting next to Lisandra at breakfast, watching in horrified fascination as her near braid unplaited itself before my eyes. Somehow I knew I was making it happen. I tried desperately to stop it; I stared at the hair, willing it to stop unbraiding, but that didn't help. I looked away, thinking my stare might be causing the problem, but when I glanced back it was too late. The loosened mane twitched itself and dunked itself in Lisandra's bowl of porridge. I snatched at it without thinking, to get it out.

"You pulled my hair!" she yelled, bringing down a reproving glance at both of us from our nurse.

"It was to try to stop it going into the porridge," I explained in a low voice.

"You made it happen."

"I didn't mean to. I tried to stop it. I don't know how."

She turned away from me and scowled as she started cleaning up the mess. I don't think she believed I hadn't done it on purpose until we got up from the table and I tripped over an untied bootlace.

"You're doing it to me, too," I said.

Even after that it was a long time before the grown-ups believed us. As puberty approached and we began to develop telepathy, we knew with greater and greater certainty that each of us was causing telekinetic mishaps to the other without being able to control it in any way, though both of us were searching desperately for some means of control.

Finally one day the tips of Lisandra's braids burst into flame before our parents' eyes. We smothered the fires without real damage, but it was clear to everyone that it was time for us to go to the Towers. Separate Towers.

It seemed to be the perfect solution. Lisandra became an under-Keeper at Neskaya. I learned to control and develop my own *laran* here at Dalereuth, and since males can't become Keepers any more these days, started as a monitor and went on to become a competent matrix technician. All went well for ten years.

When disaster struck, it didn't first strike my sister—or me, except that the loss of one's Keeper is devastating. Our Keeper, Inessa, died suddenly and unexpectedly when her young successor was only half-trained. In all the Towers, the only person who had the skills and power to be sole Keeper, yet who could be spared from her present position, was Lisandra. That's what proved to be the real disaster.

I was looking forward to seeing my sister again, confident that our years of training and maturing had left both of us free from the poltergeist phenomena that had plagued our youth. We gathered to meet her in our common room, and she came forward to greet us: a tall, graceful woman with hair like spun copper, who walked like a dancer—until, as she turned to speak to me, she tripped on her crimson robe and went sprawling. I moved instinctively to help her up, remembered not to touch her and checked abruptly. A small table skidded across the floor—which is stone, not polished wood—and caught me neatly on the shins, to send me flat on my face beside her.

"No," we both said. "Oh, no. Not again!"

It went on like that, and we were as powerless to stop it as if we were still untrained children. Clearly, we couldn't be together. And just as clearly, I was the one who had to go. Of course I felt grief and resentment at having to leave the best friends and most comfortable living circumstances—for a telepath like me—that I've ever known. But I knew I would be going to a similar life and similar work with other sympathetic people; I would be facing only what Lisandra had already just faced. That wasn't what triggered some awful thing in my unconscious mind and let loose that blast of destructive psychic energy.

It was what Lisandra said as I was leaving: "I'm not my brother's Keeper."

MARION ZIMMER BRADLEY

THE DARKOVER NOVELS

The Founding
☐ DARKOVER LANDFALL   UE2234—$3.95

The Ages of Chaos
☐ HAWKMISTRESS!   UE2239—$4.99
☐ STORMQUEEN!   UE2310—$4.50

The Hundred Kingdoms
☐ TWO TO CONQUER   UE2174—$4.99
☐ THE HEIRS OF HAMMERFELL   UE2451—$4.99
☐ THE HEIRS OF HAMMERFELL (hardcover)   UE2395—$18.95

The Renunciates (Free Amazons)
☐ THE SHATTERED CHAIN   UE2308—$3.95
☐ THENDARA HOUSE   UE2240—$4.99
☐ CITY OF SORCERY   UE2332—$4.50

Against the Terrans: The First Age
☐ THE SPELL SWORD   UE2237—$3.95
☐ THE FORBIDDEN TOWER   UE2373—$4.95

Against the Terrans: The Second Age
☐ THE HERITAGE OF HASTUR   UE2413—$4.50
☐ SHARRA'S EXILE   UE2309—$4.99

THE DARKOVER ANTHOLOGIES with The Friends of Darkover

☐ DOMAINS OF DARKOVER   UE2407—$3.95
☐ FOUR MOONS OF DARKOVER   UE2305—$4.99
☐ FREE AMAZONS OF DARKOVER   UE2430—$3.95
☐ THE KEEPER'S PRICE   UE2236—$3.95
☐ LERONI OF DARKOVER   UE2494—$4.99
☐ THE OTHER SIDE OF THE MIRROR   UE2185—$3.50
☐ RED SUN OF DARKOVER   UE2230—$3.95
☐ RENUNCIATES OF DARKOVER   UE2469—$4.50
☐ SWORD OF CHAOS   UE2172—$3.50

Buy them at your local bookstore or use this convenient coupon for ordering.

PENGUIN USA   P.O. Box 999, Bergenfield, New Jersey 07621

Please send me the DAW BOOKS I have checked above, for which I am enclosing
$_____ (please add $2.00 per order to cover postage and handling. Send check
or money order (no cash or C.O.D.'s) or charge by Mastercard or Visa (with a
$15.00 minimum.) Prices and numbers are subject to change without notice.

Card #_____ Exp. Date _____
Signature_____
Name_____
Address_____
City _____ State _____ Zip _____

For faster service when ordering by credit card call **1-800-253-6476**

Please allow a minimum of 4 to 6 weeks for delivery.

DAW

MARION ZIMMER BRADLEY
NON-DARKOVER NOVELS

- [ ] HUNTERS OF THE RED MOON   UE1968—$3.99
- [ ] THE SURVIVORS   UE1861—$3.99
- [ ] WARRIOR WOMAN   UE2253—$3.50

NON-DARKOVER ANTHOLOGIES

- [ ] SWORD AND SORCERESS I   UE2359—$4.50
- [ ] SWORD AND SORCERESS II   UE2360—$3.95
- [ ] SWORD AND SORCERESS III   UE2302—$4.50
- [ ] SWORD AND SORCERESS IV   UE2412—$4.50
- [ ] SWORD AND SORCERESS V   UE2288—$3.50
- [ ] SWORD AND SORCERESS VI   UE2423—$3.95
- [ ] SWORD AND SORCERESS VII   UE2457—$4.50
- [ ] SWORD AND SORCERESS VIII   UE2486—$4.50
- [ ] SWORD AND SORCERESS IX   UE2509—$4.50

COLLECTIONS

- [ ] LYTHANDE (with Vonda N. McIntyre)   UE2291—$3.95
- [ ] THE BEST OF MARION ZIMMER BRADLEY edited by Martin H. Greenberg   UE2268—$3.95

Buy them at your local bookstore or use this convenient coupon for ordering.

PENGUIN USA P.O. Box 999, Bergenfield, New Jersey 07621

Please send me the DAW BOOKS I have checked above, for which I am enclosing $_____ (please add $2.00 per order to cover postage and handling. Send check or money order (no cash or C.O.D.'s) or charge by Mastercard or Visa (with a $15.00 minimum.) Prices and numbers are subject to change without notice.

Card #_____ Exp. Date _____

Signature_____

Name_____

Address_____

City _____ State _____ Zip _____

For faster service when ordering by credit card call **1-800-253-6476**

Please allow a minimum of 4 to 6 weeks for delivery.

A note concerning:

THE FRIENDS OF DARKOVER

So popular have been the novels of the planet Darkover that an organization of readers and fans has come into being, virtually spontaneously. Several meetings have been held at major science fiction conventions, and more recently specially organized around the various "councils" of the Friends of Darkover, as the organization is now known.

The Friends of Darkover is purely an amateur and voluntary group. It has no paid officers and has not established any formal membership dues. Although the members of the Thendara Council of the Friends no longer publish a newsletter or any other publications themselves, they serve as a central point for information on Darkover-oriented newsletters, fanzines, and councils and maintain a chronological list of Marion Zimmer Bradley's books.

Contact may be made by writing to the Friends of Darkover, Thendara Council, Box 72, Berkeley, CA 94701, and enclosing a SASE (Self-Addressed Stamped Envelope) for information.

MARION ZIMMER BRADLEY'S FANTASY MAGAZINE

Fans of Marion Zimmer Bradley will be pleased to hear that she is now publishing her own fantasy magazine. If you're interested in subscribing and/or would like to submit material to it, write her at:

P.O. Box 249
Berkeley, CA 94701

(If you're interested in writing for the magazine, please enclose a SASE for her free Writer's Guidelines.)

(These notices are inserted gratis as a service to readers. DAW Books is in no way connected with these organizations professionally or commercially.)

DAW

JO CLAYTON

☐ A BAIT OF DREAMS   UE2276—$3.95
☐ SHADOW OF THE WARMASTER   UE2298—$3.95

DRINKER OF SOULS SERIES
☐ DRINKER OF SOULS (Book 1)   UE2433—$4.50
☐ BLUE MAGIC (Book 2)   UE2270—$3.95
☐ A GATHERING OF STONES (Book 3)   UE2346—$3.95

THE WILD MAGIC SERIES
☐ WILD MAGIC (Book 1)   UE2496—$4.99
☐ WILDFIRE (Book 2)   UE2514—$4.99

THE DIADEM SERIES
☐ DIADEM FROM THE STARS (#1)   UE1977—$2.50
☐ LAMARCHOS (#2)   UE1971—$2.50
☐ IRSUD (#3)   UE2416—$3.95
☐ MAEVE (#4)   UE2387—$3.95
☐ STAR HUNTERS (#5)   UE2219—$2.95
☐ THE NOWHERE HUNT (#6)   UE2388—$3.95
☐ GHOSTHUNT (#7)   UE2220—$2.95
☐ THE SNARES OF IBEX (#8)   UE2390—$3.95
☐ QUESTER'S ENDGAME (#9)   UE2138—$3.50

SHADITH'S QUEST
☐ SHADOWPLAY (Book 1)   UE2385—$4.50
☐ SHADOWSPEER (Book 2)   UE2441—$4.50
☐ SHADOWKILL (Book 3)   UE2467—$4.99

THE DUEL OF SORCERY TRILOGY
☐ MOONGATHER (#1)   UE2072—$3.50
☐ MOONSCATTER (#2)   UE2071—$3.50
☐ CHANGER'S MOON (#3)   UE2065—$3.50

Buy them at your local bookstore or use this convenient coupon for ordering.

PENGUIN USA P.O. Box 999, Bergenfield, New Jersey 07621

Please send me the DAW BOOKS I have checked above, for which I am enclosing
$_____ (please add $2.00 per order to cover postage and handling. Send check
or money order (no cash or C.O.D.'s) or charge by Mastercard or Visa (with a
$15.00 minimum.) Prices and numbers are subject to change without notice.

Card #_____ Exp. Date _____
Signature_____
Name_____
Address_____
City _____ State _____ Zip _____

For faster service when ordering by credit card call **1-800-253-6476**

Please allow a minimum of 4 to 6 weeks for delivery.